JENNIFER S. ALDERSON

A Statue To Die For

Contents

1

Break-In Gone Wrong

I stared at the perfection of a painting before me, taking in the joyful expression of the young woman staring back. Her eyes twinkled as her facial muscles pulled back over her teeth, as if the painter—Peter Paul Rubens—had caught her a moment before a laugh took over her face. Despite the pressure I was under, I couldn't help but stop for a moment and admire her curly brown locks, so similar to my own, cascading over her slender shoulders, and her full lips, painted a sultry burgundy.

This *Portrait of a Young Woman* had been listed as missing since 1941, taken along with five other masterpieces from a German-Jewish family's home shortly after they had fled to the United States. The painting's provenance had been whitewashed so many times, the forged documents were virtually impossible to separate from the real ones anymore. Unfortunately, Igor Thumpkin, its current owner, had also been fooled by its fake pedigree and refused to believe that his Rubens was a piece of Nazi-looted art, despite the overwhelming evidence provided by my employer's lawyers that proved otherwise.

Soon after my employer—an art recovery firm called the Rosewood Agency—reached out to him, the painting disappeared from the private museum it had been hanging in and Thumpkin broke all contact. We feared he had sold it to an even less scrupulous collector, but it was my job to find out for certain. Which is why my partner, Baroness Sophie Rutherford, and

I were at this charity fundraiser being held in his country estate a few miles outside of Ypres, Belgium.

Our host's infatuation with my lady friend had enabled her to locate our missing painting, hidden away in a private gallery inaccessible to most guests, shortly after we had arrived. Given the fact that he had tried to hide it from our legal team by lying about its current whereabouts, my employer had given me permission to recover it, at least if I could do so without getting caught.

The antique chair that I was standing on, a rare William Morris-style wingback armchair covered in a glorious floral pattern and easily worth seven thousand dollars, wobbled under my weight. As much as I hated sullying fabulous furniture such as this with my Prada stilettos, it was the only thing that could get me up high enough so that I could reach behind the painting's frame. My fingers were still searching for the wire holding it to the wall, when the crack of a heel on the parquet floor by the gallery's entrance directly behind me made me freeze.

"Hello, is anyone there?" I asked in the meek voice of a lost guest, not an art recovery specialist.

Before I could step away from the painting or hide my wire cutters, a barking voice rose up from behind me. It belonged to Igor Thumpkin, our host for the evening and a celebrated kickboxer turned art investor.

"What are you doing in here? This space is private!" From his voice's high pitch, I'd say he had already spotted me standing on his armchair.

Silently, I cursed this turn of events. He was supposed to be giving my partner a tour of his public gallery, two floors above this private space. I must have tripped a silent alarm without realizing it, and inadvertently alerted our host to my presence.

The rapidly intensifying footsteps told me that Igor was bearing down on me—and fast. Given the former kickboxer's broad posture and tall stature, I knew a fight with him would end badly, probably for both of us. Even at sixty-five years of age, the man was in phenomenal condition and had boasted earlier tonight about how he still trained daily. I was a decade younger and in good enough condition that I could usually hold my own. Yet karate and jujitsu only took me so far, and I couldn't expect him to fight fair. Once street fighting entered the mix, things got ugly fast.

I silently cursed my cockiness, wishing I had laid down a trap of some sort, so that I would have heard him entering the space, instead of allowing that hulk of a man to sneak up on me and block the door. Maybe it was the success of the previous four recovery missions that had made me heady and less aware. On the other hand, it had only been a month since I'd come out of retirement. I probably shouldn't have been too hard on myself.

I looked for a place to hide, but came up empty. The walls were covered with several paintings of dubious provenance that I had already photographed for my employer, but save for a few pedestals topped with pop-art sculptures, the rest of the space was empty.

So I ducked down behind a Doric column holding a balloon dog made of blue porcelain, hoping my attacker's love of art would outweigh his need to catch a thief. Unfortunately for me, they were not exclusive. His beady eyes seemed to anticipate my every move. He snapped his arm out and around the pedestal so quickly that neither the mass of marble nor the delicate statue resting on top moved. However, his iron-fisted punch landed hard against my thigh, causing me to fall forward and into the column anyway. As the statue tumbled towards the ground, my assailant threw himself onto the floor and held up his arms, just in time to rescue Jeff Koon's balloon dog statue.

I couldn't help but smile as I ran for my life—art had won out, after all.

While my attacker cradled his statue in his arms, I raced past him towards the entrance, holding my camera close to my chest as I did. When I reached the door before he could set the dog down, I thought I was home free. But then a marble statue of a monkey eating grapes whizzed past my head, smashing against the door and forcing it closed again.

I turned towards my attacker, trembling in fear, as he glared down at me. "I recognize you—you're Lady Sophie's guest! How did you con her into allowing you to join her here tonight? She must not know that you are a thief. As soon as I tie you up, I'm calling her down here so you can explain yourself to her."

My relief that the Baroness's cover hadn't been blown by my actions slightly overshadowed my fear of being crippled by this angry hulk of a man. I knew he was infatuated with my lady friend, and it was only thanks to that his unrequited crush that I was able to attend this private party, as her "plus-one." In reality, I was the brawn and brains of this operation; the Baroness was simply my way in—a fact that brought me no joy at that moment. Under normal circumstances, it was my task to keep her dainty hands clean of anything remotely suspicious.

A burning sensation in my arm told me that I'd been hit. Yet before I could pull a shard of marble out of my forearm, Igor was in front of me, blocking my path with his bulky figure. I considered trying to talk my way out of this mess, but he seemed to be more of a "punch first, ask questions later" kind of guy.

When he lunged for my bloody arm, I grabbed the closest thing my hands could wrap around—an art deco floor lamp with a painted-glass shade worth a few thousand to the right buyer. As much as it pained me to destroy something so beautiful, I willingly swung the heavy metal fixture towards him with as much power as I could muster. With ease, he grabbed ahold of the metal rod and pulled it out of my hands—and me off balance. Before my body hit the floor, he was already on top of me, his hands around my throat.

When his thick fingers found my esophagus, I dug my nails into his arms and threw my knee up towards his groin, refusing to give up without a fight. But my jabs didn't lessen his grip. Just as my vision began to blur, a scratching noise coming from the entrance distracted him, causing his fingers to loosen a smidgen, long enough that I could get a breath in.

Seconds later, the door swung open, startling us both. From my position, I could easily see who was entering, and her presence thrilled and scared me simultaneously. Before my assailant could turn to face the new arrival, I grabbed the man's head with both hands, to try to prevent it from swiveling. As if I stood a chance. It was like trying to hold onto a moving granite sculpture.

Still, it gave the new arrival a chance to enter, before he bore down on her. The tell-tale sparkle coming from her diamond-studded tiara told me my partner was now standing behind him. When the Baroness grabbed a vase off of the nearest pedestal, raised it above her head, and yelled out, "Get off of my guest," I wanted to cheer aloud.

Unfortunately, Sophie's arms were not used to lifting anything heavier than a champagne glass. The chunky vase she'd chosen could not have weighed more than ten pounds, but it was apparently too much for her biceps to handle. Instead of connecting with our host's head, the vase glanced off of his neck, before rolling down his back and right onto her foot. The crunch was sickening, and the following scream soul-piercing.

Just as the Baroness's shrieks filled the room, the man's balled fist swung back behind him, and right into Lady Sophie's jaw. The glint of her tiara falling to the floor told me that my partner was down.

When he finally turned to face his attacker and saw her lying crumpled on the floor, his anger turned to panic.

"Lady Sophie—*mon amour!* What have I done? I didn't mean to hurt you."

My partner held one hand to her jaw as tears rolled down her heavily-powdered cheeks. The kickboxer bent down to get a better look at her foot, gagging as he did. Sophie's blue ball gown was growing more purple by the second as it soaked up the blood streaming from her wounds.

"Call an ambulance—*tout de suite!*" he screamed.

The giant of a man then bent down and stroked Sophie's hair while murmuring gentle reassurances, the Rubens forgotten. My partner did her best to control her emotions, but if my foot had looked like that, I would have been screaming like a banshee. Instead, she trembled slightly from the pain and kept her eyes snapped shut, but nothing more. Her jaw had already begun to swell badly, which was no surprise given the man's fists were like concrete blocks. The chance was high that she would be eating through a straw for a few weeks.

Only after the paramedics had filled Sophie up with painkillers and rolled her away did Igor turn on me. "This is all your fault. If you hadn't tried to steal my painting, Lady Sophie would not have been harmed—you thief!"

Igor had no idea how right he was. That was exactly why I was meant to keep Sophie away from the rough stuff. Yet in my eagerness to find this missing Rubens painting, I had placed my partner in danger, and possibly jeopardized her future. Her getting injured in this way might cost her more than just a stay in the hospital—it could mean the end of her employment for the Rosewood Agency, if Igor blew her cover.

Part of me wanted to let him keep thinking that I was simply a thief out to steal his painting, yet after what had happened to my husband, Carlos, I couldn't stand having corrupt collectors lie to me. It was the hard-headed ones, like Igor, who thought they were above the law that upset me most.

I puffed up my chest as best as I could, but still didn't come close to reaching his shoulders qua height. "I'm not a thief; you are! This Rubens was stolen from a Jewish family in 1941. When the family's lawyer contacted you, you hid it away, instead of returning it. If you had done the right thing, Lady Sophie would never would have been in harm's way."

"Who do you two work for—an insurance company?" He stared at me in horror.

I had to convince him I was working alone; Sophie would never forgive me otherwise.

"I work for an art recovery agency, and my employer arranged for me to accompany her to this party. Lady Sophie had no idea that I was using her connections to get into your home, or that I was actually here to recover the painting," I lied.

"I can't believe this! My darling Sophie. Will she ever forgive me?"

"I don't know about that. But I do know that that Rubens is going back to its rightful owner, whether you like it or not."

2

That Woman

When my partner awoke several hours and two surgeries later, I made certain the first person that she saw was me.

"Thank goodness you are alright. You really had us all worried, Sophie," I said, using her given name instead of my nickname for her, the Baroness. She looked so frail and much older than her sixty years, thanks to her swollen jaw. It didn't help that her foot was in a cast and raised up above the bed in a sling.

My partner's eyes widened as she took in her bandages and the tubes sticking out of her arm, her confusion evident. She'd passed out before the paramedics could get her into the ambulance; I could imagine she was in a state of shock, as well as in a whole lot of pain.

I choked back a tear. "I am so sorry about what happened to you, but I cannot thank you enough for rescuing me. If you had been a few seconds later, I think our host would have strangled me with his bare hands."

Sophie tried to smile, but the movement apparently only brought her pain. "How am I doing?" she asked, her voice groggy and difficult to understand because she was attempting to speak through clenched teeth. Igor hadn't broken her jaw, but had bruised it quite badly, as the deep blues and blacks coloring her chin and cheek attested to.

"You'll live, but you're going to have to stay off of your feet for a while. That vase fractured your foot. Thankfully the surgeon said you should have full mobility once everything heals."

The Baroness averted her face just as tears began rolling down her cheeks. "I am so sorry. This is going to jeopardize the mission. And you were just getting into the swing of things again."

I knew her tears were not fake. She truly wanted to do something good for society, by any means necessary, which usually entailed using her social standing and extensive network to get me close to a target. That's why she had offered to assist the Rosewood Agency with any future cases, after we had helped her recover a portrait of her late husband, stolen from their home shortly after his death.

I'll admit, before my husband was murdered, I used to do this work for the shot of adrenaline that came with finding a stolen object. Since Carlos's death at the hands of an antiquities smuggler working for the Mafia, the thrill was gone. My motivation to see justice served, however, had increased tenfold.

"Hey, don't cry. If everything heals as expected, you'll be back in action in no time," I fibbed.

"Oh, please!" she cried through clenched teeth. "I can barely open my jaw, and my leg is immobile. I don't see myself dancing a waltz at anyone's ball anytime soon."

As much as I hated to admit it, her incapacitation created a huge problem. In a week's time, we were supposed to attend a gallery opening in Luxembourg, where I hoped to gain some intel on the inner workings of a possible art smuggling operation. But if the Baroness had to remain hospitalized, we would have to skip that assignment. I wasn't interesting enough on my own to be granted admission to such an exclusive party. Only those who were filthy rich and had the right social standing had been extended an invitation.

And without getting into that party, I wouldn't be able to get a closer look at the gallery's storeroom and search for any clues that might help me and my colleagues figure out how the owner was moving stolen art across international borders. He was quite a recluse, and his gallery was nothing more than a popup store that appeared whenever he had something interesting to sell, then disappeared once the transactions were concluded.

This was the first time in months that anyone had heard from him, and I would hate to miss this chance to get a closer look at his operation and clientele.

Yet I knew that as soon as I told our boss about the Baroness's accident, he would tell us to pack up and come home. What frustrated me most of all was that I considered this to be the most important of the eight assignments we hoped to complete during our whirlwind tour of Europe. Not that the others were far less significant. Luckily, we had five successful missions behind us, so I could still go home with my head held high. I had already verified the condition and location of a stolen medieval prayer book, a portrait by Manet, a sketch by Picasso, and a Murano glass vase. I'd also gotten close enough to another painting to know that it was not the piece we sought—it was the same period and artist, but a different version of a similar scene. Rosewood's lawyers had already arranged for the Avron Book—my first case back out of retirement—to be returned to the museum it had been stolen from in Ohio. It was only a matter of time before the portrait, sketch, and vase were on their way home, as well.

But what irked me the most about this unexpected turn of events was that I wanted to discuss with my boss, Reggie, the possibility of working for Rosewood full time again, because I was having so much fun being back in the field. I had a feeling that he still wasn't certain whether I was fit enough—mentally and emotionally—to come back to work on a permanent basis. One or two more successful recoveries would support my argument that I was more than ready to return.

So instead of packing my bags while waiting for Sophie to come out of surgery, I had spent those hours in the hospital cafeteria, sipping stale coffee and wracking my brain for a way to fix this mess. After approaching the situation from every angle, there was only one viable option, as far as I could see. However, it was so off-the-wall, I didn't know whether I could convince my boss to agree.

I grabbed Sophie's hand and squeezed. "Hey, don't you worry! I have an idea of how to fix this, I just have to run it by Reggie first."

Sophie's face cleared a little. "You do? I hope you don't mean partnering with a current agent. The only reason why our boss let me call you back in was because we are so short-staffed right now."

"You'd both mentioned that before. No, I have a civilian in mind, but a highly qualified one. She's the only person I can think of that could fill in for you—just until you're feeling better, of course," I rushed to add, knowing she would not like the suggestion that another could so easily replace her.

A slight frown crossed the Baroness's face. "Do I know this person?"

"Sort of. You remember my best friend, Rhonda Rhodes? She's been moaning for months that she needs some excitement in her life. I just hope she wasn't joking around."

The Baroness leaned back into her hospital bed. "Do you mean that woman from the television?" Her deepening scowl told me she didn't think it was a good idea. "Why, pray tell, do you think a television celebrity could take my place?"

"No one could take your place," I soothed. "But Rhonda is rich, knows a lot about art, and is famous because of her show. She should be able to get me in the door, especially if we tell the gallery owner that you are unable to attend, but trust Rhonda enough to give her your invitation," I added, afraid to step on her toes any further. In order to make my plan work, I would need my partner's full cooperation. I was meant to accompany the Baroness to the party as her personal assistant. It was plausible that Sophie had "lent" her assistant to Rhonda, as well as given her the ticket.

Thanks to the swelling, I couldn't be certain that the Baroness was pursing her lips, but she was certainly glaring at me. I knew her pride had been deeply injured already, and me assuming that a TV personality could take her ladyship's place must have felt like another kick in her royal backside. Yet right now, I couldn't worry about her feelings. The simple fact was, she could not help me get into the party, and Rhonda could. Or would hopefully be able to. Considering her state of mind the last time we'd talked, she'd probably already booked a trip to Tahiti by now.

I hesitated a moment before asking the question I really wanted an answer to. "Do you think Reggie will go for it?"

"No, I do not. You know how he feels about involving civilians," she said in the smuggest of tones, finally allowing her frustration and irritation out. "I know you are going to ask him anyway, but if he agrees, I'll eat my tiara."

3

Plan B

After promising the Baroness that I would return as soon as I'd spoken with our boss, I wandered down to the hospital's front entrance and stepped out into the late afternoon sun before making the call. I considered calling Myrtle, my official company contact, and letting her pass the message along, but I knew my boss would want to hear this firsthand.

Reginald Pinky Rosewood, or Reggie to his friends and employees, was a fairly relaxed person to work for—probably because he had become a billionaire at thirty-five and meditated as much as your typical Buddhist monk. There was very little that fazed him, and almost nothing that he couldn't fix by throwing a whole lot of money at it. That was why he had originally founded the Rosewood Agency: so his handpicked team of specialists could recover his collection of stolen paintings after the police could not.

After I had explained the situation and Sophie's condition, Reggie's initial reaction was to order us to pack up and fly home—as I expected. "No piece of art is worth either one of you getting harmed," he insisted. "After what happened to your husband, I should expect that you would agree wholeheartedly."

"That was a low blow, Reggie. No one was out to get Lady Sophie. In point of fact, she hurt herself when she dropped the vase onto her foot, instead of our target's head."

"Yes, but she did so in order to save you from being choked to death, and got injured as a result. I refuse to allow you to continue on alone, but there is no one available to take her place right now; I've already checked into it. Perhaps in a few weeks, depending on how long it takes our other operatives to wrap up their current assignments."

"But the Luxembourg party is next week," I pouted. Before I could explain that I was an adult and could decide for myself, Reggie talked over me.

"Before we talk about that party, I need you to explain to me why Baroness Rutherford was attempting to hit the target over the head. You know that your top priority is keeping her connection to our organization a secret. If her friends know she's inviting you along so you can search for stolen artwork, she won't be able to get you into those fancy parties you love so much."

We both chuckled into the phone, knowing he was teasing me. Neither of us was a fan of those fancy dress balls. In the fifteen years I'd known Reggie, I had yet to see my boss in anything other than a plain T-shirt, hoodie, and blue jeans. For me, getting dolled up for the party was the worst part of the job. It took me hours to twist my unruly hair into those fancy updos, apply the necessary layers of makeup, and squeeze into those ridiculously tight-fitting ball gowns I was expected to wear. Sure, I was trim from years of teaching self-defense classes at the YMCA. Yet the waist- and bustlines envisioned by your typical haute couture designer were not for normal body proportions, but those of living Barbie dolls.

Still, as much as I abhorred those shindigs and the snobby attendees they tended to attract, I adored recovering pieces of stolen art from the devious guests among them—those hypocritical collectors who, either out of laziness or a deep-seated desire to possess something others could not, purchased stolen artwork. If they truly cared about the thing they were buying, they would have taken the time to research its provenance or history, and could have figured out for themselves that their book, painting, or sculpture was stolen. There were enough art loss databases online these days that it wouldn't take more than a few minutes of searching to find out for certain.

"You're right. Involving Lady Sophie was a huge mistake, and one I will not make again. Look, Reggie, please listen to me before you make up your mind," I pleaded, my voice taking on a whiny tone that even I despised. "It took my partner quite a bit of time and several favors from important people just to get an invitation. And all she usually has to do is pick up the phone. It would be a huge waste of time and effort to let this opportunity pass us by. This smuggling ring has been operating for so long and is so elusive, this might be our only shot in the coming year to get close to one of the key players. I'm not a threat to anyone at the gallery, so there's no reason to assume anyone would want to harm me."

"I refuse to let you continue alone. And even if I did allow it, the gallery's security wouldn't let you inside. You aren't interesting enough to take Lady Sophie's place, and you know it."

Not only was I not rich or intriguing enough to get in the door on my own, I had already video-chatted with the gallery owner's party planner while in the role of Lady Sophie's assistant. It would be strange if I suddenly pretended to be someone regal or important. And my unruly hair tended to pop out from under wigs at the most inopportune times.

Yet Reggie's words gave me a spark of hope. He had just admitted that his issue was with me working alone—not *per se* me going to the party. Which should make it more difficult for him to refuse my next idea, I figured. "I know someone who is available and could fill the Baroness's shoes. I'm sure of it."

"You mean Lady Sophie, don't you?" Reggie growled. I forgot that our boss was unaware of my penchant for calling her the Baroness, instead of using her title properly. "Who do you know that can get you into the gallery's party?"

"It's a little out-of-the-box, but I really do think it will work."

"I'm all ears."

I sucked in my breath before blurting out, "Do you watch much television? Have you ever seen *Antiques Time*?"

"With Rhonda Rhodes? Myrtle and I love that show. But I don't see what that has to do with this…"

My heart skipped a beat—*he knows who Rhonda is!* That was going to make this conversation go much more smoothly. "Rhonda Rhodes is a good friend of mine. Her show is on hiatus for another three weeks, and the last time we spoke, she was complaining about wanting to go on an adventure. I'm certain she would fly over, if I asked her to. Surely she would be interesting enough to get me in the door."

Whereas the Baroness had the title and old money network to get us invited to the right parties, Rhonda had something she did not—celebrity status and enough charisma to melt an iceberg. It did help, at least as long as the host was male and heterosexual, that she also had a bustline to rival Dolly Parton's. But she wasn't overtly sexual and had a folksy, down-to-earth way about her that endeared her to both sexes. The network her show appeared on regularly received emails from male viewers who wanted to date her and women who wanted to befriend her.

Best of all, Rhonda was one of those naturally charismatic people who drew others to them, simply by walking in the room. With her by my side, no one would pay attention to what I was doing.

"Wait, are you suggesting we bring a civilian in on this? That seems like a bad idea to me. One word to the wrong person, and she could accidentally blow other operations we are working on. Or expose you for who you truly are, and render you useless to us. Are you really willing to take that chance?"

I could hear my boss's lips turning downwards. I had to change their direction again. "Yes, I am. Rhonda is brilliant with art and collectibles, but socially, she is as inept as they come. She firmly believes that everyone is kindhearted and good, which makes her an easy mark and means that I should be able to keep her in the dark as to my true motives. It's only one assignment, the gallery show, and all she has to do is get me in the door. I can handle the rest without involving her."

"I don't know, someone that naïve may also accidentally ruin your cover. Have you considered that?"

"Of course I have! But I don't want to give up, not when we are so close. You said the Luxembourg gig was the most important assignment of the bunch, and we're only a week away from it taking place. All I need is for her to get me into that party. There's no reason for her to know what I really am doing there. With a little luck, the gallery owner will be a fan of *Antiques Time*, too, and Rhonda can keep him occupied simply by chatting him up. Trust me, if you've ever met her, you'd know she can talk your ear off."

I crossed my fingers behind my back as I lied, knowing it was going to be a challenge to complete the assignment without alerting my friend. Rhonda was not the most observant of people, but she wasn't obtuse, either.

My best friend still did not know that I had worked as an art sleuth for the Rosewood Agency for fifteen years, until my husband's death sent me into early retirement. If Rhonda exposed me to the wrong socialite, I wouldn't be able to go undercover ever again. Was I really willing to take that chance? If it meant I could continue pursuing the art smuggling operation, instead of going home now with no assignments on the horizon, then yes. I was willing to trust that my best friend would not inadvertently destroy my career.

"It's not worth it—we'll have another opportunity somewhere down the line."

"Come on, Reggie, you know that's not true. This gallery owner has been slipping through our fingers for years. This is the best lead we've ever had, and it would be a shame to pass it up. We can let the last two assignments slide, but this is an incredible chance to potentially break up a smuggling operation!"

Reggie was quiet a moment, before answering in a calm voice. "I can tell from your tone that your mind is made up. I guess I have no choice but to agree with you, don't I?"

The resignation in his voice was music to my ears. If this was going to be my last mission as an art sleuth, then I wanted to go out with a bang. And having the chance to expose an art smuggling ring sounded like the perfect opportunity to do so.

"However, I do insist you be careful—no piece of art is worth your life. What happened to Carlos is a tragedy I do not want repeated."

I gulped and thought of my darling husband, killed on a similar assignment for the Rosewood Agency. "Of course not. And just so you know, Rhonda Rhodes is my best friend. You may think I would gamble with my own life, but I'm not going to do so with hers. You have my word on that. I'll call you back as soon as I've talked to her and let you know what she says."

4

Adventure Time

"Great," I muttered, glad no one was around to hear me grumbling to myself. Technically, Reggie had granted my wish. I would get to complete my next assignment and hopefully solve one of the biggest cases of my career. Yet now I had to figure out how to invite Rhonda over, without alerting her to my real reason for needing to attend that gallery show. How I would manage to sneak away from her and search the gallery's storeroom was a problem for later.

Ultimately I realized there was no amount of preparation that could ready me for this next challenge. It didn't matter how many variations of our conversation that I ran through in my mind; all I could be certain of was that it would not go as I expected it to.

However, I did know that I couldn't wait too long to call my bestie because she may have already booked herself a trip to an island destination, so she could spend the rest of her vacation in the sun. During our last few chats, her desperation to do something other than hang around her pool had increased dramatically, in part due to my heavily edited stories about my own adventures in Europe.

As if she was reading my mind, my telephone pinged with another photo of Rhonda sitting poolside in a neon pink bikini with fluorescent green fringe. The outfit barely covered her ample bosom or voluptuous hips.

Although lying was part of my job description, I still hated having to do so, and especially to my best friend. I ran through my least harmful lie once more, then picked up my phone and called Rhonda.

"Well, hello, stranger!"

"Hello to you, too," I answered in a similarly chipper voice. After a few minutes of casual chitchat, I turned the conversation to my real reason for calling.

"Remember how you were saying that you wanted to have an adventure? Were you joking?"

"I was dead serious—I'm going crazy here at home. The show's on break for another three weeks, and my youngest and her family just left to go on vacation."

"That's nice that Samantha is taking a break. With her newborn, I bet she could use a change of scenery. What about Julie? Is she back home, or still abroad?"

Rhonda's sigh told me that it was the latter. "Is she ever home? I was just looking at booking a holiday package to Hawaii. I don't want to be the only one stuck at home, doing nothing special."

I sucked in my breath, knowing it was now or never. "Alright then, I have a proposition for you. As you know, I'm in Europe to report on several auctions and gallery openings that Lady Sophie Rutherford wanted to attend. But she's been injured and can't go to a viewing that's taking place next week in Luxembourg. It's a pretty exclusive event, and my magazine editor is really upset that I won't able to attend. At least, not unless I find someone to take Lady Sophie's place."

"Your magazine—is this all part of your cover?" she whispered into the phone, as if that would help disguise her voice in case the line was tapped.

My first instinct was to ignore her question, knowing my boss would not be alright with me disobeying him from the outset. But then I changed my mind, figuring it was better to wipe that notion from her head with a simple white lie, now, than to let the idea simmer that I was working for a clandestine organization.

"No, silly, I'm writing a series of articles for *Hidden Treasures*. That's the same magazine I've been working for since I retired. It's just that this assignment is a little more secretive than others because of the exclusiveness of the events. Not all of the hosts would be happy to know that a journalist was also in attendance. That's why I've been so scarce on the details, when we've spoken."

I felt a wave of nausea as I spoke, hating having to tell these half-truths to my bestie. Technically, this whirlwind trip around Europe with the Baroness would result in an influx of new articles in *Hidden Treasures* that sported my byline; however, that was definitely not the reason for our visit.

My favorite way to go undercover was to crawl into the skin of an antiques journalist working for *Hidden Treasures* magazine. The magazine was real, and the large circulation helped solidify my cover by giving me a credible employer that could easily be verified as real. Each issue contained a few articles with my byline, ghostwritten by a professional journalist. Now and again, one of my photographs did make it into the magazine, so it wasn't a complete lie.

"Well, why didn't you say so straight away? I'd be happy to attend. But what makes this show in Luxembourg so special?"

I cleared my throat and lied to my bestie some more. "Well, it's kind of a hush-hush situation. I'm on the trail of an art smuggling ring, and we think one of the gallery owners is somehow involved. I couldn't tell you earlier because my editor is super paranoid about our competition finding out. It's important that I attend this show, in case the owner is involved and does try to move something stolen via the sale, but I'm simply not rich or interesting enough to be let inside on my own. I need to be the 'plus one' of someone wealthy and fascinating, and that sounds right up your alley. That's the only reason why my editor has given me the go-ahead to tell you the truth." I squeezed my eyes shut, hoping she'd buy my lies.

"So let me get this straight—you want me to fly over and escort you to a gallery opening in Luxembourg, where there might be art smugglers present?"

I held my breath when Rhonda paused, uncertain which way she was going to go, until she shrieked into the phone, "Are you kidding me? Honey, that sounds like a real adventure."

My dear friend had taken the bait—hook, line, and sinker. "So you'll help me out?"

"You bet! I knew you were holding something back the last few times we talked, but I never would have guessed it was because you were on the trail of smugglers!"

I did a little two-step, to stop myself from cheering aloud. "That's truly wonderful, Rhonda, but you know you can't say anything about why I'm really there, right? It will blow my cover and alert the bad guys. It sounds like several have been invited to the show, which is why I need to be there in person and see how they interact with each other. It might help me expose their network. I don't think they are stupid enough to harm a journalist, but I would rather not find out."

"Carmen, I would never do anything that would put you in jeopardy. My lips are sealed! Oh, boy, this is exactly what I hoped for—a real adventure! But wait, why would they let me take your partner's place, if the guest list is so exclusive?"

"Because you are Rhonda Rhodes!"

"That's true." I could hear her blushing as she replied. I loved that Rhonda had remained so down-to-earth, despite her enormous fame.

"How long would I be gone?"

"Well, the Luxembourg show is next Friday, so in eight days' time. It's only one night, so you could come over for the weekend if you prefer."

"No way! If I'm flying all the way over to Europe, then I expect to see more than one tiny country while I'm there. Do you think we could visit the French Riviera after the gallery show?"

"Are you kidding me? If you're willing to come over here and help me out with this assignment, I will make time for the Riviera."

"Fabulous! This sounds like a whole lot more fun than flying off to Hawaii all by myself. Thanks for inviting me to tag along."

"Thank you for saying yes, Rhonda," I cried, as relief flooded through my veins and calmed my heart rate. If I could pull off this next assignment, especially without company backup, Reggie couldn't turn down my request to come back to work on a more permanent basis. At least, I hoped he would not.

"So, where should we meet?"

"Brussels or Amsterdam would be the easiest."

"Got it. I'll call you back as soon as I have something booked."

"That is wonderful. I cannot wait to see you," I gushed, not lying this time. The Baroness was a good partner, but this was a good friend. Taking in the sights with her would be a lot more fun. "You're the best, Rhonda."

"I know, sweetie," she chuckled before hanging up.

I smiled at the phone in my hand, thinking that the conversation had gone better than I had expected. Now all I had to do was inform my partner.

5

Celebrity Woes

I stared up at the rows of screens announcing the arrivals at Schiphol Airport, searching for Rhonda's flight number. My knees trembled slightly, knocking together as if I was a rookie agent again. I never thought I'd be working with my bestie, even if she wouldn't know that I was actually on the job.

It helped to know that I could rely on her to follow my instructions, even if she didn't know why she was doing so. Her physical prowess also set my mind at ease. In contrast to my usual partner, Rhonda was pretty strong, thanks to her daily swims and weight-lifting routines, all recommended by her television show's personal trainer. However, the workouts didn't get her down to skinny. She was still a curvaceous, full-bodied woman, thanks to her healthy appetite for vintage wines, rich pastas, and many other high-carb foods.

When Rhonda waltzed into the arrival hall an hour later, I was standing by the gate, holding a large bouquet of dahlias. Thanks to her bouffant hair pieces, pink cowboy hat, and matching jacket, Rhonda was easy to spot. Whereas the Baroness had a penchant for ball gowns, Rhonda was more country-chic. Bright colors, floral patterns, and a whole lot of fringe were her trademarks.

"Dahlias! My favorite," she cried and sniffed deeply, before throwing her arms around me, effectively crushing the bouquet against my neck. The orange and red petals fluttered around our feet as she rocked me to and fro.

Back at home, we saw each other weekly, but her heartfelt hugs always made it feel as if we were being reunited after months of separation.

Rhonda pulled back, but kept her hands clamped onto my shoulders. "Look at you! You look great. Travel's been good for you, I see."

I'd had two days alone to recover from that last hairy assignment and did feel refreshed. The spa treatments and mani-pedi had done wonders. "Thanks. What do you think of my manicure?"

She grabbed my nails and brought them up close to her eyes. "I love the red. It's a little too bloody for my tastes, but it suits you somehow."

When she released my hands, she immediately used one of her own to cover her yawn. "Boy, I am pooped! I didn't sleep a wink on the plane. When I wasn't chatting with fans, there was an adorable man next to me who kept me awake."

"What are you talking about?" I asked, my voice laced with confusion. My routine on airplane rides consisted of completely ignoring my fellow passengers for the entire flight. I wasn't beyond being rude, if it meant they would leave me alone.

A good-looking, middle-aged man sauntered past and waved at Rhonda as he did. He had a deep tan, as if he was often out on the golf course, and wore a tailored Armani suit that must have cost a few grand. Based on the conversative pinstripe, I would guess he did something in finance. His pepper-and-salt hair was cropped close to his skull, and it looked as if he regularly plucked his eyebrows. I squinted, trying to get a better look at his eyelids. Had he had work done? From this distance, it was hard to tell. If you put a gun to my head, I would say he was in his mid-fifties, but couldn't be certain without asking.

"Speaking of which..." Rhonda waved both arms and her cherry-red Alexander McQueen bag in his direction. "Yoo hoo, Colin, over here!"

He smiled as he approached, before drawing Rhonda's hand up to his lips and kissing it for several seconds longer than necessary, as she tittered softly under his gaze. My hackles rose, until I recalled that though Rhonda and I were both widows of three years, unlike me, she was ready to find a new love.

"Ah yes, my darling seatmate, Rhonda Rhodes. It was a pleasure conversing with you. My offer still stands. I do hope you'll join us."

When he looked over at me, his eyes glanced over my James Perse blouse and baggy trousers, nodding when he noted my Gucci sandals. Apparently my designer clothing received his approval for he finally added, "And your friend, too."

"Are you sure? Maybe you should call your buddy first and ask," Rhonda replied.

"Alistair? There's no need. McPhee loves meeting new people, especially interesting ones like you. He also has a passion for collecting movie memorabilia, which means he's probably seen your show. I am certain he will be thrilled to meet you."

"Isn't that fantastic! Where do we meet up?"

"Let me send you the coordinates." He took out his phone and sent Rhonda a text message, before putting it back in his pants pocket. Seeing as he already had her number, I had to guess that they had exchanged contact information before leaving their flight. *She must like the guy*, I realized.

"It's a dock close to Amsterdam's Central Station. We'll meet there tomorrow evening at six. A boat will pick us up and take us to the party. We were warned to bring an overnight bag, so you should do the same. Do you think you can find it on your own?"

"Yes, I'm certain we can," I replied for Rhonda, knowing I was going to be doing the navigating during this trip. As intelligent as my friend was, I'd learned from many a road trip together that she was navigationally challenged.

A soft ping coming from his pants caused his suave expression to transform into one of light irritation. A glance at the screen caused him to sigh deeply. "I do apologize, but I must leave you. My limo has arrived. I hope to see you two tomorrow evening."

He released Rhonda's hand, then strode outside the airport terminal, presumably to meet his awaiting ride.

As soon as he was out of sight, Rhonda began waving an imaginary fan in front of her face before pretending to faint. "Oh la la—that man is almost too much! He's not just easy on the eyes; he was a fascinating conversationalist, too."

"Hum, I'm sure. But what party is he talking about, and who is Alistair McPhee?"

"All I know about Alistair is that he is hosting a party Colin is attending, and that he used to be a Hollywood director, but retired several years ago."

"Alright. What do you know about Colin?"

"Well, that his name is Colin Worchester and he's here in Amsterdam to attend a friend's party." She eyed me sideways as she spoke, a hint of a smile on her otherwise impassive face.

When my brow furrowed, she slapped my shoulder. "Relax a little! He's just some guy I met on the plane. All I know about him is that he's a corporate investor based out of Los Angeles. We didn't really talk much more about work, or at least not his job. He was sitting next to me in first class, recognized me from my show, and started chatting me up as soon as we boarded. It did make the flight go by faster."

Rhonda paused a moment, as if she was thinking back on their conversation. "The way he looks at you when he speaks makes you feel like you're special somehow. But he was flirting shamelessly with every woman on that flight, so I don't think he's really taken a shine to me. Still, it was fun to be the center of his world for a few hours." Wistfulness colored her voice. I knew she missed her husband, Ralph, as much as I did mine. Yet, she desperately wanted to find a new partner to share her twilight years with, whereas I was happy to go it alone.

I grabbed her hand and squeezed, knowing I needed to tone down the interrogation techniques. "It's not the same, but I'll see to it that you're pampered during your entire trip. You haven't been out of the States in how long?"

"Since my honeymoon, thirty-two years ago. Can you believe it's been that long?"

"No, I cannot," I said honestly. "Now I'm even more glad that I called you. Thanks again for coming all the way over here to help me out."

"Sure thing. But considering your gallery show isn't until later this week, would you like to go to Alistair McPhee's party with me?" Rhonda asked, hesitation in her voice. "Colin said there will probably be famous actresses and producers there. Who would have thought we would run into Hollywood types, here in Europe! It sounds like it could be fun, and it's the silly sort of adventure I was craving."

I bit my lip, hesitant to say yes. "Let me think about the timing, alright? I'm a little nervous about the upcoming assignment."

"Even if we do end up spending the night at Alistair's house, we'll still have plenty of time to get you to Luxembourg and prepare. Please?"

"I had hoped to see the sights with you before we leave for Luxembourg in four days. Could we maybe catch up a little first, before we decide?"

"Sure, that sounds good. Where can we get a cup of strong coffee? I could use a jolt of caffeine, otherwise jet lag is going to win out and I'll crash out on the bed as soon as I enter my hotel room."

"I know just the place. It's a few minutes away. Do you want to walk?" I took another look at her three cotton-candy-colored suitcases. "Or we could take a taxi."

"Taxi, please. I know it's lazy of me, but I really need to put my feet up for a spell."

"How can your feet be tired?"

Rhonda suppressed another yawn. "Once I have a coffee in my hand, I'll tell you whatever you want to know."

6

Star Allure

The taxi driver whisked us through Amsterdam at speeds that seemed simultaneously slow, yet too fast considering all of the bicycles and trams vying for space on the narrow strips of road crisscrossing the city center. There was something so magical about the seventeenth-century homes lining the canals that circled the city, I didn't mind him keeping it around fifteen kilometers per hour.

He dropped us off a short distance away from Central Station, next to a gigantic bust of a man. The bronzed figure's hair was sticking out at all angles and sported a mustache that reminded me of a famous scientist.

"Is that Albert Einstein?" I asked our taxi driver before paying an absurd amount for our brief ride.

"No, it's a Dutch writer named Multatuli," he said as he seemed to study the statue through the open window. "But I see what you mean about Einstein."

On our right was our destination, a tiny espresso bar called Caffè il Momento that looked out onto the statue. The reviews of the coffee were so good, I figured it would pack the right punch. Whereas the Baroness was a tea drinker, both Rhonda and I preferred our caffeine black. Well, sometimes with a sugar or two.

We ordered our drinks and squeezed onto the tiny terrace, turning to face the morning sun like sunflowers.

Since Rhonda had said yes, I'd spent every waking minute trying to work

28

out how to explain what I needed her to do, without revealing what I was intending to do. Yet the words changed each time. Now that Rhonda was here, sitting in a chair across from me and expecting answers, I was still tripping over my tongue to find the right words. So instead of jumping right in, I decided to start with something lighter and work my way up to it.

"So, tell me, how are your feet tired? You were just stuck on an airplane for eleven hours. Most people want to stretch their legs after such a long flight."

"Oh, that was because the stewardesses stopped letting passengers from the economy class into first class so they could chat with me."

I stared at her, trying to process her words. I'd known her practically all of my life, and to me she was just Rhonda. I often had trouble remembering that she was a seriously famous person. "What now?"

"When we were waiting to board, a few passengers recognized me and before I knew it, the whole flight seemed to know I was on it!" Rhonda chuckled, her cheeks glowing with the memory of all of those people recognizing her.

That was where my bestie and I differed greatly. Whereas she sought the spotlight, I did everything in my power to stay out of it. I would have gladly asked the stewardesses to keep the others at bay. On the other hand, I had no plans to star in a national television show, so I really didn't have to worry about being besieged by fans.

"That uppity behavior doesn't sit right with me, so I ended up walking the aisles of economy class and taking selfies with fans of the show for most of the flight. A few even had antique jewelry with them that they wanted me to appraise, bless them!" Rhonda giggled as she leaned back against the wooden bench and tilted her head up towards the sun's warm rays. "Boy, it sure does feel good to feel the sun on my face. It was raining cats and dogs when we flew out of Seattle."

"It's always raining in Seattle," I grumbled, before adding in a louder voice, "That doesn't seem right that you had to walk around the whole time. You paid a lot of money for your ticket."

Rhonda waved it off. "I thought it was sweet that so many people wanted to talk with me about their treasured objects. It's fascinating what some people collect. One passenger told me he had a whole cabinet full of disposable vomit bags from airliners from all around the world! I never would have thought to collect those."

"Wow, me either," I laughed along, glad to have a few days to see Europe with my bestie. The Baroness was a good partner, but she wasn't nearly as fun as Rhonda, or as easy to talk to.

After I had proposed this trip, it had taken Rhonda a half hour to call me back and let me know she'd booked a flight to Amsterdam via Los Angeles, leaving the next day. We could have hopped into a car and driven straight through to Luxembourg City in five hours' time, but I didn't want any of the potential players in that smuggling game to recognize me as being that woman they'd seen sneaking around town the past week. Besides, Amsterdam was one of Europe's most popular destinations for a reason. I figured if we were going to spend a few days seeing the sights, Amsterdam was as good a place as any.

Before I could figure out a way to broach the reason for her being here, Rhonda beat me to it. "So, who is this Baroness Sophie Rutherford, exactly? You'd not mentioned her before. And why did you need her to get you into these parties? Is this for your freelance work, or your old job that you'd said you'd retired from? Wink. Wink."

Because I had signed a confidentiality agreement when I'd joined the agency, I'd had to create a fake identity believable enough to fool my friends and family for decades. To simplify my life, I had embellished the truth, instead of inventing a completely fictious background, as some operatives did. So my friends and family thought I was a former art history professor who, after suffering a nasty burnout, left her full-time job to work freelance as an antiques appraiser and journalist for *Hidden Treasures* magazine.

But Rhonda knew me too well, and after years of hearing my increasingly ridiculous excuses as to why I spent so much time abroad, she began to get suspicious. When I refused to tell her exactly what I was doing, she just assumed I was working for the CIA or something similar. To her credit, she had never pushed me to tell her the truth, though she often took stabs in the dark to see how I would react.

I'd never dispelled that notion because I had nothing better to replace it with. Although deception was an integral part of my job, it was extraordinarily difficult to lie to someone who knew me as well as Rhonda did. So I held my tongue each time she made some wild reference to my supposed employer, figuring she would eventually stop asking questions if she knew I wouldn't answer them. And it had worked. Until I was suddenly home a whole lot more than could be justified simply by the death of my husband. That's when I'd told her that I'd retired from my clandestine job; yet to this day I have refused to tell her exactly what I had done for a living. Not that I wasn't proud of my work or worried that she would gossip about it with our friends. I just took that confidentiality contract seriously.

Rhonda grabbed my hand. "Do you swear that you are not working for your former employer?"

It took all of my training to keep my expression and tone relaxed and jovial. For someone who was terrible at reading people, Rhonda could sometimes hit the nail right on the head.

With as much fake sincerity as I could muster, I replied evenly, "I am here on assignment for *Hidden Treasures*, and nothing more. Lady Rutherford was willing to help my employer get me close to the potential smugglers, which is why she graciously used her connections to wrangle an invitation to this gallery show. Thanks to her title and social network, she hears about parties and exclusive events that normal people are not privy to."

"Is Lady Rutherford really royalty?" Rhonda whispered, wide-eyed.

Considering the circumstances, I owed my friend an explanation, even if it was not one hundred percent true. "She is, but a baroness is one of the lower ranks of royalty, and her title is more ceremonial in nature, from what I've understood from her."

I was one of the few who knew the Baroness's deepest and darkest secret, but I sure wasn't going to tell Rhonda the whole truth. If she somehow slipped up and repeated it to Sophie, she would never work with me again. And if Rhonda found out that the Baroness's title was in name only, that her family had gambled away their land generations ago and her money really came from her stockbroker husband, she probably would be less impressed with my royal partner.

"Huh." I could tell from her intonation that she wasn't really impressed, anyway.

"She does wear a real tiara, though," I added. "She inherited it from the original Lady Sophie Rutherford, like three generations ago."

"Oooh, with real diamonds and everything?" Based on how quickly her eyebrows shot up, I'd say that tidbit piqued her interest.

"Yep, a whole bunch of little ones. It's quite beautiful."

"I sure would like to meet her. Lady Sophie does sound like a fascinating person. Maybe we can stop by the hospital before we leave for Luxembourg."

"Oh, gosh," I stuttered, knowing my partner wanted nothing to do with this civilian, as she insisted on calling Rhonda. Heck, if we had met outside of work, the Baroness would not have tolerated me, either.

"I don't know if that's a good idea. She's in a lot of pain right now and they've got her heavily sedated. I am certain she wouldn't want you to see her like that, at least not the first time."

"What happened to her?" Rhonda's voice dripped with concern, which I knew she truly felt. I squeezed her hand, grateful to have such a caring person as my best friend.

"We were at a black-tie event when a Ming vase got knocked over and fell onto her foot and fractured it," I half fibbed. "She hit her jaw pretty badly, as well, when she fell, and her face looks like a puffy grape. It's going to take a couple of weeks before she's back to looking normal, and maybe a few more before she's mobile again."

"Oh my—that sounds painful!"

"I agree. The vase crushed her foot, which means she's in a cast for the coming few weeks and needs to keep it elevated as much as possible. Going to a party, even one with possible smugglers present, isn't really enough reason to risk permanent damage to her foot, I think."

Rhonda patted my hand. "I agree. Well, it's a good thing you called me."

"Speaking of which, I want you to know that she is thrilled you are taking her place. She felt like she'd let me and the magazine down by getting injured. It's a weight off her shoulders to know you're here," I lied.

It was important to me that Rhonda feel appreciated. The Baroness was not happy to have Rhonda here; in fact, she became downright livid when I'd told her the good-to-me news. I still wasn't certain whether she was upset that she couldn't attend the Luxembourg show or that a television celebrity, the type of person Sophie detested on principle, could take her place.

"So what exactly are we going to do at that show in Luxembourg? How are you going to flush out the smugglers?"

"*We* aren't doing anything. You are going to have fun and show everyone what a fabulous person you are. Hopefully, you'll distract our host enough that I can sneak into his gallery's storeroom and take a look around. Don't worry, I'm not going to remove anything from the space. If I find anything I believe to be stolen, a photograph of it will be enough to satisfy my editor, and hopefully give the police a reason to arrest the gallery's owner."

"Then what do you need me for?" Her voice dripped with disappointment.

"I need you to attend the party, so I can join you as your personal assistant. That's my way inside."

"But you're a journalist."

"As you can imagine, the would-be smugglers don't want any journalists attending their sale of possibly stolen artwork, so I had to reinvent myself as the Baroness's PA."

Rhonda gasped. "You mean Lady Sophie, right?"

"Yeah, er, that's what I meant. And since I was meant to be Baroness Rutherford's plus one, I'm now yours."

"I guess that makes sense. But why would I be a good replacement? I'm not from old money, and I don't have a royal title. Are you sure my show's well-known over here?"

Maybe it was because she had never set out to be a television star, but Rhonda couldn't seem to wrap her head around the fact that her show was incredibly successful, at home and abroad. Or perhaps it was because she just wasn't wired to be arrogant enough to let fame go to her head.

Fine arts had always been her passion, and if she hadn't gotten married and fallen pregnant during her first year of college, she would have made a wonderful art history professor. But she chose to stay home and raise her children, instead of finishing school or working full time. To keep her mind occupied, she'd read pretty much everything she could get her hands on that had to do with art, antiques, and collectibles. That solid foundation of knowledge built up over twenty-four years had proved to be incredibly useful—and perhaps even instrumental—to the success of her business and career as a television personality.

It was only after her youngest started high school that she had opened a small antiques shop in town, to keep her mind busy, she'd said. Her business had grown rapidly, thanks to her sharp eye and gift for marketing, so much so that she'd had to rent a larger location within a few months of opening. But business really took off when she began organizing a monthly appraisal day in her shop. It turned out that she had a knack for it. Few other antique dealers could eyeball-estimate an item and get it right as often as she did.

A local television producer happened to stop by during one such day and was so impressed by her quick wit, charismatic personality, accurate estimation, and almost photographic memory when it came to antiques and collectibles that he asked her to host a new show that was basically an American rip-off of *Antiques Roadshow*. Within six months, it got picked up by a national television channel that renamed it *Antiques Time with Rhonda Rhodes*. The rest, as they say, was history.

She still had her shop, but two of her nieces were running it. From what I'd seen last time I stopped by, they had as sharp of an eye for antiques as their aunt did.

"Oh, yes, *Antiques Time* is really popular over here. It's on BBC and seen all over Europe. If our host watches television, I am certain he will recognize you."

My bestie's chest puffed out. "That's amazing! I never thought to ask my agent about our viewing audience outside of the States, but I should have. I'll have to ask her for stats when I get back. Maybe we can film a few shows over in Europe."

"Oh, wow, that would be great! I bet you would get some fascinating objects across your desk."

"I bet I would." Rhonda cupped her hands against the shop's window, looking towards the back of the espresso bar's rather narrow interior. "Say, the coffee's gone right through me. I need to powder my nose. I'll be back in a jiff."

"Sure thing." When I noticed the long line of women already waiting for the restroom, I knew it was as good a moment as any to reach out to my employer. During our ride over, the name Alistair McPhee kept niggling at my brain. It seemed so familiar, but I couldn't place it. Had he directed a few movies I liked? Or was he a former target we had once recovered an object from?

If so, I wanted to stay well away from his party. Most collectors were not happy to hand over the painting, book, or sculpture they had spent millions to acquire, even if Rosewood's lawyers could prove it had been stolen. They tended to hold a grudge. If I had taken something from him, then I would not be able to attend, no matter how badly Rhonda wanted me to go.

I texted Alistair's name to Myrtle, my company contact, to see whether she recognized it, before letting her know that Rhonda wanted to attend his party. I didn't bother checking the time; she was an insomniac and most likely awake, whatever the time in Seattle. Myrtle Rosewood was a seventy-something computer whiz and mother to my boss. She was as feisty as she was smart, but with a mouth that would put a sailor to shame. Luckily, the company-mandated swear jar on her desk did help to temper her choice words.

Far faster than expected, my phone pinged with a reaction from Myrtle. Her message's tone and contents were not at all what I was expecting.

"Are you kidding me—Alistair McPhee, the Hollywood director? That guy's a ghost! We've been searching for him for years. I'll send you a list of the movie props he's suspected of having stolen ten years ago. If Rhonda really did get you an invitation to a party he'll be attending, then you better get your butt to it! Are you with Rhonda now? Call me as soon as you're free."

To my utter shock, Myrtle signed off with a smiley emoji—something she had never done before. I guess she truly was happy with this news.

"Movie props?" I mumbled. It took all of my willpower not to stick out my lower lip. My major was art history, not pop history. Movie props didn't sound that enticing, and were definitely nothing the Baroness would have flown over to Europe to purchase.

When Myrtle's second message arrived with the list of stolen items, I had trouble keeping my jaw from falling open. Audrey Hepburn's necklace from *Breakfast at Tiffany's*, James Dean's switchblade from *Rebel Without a Cause*, Marilyn Monroe's white dress from *The Seven Year Itch*, and the Maltese Falcon statue from the film of the same name jumped out on a list of thirty-three items.

Luckily for me, Rhonda was taking her time in the restroom, giving me plenty of time to process my shock and surprise. Alistair McPhee was a huge find, and it was all thanks to my bestie that we were welcome. It was only too bad that I had to keep her in the dark as to my true reason for wanting to attend.

I scanned the list once again, wondering whether Alistair still possessed any of them. If he did, he would be foolish to leave them out for all to see. Several of these pieces were quite unique and would be recognized by even the most casual movie fan.

I bit my lip, considering the possibilities. Even if this was a fruitless assignment, I couldn't pass this chance up. He was apparently hard to track, meaning this off-chance to get close to him was not to be missed. Besides, I'd never seen Myrtle so happy about finding a new lead and didn't want to disappoint her by skipping the party.

When Rhonda returned several minutes later, a new layer of makeup freshly applied, I added a bit of sparkle to my voice. "Say, I was thinking, that party does sound like a lot of fun. I mean, how often do you get invited to a shindig hosted by a Hollywood celebrity? I only attend boring artsy-fartsy events for the magazine."

"Yeah, right? That's what I was thinking. I'll text Colin and let him know we do want to come." Rhonda's face lit up, as I knew it would.

Her telephone beeped a few minutes later, and after reading the incoming message, Rhonda began to cheer in delight. "Colin says we are more than welcome! But we'd better not be late tomorrow. The boat leaves promptly at six. We can make that, can't we?"

She looked over at me with pleading eyes, not realizing how happy her news made me. We couldn't miss the gallery show in Luxembourg, but that was taking place later this week. Even if we spent the night at Alistair's, we'd be back with four days to spare, giving us plenty of time to take in a few sights before duty called again.

I patted her hand. "Of course we can."

7

Fan Girl Myrtle

After I'd gotten Rhonda settled into her hotel room, I offered to get her some bottled water from the front desk while she unpacked. In actuality, I wanted a moment alone to call Myrtle.

"Are you certain Alistair McPhee is hosting the party?" my company contact barked into the phone as soon as the call connected.

"That's what the guy who invited us said, and he'd even mentioned Alistair being a Hollywood director. He was sitting next to Rhonda in first class, so he's probably got money."

"Incredible. We suspect that McPhee stole five million dollars' worth of film props from a WorldWide Studios warehouse ten years ago. He vanished shortly after. There was a blip on the radar a few months after the robbery, when he was spotted on a film set in Spain, but he disappeared again before anyone could verify that it was really him. This is the first time he's stuck his head up in all that time!"

"That's amazing. What a coincidence that Rhonda was sitting next to one of the invitees."

"Lady Sophie does have an extensive network of informants and friends, but none that would have known about this party. She couldn't have gotten us close to someone like McPhee. I like this Rhonda already."

Inwardly, I cheered for my friend, secretly thrilled that Rhonda had done something my real partner could not. It confirmed for me that I had done the right thing by inviting her to come over and help on the Luxembourg mission, despite the Baroness's objections.

"Are we certain McPhee stole all of the props on your list, and that he still has them in his possession? Ten years is a long time to hang on to so many ill-gotten goods," I reasoned.

I knew from my years with Rosewood that not everyone suspected of harboring stolen items was really harboring stolen items. That was why we didn't alert the police as soon as we received a new lead to a missing object. Sometimes our intel was wrong, and we didn't want to offend the art-loving elite without good reason. Worming my way into a suspect's inner circle and getting them to let their guard down was usually the best way of discovering where the item had been hidden away and how the person had acquired it. It did help to have a woman's touch, but I would never do anything I couldn't tell my mother about.

"I have no idea if he still has all of the stolen items or not—that's why we're asking you to go to his party and try to find out," Myrtle barked, before continuing in a calmer tone, "We are ninety-nine percent sure that Alistair is the thief. The man they arrested for the crime, a property or 'props' master named Gary Thompson, maintained that Alistair was the mastermind, and all he had done was let McPhee inside. But his own lawyer couldn't prove that McPhee was involved, and Gary ended up being sentenced to nine years. Shortly after, Alistair popped up in Spain and tried to sell a few of the props that had been stolen during that robbery to our contact, which is why we suspect Thompson wasn't lying, after all. But Alistair disappeared again, before we could send anyone over to check out the lead."

"I see why you are so eager for me to attend."

"I could kiss Rhonda for getting you invited to his party, and I've never even met her." Myrtle paused a moment before adding in a shy voice, "Did Reggie tell you that we watch her show, *Antiques Time*? I hope that after this is all done, we might be able to meet her in person."

I pulled the phone back from my ear and stared at the receiver, confused by her fan-girl tone. Myrtle was always so tough, it was adorable to see her melting at the mention of my best friend's name. "I am certain we can arrange a meeting."

"That's wonderful," she half whispered, before adding in a louder and gruffer tone, "Did you catch the man's name, the one who invited Miss Rhodes to the party?"

"You can call her Rhonda, and yes, it's Colin Worchester."

"You should have sent it over with your first message," she scolded as I heard her fingers flying across her keyboard. "Give me a second to look him up."

And we're back, I thought. Myrtle usually treated me as a helpless rookie, not the senior agent that I was.

Ten second later, she picked the receiver back up. "He's not mentioned in our databases, so your focus is on the host, Alistair McPhee. Where's this party being held?"

"I'm not certain. We are being picked up from Central Station in Amsterdam tomorrow evening, by a boat that will take us to the party's location."

"Alright. Well, get us any intel you can about the host, his collection, and especially his location. Leave your phone on so we can track you, and we will arrange for backup if you request it."

"You mean local law enforcement, I hope?"

"If you can verify for us that it really is McPhee, then yes, we will do everything we can to get Interpol to your location. You have no idea how much Reggie and I want to catch this guy. But you need to be certain it really is him and not some schmuck masquerading as McPhee."

"And how am I supposed to do that? The last known picture of him is ten years old. A man's appearance can change quite a bit in that span of time."

"Then you'll have to watch the other guests, zero in on those who knew him intimately, and see how they react to his appearance and behavior. Unless you can manage to pull his fingerprints, of course. With that new app I installed on your phone, you should be able to scan any prints in and check it against our databases."

"Excellent. Will do."

8

High As A Kite

When I returned to Rhonda's hotel room, she didn't answer her door. Luckily, I had taken up the receptionist's offer of a second key card, allowing me to find my friend sprawled out on the couch, snoring like an old man.

"Your neck is going to hurt, if you stay like that," I muttered as I shook her awake, or at least enough to get her up. She hadn't traveled abroad in so long, the jet lag must have gotten to her. Seeing as she was clearly too tired to see the sights and enjoy them, I figured letting her sleep for an hour or two would be better than trying to keep her awake. We could always take a walk around Amsterdam's gorgeous historical center, once she was feeling more fit.

After helping my bestie into bed and a more comfortable position, I decided this was the perfect moment to visit my partner and update her on this new situation, before we left town.

"If you don't mind, I'm going to go see how Lady Sophie is doing," I said in a soft voice, not wanting to jar Rhonda completely awake. "I'll be back within the hour to wake you up, otherwise you might not sleep tonight."

She turned on her side and yawned into her pillow, yet her eyes remained closed. "Jet lag is a killer. Please do give my regards to Lady Sophie."

"That's sweet. I will."

When I arrived at the hospital, the Baroness was awake. She looked so sad, propped up with cushions in that hospital bed. But her head was held high, and her trademark tiara rested comfortably on top of her somewhat disheveled bob.

"My dear Carmen, it's lovely to see you." Her voice's pitch was higher than normal and her pupils seemed to be dilated. A glance at the medical chart hanging off the back of her bed made clear that she was receiving a pretty substantial dose of painkillers through that intravenous line.

She leaned forward, her arms spread wide, as if she was waiting for an uncharacteristic hug. Yep, she was high as a kite. I responded by leaning in, gently hugging her fragile shoulders, afraid to harm her further.

"I'm not made of porcelain," she replied gruffly and squeezed back, quite hard. Was she trying to prove a point, that she wasn't as weak as she appeared, or was it the painkillers that made her do it?

When she patted the side of her bed, I sank down onto the fluffy mattress and took her hand.

"So, do tell me that you've come to your senses about that film director's party and are going to decline the invitation. Reggie and Myrtle told me about it, but it really does sound like a waste of time. Shouldn't you be focusing on the Luxembourg assignment?" Her words were difficult to understand, thanks to her clenched jaw.

I eyed her tiara, wondering how it would taste. Luckily for the Baroness, I wasn't planning on making her keep her word. "Actually, I just spoke to Myrtle about it. She and Reggie really want me to attend. It turns out Alistair McPhee is suspected of having stolen several million dollars' worth of collectibles."

"You mean movie props. What a load of nonsense. Most of them look as if they could have been purchased over the counter. It's not as if they are handcrafted works of art." The Baroness dismissed McPhee's collection with a wave of her hand. It must be the medicine, I figured, because she was usually more tactful about such matters. At least, in my presence.

"It's the story that makes them unique." I'd spent a few minutes on the tram over here searching the internet, trying to address the same concern Sophie raised. Why were these props worth so much? And was there really a black market for stolen items such as these?

It turned out to be yes to both questions. Apparently certain kinds of movie props, especially more iconic ones such as Luke Skywalker's lightsaber, the Scarecrow's costume from *The Wizard of Oz*, or a dress worn by Marilyn Monroe, were worth millions. And as such, theft was a real concern for the major studios and private collectors. If Alistair had stolen millions of dollars' worth of props, then it was worth my time to find out whether he still had any of them in his possession. I could only hope that the party was taking place in his home or wherever he kept his collection.

"Yes, but anyone can buy a replica of it at a shop. Why would someone pay more, simply because it was seen on screen?"

"Why would someone pay millions for an Andy Warhol print? There are several hundred copies of them in circulation, but originals still go for seven figures or more."

"That's different. These things were made for a movie, not a museum," the Baroness said and looked away.

"Are you really upset about the props? Or is there something else going on?"

"Reggie seems tickled pink with your friend Rhonda."

Aha, so her nose was out of joint, I realized. "It was pure luck that Rhonda was invited to this party—"

"What's your cover?" she snapped, cutting me off.

I shifted uncomfortably, my discomfort caused more by the answer I was about to give than the mattress. "I'm going as myself, just plain ole' Carmen De Luca."

The Baroness was aghast, as I was afraid she would be. "What if one of the guests also attends the gallery show in Luxembourg? Won't it compromise your cover?"

"I don't think so," I stated confidently, only because I'd had time to work out the answer to her valid question.

"For this party, I'm simply Rhonda's childhood friend. Seeing as how you gave Rhonda your ticket, it's not strange that I would also be at the Luxembourg show."

"As if I would know someone like Rhonda Rhodes," Sophie muttered.

I cocked my head at her. "What did you say?"

"Nothing," she growled.

Yes, her nose was definitely out of joint. As much as I wanted to talk it out with her, now was not the time to do so. Not only because I had my friend waiting for me back at the hotel room, but because the Baroness was high on painkillers and probably wouldn't even recall the conversation, once she'd come down.

So instead, I rose from the bed and patted her shoulder. "I'm glad to see you're feeling better. I'll call every day to check in on you, alright?"

The Baroness's lips turned downward, but otherwise she ignored my last remark. "Oh, did you see the doctor on your way in? He should be able to fit me with a walking cast in a few days. We may not need Rhonda for the Luxembourg assignment, after all."

Now it was my turn to frown. "Wait a second, you have a compound fracture in your foot, Sophie. And your jaw is as purple as a prune. There is no amount of makeup that's going to hide the color or swelling. Besides, the doctor was pretty clear that you needed to stay off your foot as much as possible during the first six weeks, if you want it to heal properly."

"Poppycock. I'm going crazy just sitting here, and it sounds like your friend is doing her best to ruin all of our hard work by whisking you off to a Hollywood party!"

"A party being hosted by a man suspected of stealing millions of dollars in collectibles. I'd say attending this party is more work than pleasure, at least for me, wouldn't you?"

Instead of answering me, she reached for the pitcher of water, placed to her left but just out of her reach. I leaned over to move it closer, when she slapped my hand away.

"I can do it," she snapped, with an intensity that made clear her refusal was more to do with pride. Before her husband died of a heart attack on the stock market floor, the Baroness hadn't worried her pretty little head about much of anything. After coasting through life all of her adult years, everyone assumed she would marry fast because she would need someone to take care of her. To everyone's surprise, she had not even dated since

Richard's passing. Instead, she'd done everything her way ever since, and had not relied on a man to accomplish any of her goals. Having several million in the bank did, of course, help further fuel her sense of self-reliance. She certainly had enough money to get herself out of pretty much any situation.

She'd tried the charity circuit, but had quickly bored of organizing endless high teas and champagne brunches. Working for Rosewood gave her a sense of accomplishment she could get nowhere else. That was probably why Sophie was so upset about her hospitalization. Yet, she'd also referred to Rhonda several times as "charming," her code word for someone beneath her.

My sympathy for the Baroness started to fade into resentment. *If that's what she thinks of Rhonda, she must think I'm a fool. I laugh at the wrong jokes, spill drinks on my favorite clothes, and am definitely not rich or stylish enough to get invited to the high-class parties our targets attend. Would the Baroness even talk to me if we weren't partners? Probably not.*

I didn't want to leave angry, but I was tired of trying to convince Sophie of this party's importance and Rhonda's goodness. I had a sneaking suspicion that she would never completely understand either, anyway. Films and pop memorabilia held no interest for her. Movies were not something she or her friends indulged in or discussed, I suspected. At least not the kinds of films that were popular in the theaters. I could see her sitting down to some sort of challenging old French movie, but not one produced by James Cameron or Steven Spielberg.

So instead of wasting my breath, I decided to let bygones be bygones and skip the argument. I gave her my usual kiss on each cheek greeting, then bid her *adieu*, only after promising to keep her abreast of our developments via telephone.

9

Meeting The Invitees

When our taxi hopped the curb and we squealed to a stop in front of the correct dock at two minutes past six, I was certain we had missed the boat.

To my relief, a cluster of well-dressed people with small bags still waited at the end of the designated pier. We had downsized our luggage and my dear friend Rhonda had trouble deciding which of her hair extensions and costume changes should be shoved into her carry-on. We had left the rest behind in our hotel room. Considering the ludicrous amount my employer was paying per night for us to sleep there, the staff couldn't complain about having to babysit our luggage.

It had taken all of my willpower to not rush her along, for fear of her realizing that I might have an ulterior motive for attending this party. Luckily, she knew that I was a stickler for being on time, which made my concern that she would make us late and we would miss the boat in character. I hated the fact that I had to double-check that my reactions fit with the personage I was playing, especially when I was being myself.

I began to speedwalk toward the group at the end of the pier, until I realized that Rhonda couldn't move so quickly in her heels. They were wedge-cut, but a touch too high for her robust frame. So I relaxed my pace and made do with studying the other guests as we approached.

There were only a handful of people on the dock, but all were quite swanky qua dress and style. I was a little concerned that our casual attire—baggy linen trousers and a loose-fitting blouse for me, and a low-cut sundress with a fringe-lined pink cardigan for Rhonda—wasn't appropriate. Luckily, we'd both brought formal wear to change into, if need be.

Apparently my bestie had the same concerns, for she leaned into my ear and whispered, "These are real Hollywood types, aren't they? I don't know about this. I've got a feeling that we aren't really going to fit in. I bet that Alistair fellow is going to be upset with Colin for inviting us. Speaking of which, where is he? If Colin doesn't show before the boat disembarks, then I refuse to go."

Her feet slowed to the point where we were barely moving. She was serious about not going, unless Colin was on board.

I refused to panic, instead reminding myself that I could manipulate my bestie, if I needed to. It wouldn't be the first time. The way she chewed on her lower lip, I was afraid she was going to bite clean through it before we reached the others. Instead of playing up her fears, I decided to shrug off her nervousness as pointless.

"Come on, Rhonda, we are all adults. Colin knows the host, we don't, and he says we will be welcome. If Alistair doesn't want us to board, he'll tell us to leave, and we'll leave. It's that simple."

Rhonda's shoulders seemed to relax a smidgeon before she gushed, "You're right. I'm overthinking this."

I sighed in relief, knowing Myrtle was champing at the bit to find out more about the party's host and the objects he may or may not still have in his possession. In the fifteen years I'd worked for Rosewood, I'd never seen her so fired up before and didn't want to disappoint her by missing the party.

Thankfully, I didn't have to manipulate anyone, for moments later, a limousine sped up to the marina and Colin stepped out. He crossed over to the group, squeezing Rhonda's shoulder before saying hello to the rest. By the way my bestie was blushing, I think she was enjoying his attention.

"Hello everyone, I'm Colin Worchester. It's been a while, but I think I recognize a few old faces."

He looked to a middle-aged woman dressed in a pencil skirt and matching jacket that must have been tailored specifically to fit over her surgically enhanced breasts. Come to think of it, her cheekbones were unnaturally high, her lips more bee-stung than what seemed normal for her facial structure, and her forehead was completely wrinkle-free.

"Divine—is that you?" Colin asked, a smile playing on his lips.

The blonde crossed over to him and kissed his cheek. "Colin, darling. It's been too long!"

"You've had some work done, I see. You look great—I hardly recognized you."

For most women, that would have been a slap in the face. But Divine seemed to take it as a compliment.

"What have you been up to these days? Are you still in the business?" she asked in a voice high enough to shatter crystal.

Colin shook his head. "No, I've moved on to international finance. I have an important meeting in London next week, otherwise I might not have come."

"I know what you mean. I wasn't really sure I wanted to see Alistair again, not after what he did."

Colin's eyes darkened and he opened his mouth to reply, until he glanced at me and Rhonda, standing close and listening in.

"Let's try to forget the past and just enjoy the company and hospitality, shall we?" Colin raised her hand to his lips and kissed it, bringing a smile to Divine's face.

However, she seemed less interested in forgetting the past than Colin. "Did your invitation explain why he's asked us all to come out here, after all these years?"

He shook his head. "No, but considering he has been hiding out for ten years and finally decides to pop up, out of nowhere, how could I say no?"

"Exactly. After all he owes me, I'm looking forward to hearing him grovel for our forgiveness."

"So, my dear, what are you starring in these days?" Colin smiled, obviously trying to keep the conversation light. "Or have you retired to a sunny island and left the film industry behind?"

"I wish, but I never did earn enough from the Massacre films to make that happen. No, I'm the face of the Maxine's Choice Shopping Channel these days. It's a great gig," Divine said as she patted her blonde bob. Her chunky bracelet sparkled in the light as she moved. I doubted it was a high-quality silver, and knew all of those gems were fakes. She probably bought it on her shopping channel, I figured.

"The Massacre films?" Rhonda whispered into my ear, loudly enough for the rest to hear.

When Divine acted as if she hadn't heard her, Colin turned to us and smiled.

"Please let me introduce you to my guests, Rhonda and Carmen."

Divine's face dropped. "Oh, I thought Alistair said no guests were allowed. My husband wanted to join me, but I told him no."

Before anyone could respond, a boat approached the dock at a clipped speed, slowing just in time to fishtail itself parallel to the dock. It was obviously not the captain's first ride. A woman sporting a uniform leaned out and yelled, "Are you the McPhee party?"

Divine waved her hand. "Yes, that's us. Ahoy there!"

The boat's steward didn't check our names or even seem to do a head count. After helping us on board, the captain announced we would arrive at our destination within twenty minutes, then ignored us. We soon set off at a fast pace down a narrow river that led to the ocean.

The seats ran down the sides and middle, and were placed to ensure that each guest could converse with as many of their seatmates as possible. I could imagine that it was primarily used for business events and private parties, where easy conversation was a must.

This group, however, did their best to ignore each other, as if they were afraid to accept that the other person was actually here. Did they know each other from Hollywood? Or were they here simply because they were connected to Alistair, in one form or another?

An uncomfortable silence descended as soon as the boat sped off, but I knew that I only had to wait a moment, and that would all change. One advantage of being with Rhonda was that she tended to get chatty when she was nervous. And based on how tight she was holding onto her handbag's straps, she was borderline panicked. It didn't help matters that Divine had confirmed her fear—that we would not be welcome at the party.

Sure enough, it only took a few minutes, and then she was off and running. She turned to the man seated closest to her, an older gentleman with slicked-back hair who looked like he'd walked off the set of *Goodfellas*. He was as wide as a bus and dressed in a shiny gray suit that seemed a bit snug.

"Hi, there. I'm Rhonda Rhodes, and who might you be?" Rhonda asked.

A flash of annoyance briefly crossed his face before his expression settled into one of bemusement. "I'm Mac Mahoney, but most people call me 'Moneybags.' I got that nickname because I've financed so many films."

Colin's eyes widened when he heard the man say his name. "Ah, yes. I didn't recognize your face, but as I recall, you were the 'private investor' who once came to our office and threatened to break my legs if I didn't tell you where Alistair was, after he did his disappearing act."

Though his tone was light, his words were pretty dark. Mac's eyelids lowered to slits. "Oh, yeah? I suppose it could have been me. There have been so many delinquent payers over the years. It's a rough business, loaning those Hollywood types money. Lots of risk involved, for both parties."

"Funny. For several years, I thought you had found Alistair and done away with him, until I received this invitation from him. I do hope he'll still be alive at the conclusion of our festivities."

"I certainly hope so. He still owes me quite a bit of money, and I expect him to make good on what he promised. Which means he's no good to me dead."

"Good. I'm glad to hear you say it aloud."

The two men glared at each other so intently, I was almost expecting one of them to start shooting bullets out of their eyes.

I was glad for my friend's assertiveness. Not only did she help to break the ice, she also helped me work out who was who. Once we got to our destination, I could pass the names on to Myrtle. I wasn't much of a gambling person, but I would bet that Moneybags Mahoney was in our company databases, as well.

I glanced over the rest of the guests, wondering whether they were also sought by the Rosewood Agency. One woman who looked to be in her mid-sixties sat apart from the rest and had turned her body so she didn't have to take part in the conversation. Whoever she was, she was gorgeous for her age, with a regal demeanor that reminded me of Greta Garbo; all she needed was a cigarette holder. Her dress was a black silk taffeta evening gown that shimmered in the light, topped with a chiffon wrap that was completely out of place on such a shabby boat. She'd twisted her long gray hair into a loose bun that was held up by a gorgeous vintage metal pin with a scroll-like handle, revealing pearl-drop earrings that fit perfectly with her outfit.

Before I could try to engage her in conversation, the mouth of the river came into view. I stood, to get a better look at the ocean before us—a flat gray expanse of white-capped waves that seemed to go on forever—when one of the stewards reappeared, a black bag held out before him.

"Your host does request that this event remain private, which is why he has asked us to secure all of your phones in this locked bag before we arrive. He does not wish to have any photos from the party posted online, until after the event has concluded."

"I'm not giving up my phone!" Divine exclaimed.

"We have orders to gather your phones before we arrive, otherwise you are not welcome to join the event."

"I just flew twelve hours to get here and now you're telling me I have to give up my phone or not come in? This is ridiculous," Mac stated and half rose out of his chair, in a clear attempt to physically intimidate the steward.

To his credit, the much smaller man did not flinch. "It is only for the duration of the event. After the party is over, your phones will be returned to you."

"Fine," Mac growled before finally consenting.

As I dropped my phone into the satchel, I was kicking myself internally for not having purchased a burner phone during my time off, for just this sort of situation. It was an amateur move, and one I hoped not to repeat anytime soon. I would have to rectify that situation before I went to Luxembourg, in case the gallery's owner made the same request.

Why did Alistair demand such extreme measures for a party, and why was he being so secretive about our final destination? Was there something more sinister going on tonight? Or did his reasoning have something to do with why he had decided to resurface again, ten years after the theft? Did he still possess any of the items on Myrtle's list, and where would he be most likely to hide them?

I tapped my chin, considering his options. Would he hide them at all? The statute of limitations had expired years ago, so technically he couldn't be arrested for possessing stolen goods.

This was my favorite part of the search, trying to anticipate the hows, wheres, and whys. I could feel my pulse accelerating as I considered how to best approach and fool my target, my mind teeming with possibilities.

10

Walk The Plank

Soon the sandy dunes of the Dutch coast and gray-blue water of the North Sea were in sight. The mouth of the small river we'd been following was filled with a lock for large boats, a dock for a car ferry to England, IJmuiden's industrial harbor, and a plethora of marinas for large boats and ships—mostly used for fishing, I gathered, based on all the nets hanging off of them. Yet we kept cruising forward at a good speed, as if we were nowhere near our destination. Were we headed towards another boat or going back to shore?

A few moments later, I got my answer when our boat's engines throttled back. The captain slowly pulled up to a two-masted ship that looked like it had just sailed away from a seventeenth-century battlefield. There were no cannon holes in the hull, at least none visible from where we were positioned, but there could have easily been.

"Wow, is that a brigantine?" Colin asked.

I stared at the vessel before me, not knowing whether it was technically a boat or a ship. Sailing was more of the Baroness's thing, though I understood she preferred skippered yachts to boats.

A dark shadow passing overhead made me look up. An elderly man wearing a pirate costume stared down at us from the ship's deck. His eye patch and large sword, along with his menacing glare, didn't make me feel welcome.

"Ahoy, maties!" he called down, his rich baritone voice rolling over me like a wave of fog. On his command, a narrow gangplank was lowered so the guests could ascend to the deck. Yet before we did, the captain of our smaller boat skipped up the plank and handed the locked pouch with our phones inside over to a scruffy-looking man with a captain's hat on. I'd guess him to be in his fifties, given the gray of his hair and size of his paunch. Only after the phones had been passed from one boat to the other and the captain had made his way back up to the bridge were we allowed to ascend.

"Alistair, is that you under there?" Divine giggled when she reached the top of the wooden plank.

"Nice costume," Mac said. Because his voice was so gruff, it made his words sounds like a threat.

The Greta Garbo lookalike drifted past without a word. So far, it was as if she was a ghost. No one seemed interested in interacting with her, nor she with the others, not even the host. So why was she here?

"What an entrance! You still got it." Colin slapped Alistair on the back when he reached the top.

Rhonda and I trailed just behind him. When my bestie was about to step onto the deck, the pirate sprang forward and pointed his—hopefully fake—sword at us. "Aargh! What do I see here—uninvited guests?"

He looked so menacing that if he told Rhonda to walk the plank, I bet she'd willingly jump overboard.

"Let them aboard, Alistair. I invited them," Colin stated loudly.

All of a sudden, our pirate transformed into a two-year-old having a tantrum. "I specifically said in my letter that you were to bring no guests! How difficult a request is that to fulfill?"

Colin started to retort, but Alistair held up a gloved hand to silence him. "Who are you two? You better not be lawyers or journalists. Speak now or walk the plank!"

I breathed a sigh of relief, glad I was not traveling as a journalist on this assignment. Yet my respite was fleeting. When Alistair sprung up and pointed that stupid sword at us again, all I wanted to do was grab it out of his hands. Instead, I cowered as if I was scared, mirroring Rhonda's real terror as I lay a hand on my friend's shoulder to comfort her.

"Colin said it would be alright if we tagged along…" Rhonda managed through chattering teeth. The narrow strip of wood we were still standing was trembling so badly, I was afraid it was going to shake loose and we would fall into the cold water below.

"For pity's sake, Alistair, let them pass," Colin said in a bored voice, clearly done with his antics.

"I said no guests," the pirate yelled out before lunging at us.

"Heavens to Betsy!" Rhonda shrieked as she covered her eyes with her hands.

I held her tight, to ensure she didn't fall off the gangplank in her fright, when our attacker suddenly froze midjab and stared at Rhonda.

"Why does your voice sound so familiar?"

He lifted up his eye patch to study her better. Our host's face went as white as the ship's sails and he stammered, "Shiver me timbers! You are Rhonda Rhodes, aren't you?"

"The one and only. That's why I invited her," Colin interjected, a smile in his voice.

"You should have told me straightaway! Here I am, in the presence of greatness and I'm acting the fool," Alistair chastised his invited guest before holding out a hand to Rhonda.

Once she'd boarded, Alistair stepped back and bowed deeply. "Dear Ms. Rhodes, please forgive the theatrics. My name is Alistair McPhee, and it is an honor to have you on board *La Vida Loca*."

"You named your ship 'Crazy Life'?" I couldn't help but ask.

"That was its name when I boarded." Alistair smiled, yet his gaze and flippant remark made clear that I was not important enough to do anything but humor.

He sought one of Rhonda's hands and slowly brought it to his lips, keeping his eyes locked on hers the entire time. Something about the scene before me made my own eyes narrow in suspicion.

Just before his pucker made contact with the back of her hand, he asked, "Is it true, Ms. Rhodes, that you have a photographic memory?"

I knew from past experience that this was the question Rhonda was asked most often. Her show was edited before it went out on air, but the appraisals were done live in front of a studio audience. Her ability to quickly and accurately recall, with almost encyclopedic accuracy, an artist's oeuvre and pinpoint a specific object's current value was uncanny. It didn't matter whether it was a salt cellar made by Meissen, or an abstract painted by Vasily Kandinsky, she knew how much it was worth.

It wasn't because Rhonda had a photographic memory, but because she had spent decades absorbing everything she could about the artists and artwork that were popular among collectors. She was just lucky enough to be able to accurately recall what she had read, decades later.

It was not only an impressive skill, it helped to make her show a resounding success. Over the years, several experts had tried to challenge her, but Rhonda's estimates were far more accurate. Once, she had even spotted a forgery that had fooled experts for years, live on her show.

"Please call me Rhonda," my bestie breathed. "I don't know if it's photographic or not, but I do tend to remember everything I've read about collectibles over the years. Though I must admit, my abilities are limited to the fine arts. I usually can't remember someone's name until I've said it about a hundred times, so I hope your guests don't get mad at me if I forget who they are!"

"I have seen every one of your episodes online. The items brought on it are often quite interesting, but you, my dear, make the show. I am constantly amazed by your expansive knowledge and quick recall. It is an honor—no, a dream come true—to have you here today!"

Rhonda blushed, clearly enjoying the attention. And why shouldn't she? My bestie was a fascinating woman and a successful television presenter, to boot. It was easy to forget that she was not simply a girl I grew up with, but a powerful businessperson in her own right.

"Who are you, you divine creature?" Rhonda gazed up at Alistair in wonder.

"A Hollywood director, or at least I used to be. My kind of films went out of fashion in the nineties, and I haven't had much work since." He paused and regarded her with a grimace, as if he was already anticipating a negative reaction to his next comment. "I specialized in horror films."

Rhonda's eyes widened, and her eyebrows shot up. "Oh, my! Horror is not really my cup of tea, but it's still fascinating to meet you."

Alistair smiled again; apparently Rhonda's enthusiastic response was good enough for him. "Tell me, dear Rhonda, do you know much about movie memorabilia? I have an extensive collection that I would love to show you later. Perhaps you would do me the honors of appraising a few of my more valuable collectibles? I wouldn't trust most experts' evaluations, but I would value yours."

My ears perked up at the mention of movie props. Something on Myrtle's list of thirty-three missing items might just be among those he asked Rhonda to evaluate. I wished I could share the list with her, but knowing she would soon be privy to the collection's location was already a huge step forward. I had to hand it to Rhonda; even without knowingly doing so, she was leading me straight to the potentially stolen goods that I was here to verify.

"Golly, I guess I could. I usually appraise fine arts, but we get enough other stuff through on our show, that I'd be happy to take a stab at it," Rhonda said, but her eyes were no longer on her host. She seemed to be studying the ship.

I did the same, taking in the large mast poles, rolled-up sails, multitude of rope ladders, and, high above, a crow's nest. It felt as if we had stepped into a *Pirates of the Caribbean* film set; all that was missing were Davy Jones and his crew.

"Alistair, you have to tell me where you found this fantastic ship," Rhonda said. "Did you rent it for the party?"

Our host laughed heartily in response. I didn't think her remark was particularly funny; the same thoughts had been swirling around my head. "No, my dear, this is my home."

My ears were on fire now. If Alistair lived on this boat, then his collection must also be on board. This assignment was going to be as easy as cooking oatmeal. Best of all, Myrtle was going to be thrilled. Now all I had to do was get my phone back and call it in.

Rhonda slapped our host lightly on the shoulder and chortled. "Are you kidding me? How do you even buy an old boat like this?"

He grinned widely. "This ship was the set of a low-budget war movie I directed ten years ago. A Spanish friend of mine was producing it, and when the original director backed out at the last minute, he asked me to take over. It's why I came to Europe. They didn't have enough cash to pay me my usual fee, so I accepted this ship in lieu of a salary. I've been sailing the seas ever since. It was never my intention to live on it for so long, but it is pretty special. I mean, how many people can say they live on a pirate ship?"

So that was why he had been in Spain ten years ago. According to Myrtle, it was at a party in Madrid that Alistair had approached one of our trusted contacts and offered to sell him James Dean's switchblade and Marilyn Monroe's white dress from *The Seven Year Itch*, for a reasonable price. The collector was quite interested, but after he asked about the items' provenance, Alistair lost interest in their conversation and, shortly after, left the party. No one knew where he was staying or working at the time, and our trusted source never ran into him again.

Rosewood's intel confirmed that Alistair had disappeared around the time of the robbery and the convicted thief, one Gary Thompson, had always maintained that Alistair had stolen the items, not him. Because no physical proof of Alistair's involvement was found at the scene, it was never confirmed. If our collector had not tipped us off to Alistair's location, or the fact that he'd offered to sell him two items that were taken during the robbery shortly after it occurred, we never would have known that Alistair was really involved.

"So that's how you've stayed hidden for so long. There were rumors of sightings now and again, but none of my people could get confirmation. They must have showed up after you'd sailed away," Mac said, surprise in his voice as if he'd just solved a puzzle that had been eating at his subconscious for years.

Alistair regarded him with half-lidded eyes and resignation in his voice. "I guess they did. I wondered if you would still be looking for me, after all these years."

"The guys I work with never forget a debt." Mac smiled, but it was not a warm and fuzzy grin. It was cold, calculating, and made me even more nervous than I already was.

Alistair smiled, but not as easily this time. "I guess I've gotten good at living under the radar."

"Oh, did you get into trouble, back in the States?" Rhonda asked, excitement and terror mingling in her tone. I held my breath, wondering how he would respond. Given her state of mind, I was afraid Rhonda might start clapping, if he did announce that he was an outlaw.

"I got into trouble with the IRS when I refused to pay what they thought I owed them. So I took off to Europe and haven't paid my taxes since," he said, with pride in his voice.

Apparently tax evasion wasn't sexy to Rhonda because she seemed indifferent to his news.

I concealed my own frown of disappointment with the back of my hand. I hadn't really expected him to tell us the truth about the robbery or his involvement, but it would have been refreshing if he had.

"Don't you miss living in Hollywood?" Rhonda asked.

"No, not really. Once you get stamped a 'has-been' and investors and the studios stop showing interest, Hollywood can be a cruel place to live. My parents passed years ago, and I never married, so there's no one left to miss me. I can go wherever I want, whenever I please." Despite the lightness in his voice, I sensed an undercurrent of sadness.

A moment later, he shook his head, as if he was wiping the thoughts from his mind. "Why are we talking about boring things such as the past? We should be celebrating the now! That's what I learned recently—how to live in the present. You can't change the past, and no one knows what the future holds. So you might as well keep your attention focused on the here and now."

"Hmm, isn't that rather short-term thinking?" Rhonda replied. While my bestie kept our host busy, I studied the other, invited guests. Divine and Colin were watching Alistair with narrowed eyes, as if they were not really happy to see him. They exchanged whispered comments, using their hands to cover their mouths as they did. Moneybags Mahoney had his bulky arms wrapped over his torso as he glared at our host. The woman who had kept to herself on the boat now stood, not surprisingly, a ways away from us, her eyes never leaving Alistair. The way they all watched our host reminded me of a hawk watching the water for its prey to surface, patiently waiting for the right moment to strike.

Alistair offered Rhonda his arm. "I can give you the grand tour of my humble abode, if you'd like."

She hooked hers through his. "I would love that!"

My heart skipped a beat, excited to soon know the location of his movie memorabilia. Until Divine stepped in front of Alistair, with her hands planted on her hips.

"Excuse me for breaking up your little fan fest, but you did invite us to this party, Alistair, and not her."

11

Why Are We Here?

"Could you spare a little attention for us?" Divine asked in her high-pitched voice.

When Alistair turned back to face Divine, he blinked as if he was surprised to see her standing there.

"You got some nerve, popping up after all these years, acting like nothing is the matter. Why did you ask us to come here, anyway?" Mac growled.

"Your invitation was quite vague, albeit pressing," Colin added. "Can you please explain to everyone why we are here?"

"Of course." Alistair's expression softened. "You are right, I owe you all an explanation."

He stepped back so that he could face all of his guests. "Firstly, I cannot thank you enough for gracing me with your presence tonight. I hope we can enjoy each other's company for the next few hours. My chef has prepared a special meal for us, and with a little luck, the skies will clear and we'll have a wonderful view of the stars."

"I didn't come here to stargaze," Mac growled.

"Fair enough. Before we eat, I have something I want to share with you. I suspect that it will keep us busy for the rest of the night. We have enough cabins for everyone, even our extra guests," he said with a slight nod in Rhonda's direction. "After we dock in Zeebrugge, we can enjoy a champagne brunch to celebrate our brief reunion before everyone parts ways."

"Wait, that's in Belgium," Colin exclaimed.

"I'll have a taxi take you to wherever you desire after we dock. It's only a few hours' ride back to Amsterdam. The Lowlands are quite small. You'll be back in your hotel before you know it."

"Why can't we sail back, like in a loop?" Divine asked.

Alistair smiled. "I seldom visit the same port twice. It simplifies my life."

"This is all well and good, but why are we here?" the quiet woman asked.

"Indeed, that is the question of the hour, dear friends."

Mac snorted loudly at "friends," but Alistair simply nodded.

"You're right, Mac. Perhaps 'friend' is too strong a word. I know that I've wronged you all in the past and hurt each of you with my selfishness. I invited you here to try to make amends for all the pain I've caused. I know you can't just put a price on what I've done, but that's exactly what I've tried to do."

"Penance is not enough—you ruined our business and my career when you disappeared. I had to declare bankruptcy because you'd drained our bank accounts before you left," Colin seethed.

"You still owe me my cut of the last five films we made together," Divine added.

"Why now, after all these years?" Greta Garbo's lookalike asked.

Alistair held up his hands as if he was making clear that he was not holding a weapon. "I recently found my spiritual center thanks to my guru, Fred. Bringing you all together here was his idea."

"Fred?" I whispered to Rhonda, who covered her laugh with her hand.

"In order to become truly whole—spiritually and emotionally—I need to seek forgiveness from those I wronged the most. And that's you. I owe you all, in so many ways. You are here so that I can make things up to you, as best as I can."

"How exactly are you going to do that?" Mac asked.

Alistair's eyes twinkled. "I'm going to sell off my most valuable possessions and use the proceeds to pay you all back."

"That's generous of you, if not ten years too late," Divine grumbled.

"Which brings us to tonight." Alistair rubbed his hands together, a silly grin on his face as he locked eyes with each of his invited guests.

"I want you to see what I'm selling, so you know that I am serious about making amends. And, of course, to give you first dibs on any of the items in my collection."

It took a moment for his words to sink in. But once they did, I could literally feel the shockwave of indignation reverberating around the space.

"Wait a second—do you mean that you expect us to buy your stuff, and you're going to use the proceeds to pay us back? Are you daft?" Divine shrieked.

"It's not like that! Because of our histories, I'm willing to give you a discount on certain items."

Divine's face turned so red, I was afraid she was about to self-combust.

"Even if you don't want to buy anything, know that once I do sell the collection off, the money will be used to pay you back, as best I can."

"No one should pay for the things you took," the quiet woman hissed. My ears went on high alert. Did she know that Alistair had stolen several movie props? If so, how did she find out about the robbery? I made a mental note to watch how they interacted with each other, and try to discern her name. So far, she'd avoided the others, as if she wanted nothing to do with them. Our host wasn't any better. Even now, Alistair did his best to ignore her and her suggestion that he had stolen anything.

"Well, I'm not giving them away," Alistair laughed off her remark before grabbing Divine's hands. "With you as the face of the sale of the sale, we're bound to make a fortune."

"What are you talking about?" Divine asked, astonishment coloring her voice as she pulled her hands out of his.

"That's why I asked you to come, to help me host the online auction next week." Alistair added hastily, "For a percentage of the profits, naturally."

Divine folded her arms over her torso. "Why would I help you?"

"You're the host of a popular show on a high-end shopping network channel that's known for only selling authentic vintage items and never replicas. You are the epitome of reliability and trustworthiness."

I rolled my eyes, instead of laughing at his rather ludicrous description of

Divine's show. In reality, it was her hawking a random selection of vintage furniture, designer makeup bags, and chunky jewelry to rich housewives.

"If you host the online auction for me," Alistair cooed, "your celebrity status and number of followers should help drum up publicity and bring in more bidders, which means more money to pay you all back with."

He drummed his fingers on his thighs before continuing in a more frantic pace, "The auction is going to take place in two weeks' time, and you can stay here—free of charge—until then. We could shoot some promotional videos around the ship to help build excitement, and then the day of, we could broadcast from up on the deck. I'll ensure we're somewhere sunny by then."

"Are your medications out of whack?" Divine's wide eyes and pursed lips made clear that she was not impressed with Alistair's proposal. "There is no way I am staying here on this ship with you for two weeks, for free or not. My show tapes every weekday, which means I am flying out tomorrow. There is nothing you can say that would make me miss a single day of shooting."

"We can talk about the specifics in a minute, but I promise I'll make it worth your while," Alistair pleaded before turning to his old business partner, his tone borderline hysterical.

"And Colin, I bet a lot of our old contacts would be interested in several of the items I have for sale. If you could send out an email and let our old network know, that would be a big help."

Colin snickered. "Are you serious? You destroyed our company when you left. There is no network, not anymore."

Alistair's face fell, but he refused to give up. His expression brightened when his eyes landed on Rhonda. "You know, you being here just gave me a wonderful idea. Perhaps I could bring something from my collection on to your show and have you appraise it live, on air? It would be great publicity for the sale."

"Oh, we make a point of not promoting any auctions or private sales on our show. And anyway, we're on hiatus for another three weeks." I could tell she didn't want to disappoint Alistair by the way she tittered as she spoke.

Our host was clearly not pleased by her remark, but he was at least gentlemanly enough not to hold it against her. "That's alright, it's still a pleasure to have you on board."

"What about me? Why did you invite me to your little soiree. You know my network isn't interested in buying any of your stuff."

"Ah yes, Moneybags Mahoney. I figured you wouldn't forget about my loan, which is why I invited you over here—to prove to you that I was serious about paying you back. Hopefully we can work something out, without you sending someone over to cause me bodily harm."

Alistair laughed as if it was a joke, but Mac did not respond in kind. "I wouldn't have to send anyone over. And to be clear, I refuse to get off this boat without what you owe me—plus interest."

Our host gulped audibly and began wringing his hands together. "I won't be able to get all of your money before you leave tomorrow, because I have to sell my collection first. But know that I am working on it."

The man grinned, his lips pulling back over his shark-like teeth, as he cracked his knuckles. "Sure. I've heard that one before. I don't know about you all, but he's owed me seven figures for the past ten years, and I'm tired of waiting for him to settle his debts."

Alistair held up his hands, as if he was fending off an imaginary attacker. "Look, I know you have no reason to believe me—I've damaged your trust too much for that. However, if you will at least take a look at what I'm selling, then perhaps you will understand that I am serious about setting things right."

12

Hiding In Plain Sight

"Everyone please follow me to the saloon," Alistair said.

He walked past the wheelhouse to the back of the boat and down a short flight of stairs to a narrow hallway. The closed doors on either side were marked "Mess," "Galley," "Cabin #1," and "Saloon."

When he reached out to open the saloon door, the brass handle fell off into his hand, and the screw fell to the floor with a loud clank.

"Oops, I'll have to have someone look at that the next time I'm on shore," our host said, as he quickly screwed the handle back into place.

When he pulled the door open, I was taken aback by what I saw. It looked as if we were stepping into the foyer of an old-fashioned movie theater, with red velvet curtains covering the walls, chunky brass railings acting as room dividers, and even a popcorn machine built into the bar at the front of the space.

"Popcorn! Oh, gosh, I haven't had a fresh bucket in ages." Like a giddy schoolgirl, I rushed over to the machine, a smile lighting up my face at the memories of enjoying the buttery treat.

Alistair cleared his throat. "I'm afraid it doesn't work. It's on my list of things to fix."

"That's too bad."

Our host approached with a smile. "You know, I was so taken aback by Rhonda's presence, I forgot to ask who you are."

66

"She's an antiques appraiser and my best friend," Rhonda piped up and wrapped an arm around my shoulder. "We're traveling through Europe together. Isn't that nice?"

"It certainly is." He quickly air-kissed the back of my hand then let it drop. "Any friend of Rhonda's is welcome on board."

He winked once at my friend then crossed over to his invited guests.

I turned back to the popcorn machine and took a closer look. It had clearly not been used in years, and the inside appeared to be moldy. When I ran my hand back over the railing separating the bar from the rest of the space, I noted how chipped and worn the surface was. Upon closer inspection, the curtains covering the wall behind me were moth-eaten and threadbare. "This ship has seen better days, hasn't it?"

"It is too bad that he hasn't kept up with the repairs," Rhonda agreed. "It would probably be worth a small fortune if it was in better shape. Well, and if you could find a buyer for it. I can imagine there aren't many people who want to own something so large."

After I got over my popcorn obsession and the fact that my craving would not be sated during this trip, I took a good look around the rest of the space. The saloon, as Alistair called it, was a large space that was as wide as the brigantine, and seemed to take up about a third of the boat's length.

My heart skipped a beat as I realized what the room contained. Glass cases dotted the floor and lined parts of the walls. Interspersed between them were life-sized mannequins dressed up in costumes that seemed familiar. Framed film posters, all sporting prominent signatures, filled in the few empty spaces. If Alistair still possessed any of the items taken during the robbery, there was a chance that they were displayed in here.

Technically, Alistair had every right to sell whatever was stolen, because the statute of limitations had expired several years ago. However, I still wondered whether he would be so brazen as to show off the objects that had been taken.

A quick look around revealed that he was indeed bold enough to do so. In the first two cases, I spotted three items on Myrtle's list. My pulse quickened as I thought of all the brownie points I was going to score with my crotchety company contact, thanks to this find.

I took a deep breath and told myself to relax, for fear of Rhonda or Alistair noticing my internal excitement. There were still several more vitrines to check. With a critical eye, I scanned the room again. It was all very theatrical and fitting for a Hollywood type, I reckoned, even if the low lighting made it difficult to get a good look at the items for sale.

The only bright light emitted from the glass cases, the planks filled with a plethora of small items—watches, eyeglasses, pens, and several framed photos of celebrities with signatures across the bottom. Next to each object was a card that stated in which film it had appeared, and in which form.

Yesterday, shortly after receiving Myrtle's list of stolen items, I had searched the internet to figure out how to best authenticate whatever I potentially found in Alistair's home. My specialty was fine arts—paintings and sculptures, in particular—and I had no real experience with collectibles such as these. Without having done that research, I would have been lost because it turned out to be more complicated than I'd expected.

It seemed that the value of a prop was partially determined by its use. An item labeled as "Made for Production" was most likely created for a scene that was edited from the final version of the film, and therefore was not seen on-screen. These were less desirable than a "Screen Used" prop, an item that was used in the film, even if it wasn't always easy to spot in the final version. However, the most valuable were those that could be "Screen Matched," which meant the item was clearly visible in the movie, most likely because it was important for the storyline or was worn by a major character.

I bent down to get a better look at the items displayed in the case closest to me. Inside were Benjamin Button's glasses, a pair of Captain Spock's fake ears, and a helmet and dog tags seen in *Band of Brothers*, according to the accompanying card. Though the glasses and ears were somewhat unique, the last two items could have easily been purchased at an army surplus store, I realized. How was Rhonda going to appraise these kinds of props—those that were not unique, but common items easily purchased in a shop? I wouldn't know where to begin, without searching online for the sales of similar items.

When I turned around, a familiar face smiled down at me, his head partially in the shadows thanks to his wide-brimmed, leather hat. I took in the mannequin dressed as an adventure-seeking archeologist, admiring his whip and jacket for a moment before realizing that something seemed off about the rest.

If Alistair was going for a Madame Tussauds vibe with his mannequins, he'd significantly missed the mark. Instead of resembling the actual person, our host had made do with old store dummies dressed up in clothes similar to those that the fictional characters wore on screen.

"Give me a break. Indiana Jones had brown hair, not blond. Alistair couldn't even get that right," Divine grumbled as she passed by, a smirk on her face. From the looks of it, she was not real excited about this auction or being the face of it.

Rhonda bounced up behind me. "Did you see Audrey Hepburn? Her dress and necklace are to die for."

When she noted who'd just passed, she called out, "Hey, it's Divine Wilkes, isn't it? I thought you looked familiar."

Divine tossed her hair and lifted her chin.

"I just love your show on the shopping channel. The hair extensions you sell are really high quality, unlike most. It's an honor to meet you."

The disappointment on Divine's face was evident. "I was also an actress for twenty years."

"Oh, yes, I heard you mention some sort of Massacre film. What is that, dear?"

"They were horror films, but ahead of their time. Now they're all cult classics."

"Isn't that lovely? It's a good thing you actors receive royalties from your films, even so many years later," Rhonda enthused.

Divine gritted her teeth. "We're supposed to—you're right about that."

Before I could try to get more information out of her, Alistair clapped his hands together. "Let me give you all a quick tour, and then I'll let you examine everything at your leisure."

Alistair pointed out a few objects in the vitrines as he walked by, sharing tidbits about the films the objects were supposedly featured in. I had to take his word for it, because I didn't recognize most of the movies he mentioned. Many of the props were smaller items from older Hollywood movies, or pieces that featured in European arthouse films and spaghetti westerns.

One corner of the space seemed to be dedicated to props used in horror films. The mannequins wielded futuristic-looking weapons and frightening masks. That was a corner I luckily didn't have to spend too much time in, for almost all of the items on my list of stolen goods had featured in a classic Hollywood film, not a slasher movie.

I had memorized the list and had already spotted several items in the vitrines during Alistair's tour, but not all of them. Frankly, I was shocked to see any of them here and on display, figuring that Alistair would have had to sell them off to support himself, given how he hadn't worked in over a decade.

Regardless of my reason for being here, seeing all of these props made me smile as I recalled the films they were featured in and the fond memories and associations I had with each. The Baroness would have hated this, which made me even more glad that I was with Rhonda, and not my official partner. She could at least appreciate these items for what they were. Movie props might not be cultural treasures in the same sense as a painting or sculpture, but I understood why some collectors fancied having them. The nostalgia that they evoked was powerful.

Alistair kept up his clipped pace, until he reached another mannequin towards the back of the space, a jolly-looking fellow dressed in green felt and holding a bow and arrow, the string pulled back as if he was about to fire.

"Of course you all remember Robin Hood, prince of thieves." Alistair placed his hand on a male mannequin's arm. Its emotionless face sported a blond mustache, and a brown felt hat complete with feathers rested on its head.

"Are you sure that's the bow and arrow used in the film?" Colin asked as he squinted at the tiny bit of text lying by the mannequin's feet.

"One hundred percent," Alistair said in a chipper voice, before turning to the life-sized figure standing next to Robin Hood. "Who recognizes this tough guy?"

It took me a second to recognize the angry young man in the cherry-red nylon jacket, white T-shirt, and blue jeans.

"James Dean!" I exclaimed, strangely happy to be the first to say it aloud.

"Spot on!" our host replied.

The James Dean mannequin had his arms outstretched as if he was about to take on a group of hooligans, his famous switchblade already open in his hand, at the ready. Next to him, a female mannequin that vaguely resembled Audrey Hepburn wore a dress and diamond necklace that could have been in *Breakfast at Tiffany's*, but something about the way the gems sparkled told me that they were probably made of glass, not pressurized carbon. Across from her, a decent Marilyn Monroe, complete with trademark mole, posed in a white dress that was supposedly seen in *The Seven Year Itch*.

That's interesting, I thought. Alistair had offered to sell our informant both the switchblade and dress ten years ago, but disappeared when the buyer asked to see the paperwork. So had Alistair hung onto the genuine items all these years? Or were they fakes to begin with?

Before I could ponder either question, Mac cleared his throat. "Look, you've got some good pieces here, but you took off with two million of my dollars. When you add ten years of interest to it, I don't think you're going to make enough off of these trinkets to pay me back." While he spoke, he looked around the room with a mixture of disgust and irritation on his face.

"Wait a second, this isn't everything. The more expensive pieces are in my office. The proceeds from those alone will pay off your debt."

"This I gotta see. Lead the way."

13

The Maltese Falcon

Alistair walked to the back wall and pushed aside the thick red velvet curtain covering it, to reveal two unmarked doors. He pointed from one door to the other. "That's my bedroom, and this is my office. I keep the most expensive pieces in here."

He pulled open the office door with a flourish, revealing nothing more than a pitch-black space. Yet when he flipped a switch close to the entrance, several display cases lit up, including a large case in the center of the room, clearly placed so he could see its contents when sitting at his desk. Under the bright lights, the object inside reflected a rainbow of colors—golden yellow, ruby red, emerald green, and sapphire blue—onto the glass case. The tiny gems were affixed to the head of a brooding bird, his shoulders hunched over as he stared out at us.

"This, ladies and gentlemen, is what dreams are made of."

That line rang a bell, but a vague one, until Rhonda clapped her hands together. "Oh, that's Humphry Bogart playing Sam Spade in *The Maltese Falcon!*"

Alistair clapped back. "Well done."

"Wait, is that *the* Maltese Falcon?" Colin gasped as he stared at the small statue.

"It is the one and only. Well, I should say, one of the few."

"It is either the falcon or it's not—so which is it?" Mac snarled.

Alistair wagged a finger at him and smiled. "Don't forget, we're talking about Hollywood. There are always several versions made of the more important props, in case they get damaged during shooting. I submit that this, ladies and gentlemen, is one of the original seven falcon statues made for the 1941 version—and I have the paperwork to prove it."

Instead of oohing and aahing in delight, his small crowd simply stared at the statue.

"What's so special about this bird?" Mac asked. "It doesn't look like it'll fetch much."

"Really? The falcon statues are all estimated to be worth somewhere between a half million and four million dollars, depending on the condition and the materials used."

"Now you're talking," Mac breathed.

Buoyed by Mac's interest, Alistair continued to share more about the statue; his voice was infused with reverence as he spoke. "Three versions of *The Maltese Falcon* have been filmed, as well as a comedic sequel brought out in 1975, and all were based on the world Dashiell Hammett created in his book of the same name. The statues used during shooting were not initially considered to be valuable.

By the time there was a market for props like these, they had been buried away in the studios' storerooms or in private collections, gathering dust. Until a Beverly Hills doctor sold his in the 1980s for four million dollars! A few others were sold at auction, shortly after. Leonardo DiCaprio's even got one in his collection—he lent it to Quentin Tarantino when they were filming *Once Upon a Time in Hollywood*. It's a good movie; if you haven't seen it yet, you should."

His smile was so smug, I had trouble believing he was telling us the truth.

Alistair patted the tinted glass case. "As you can see, this one is bejeweled and covered in gold. It may not be as richly decorated as the doctor's version, but it is a close second. Which is why I'm only asking two million for it."

His small crowd burst out into laughter.

"Good one!" Divine had to hold her belly, she was laughing so hard.

"Yeah, right. You've been holding onto a two-million-dollar statue for all these years, and never thought to sell it before now? Do you think we were born yesterday?" Mac rolled his eyes. "You could have paid off all of your debts to me ten years ago, instead of having to worry about me tracking you down."

"Mac's right," Divine added, after her giggle fit had subsided. "How do we know you're not lying about its provenance?"

"You did promise not to swindle us again," Colin growled.

"I have the documentation to prove that what I say is true, but only the highest bidder gets to see it. They will also receive this key." He pulled a thin chain from around his neck and held up the tiny key hanging off of it. "It's the only way to disarm the alarm and get the case open. I've got everything but lasers protecting that thing!" His guffaw filled the room.

"Oh, please," Greta Garbo's lookalike mumbled.

I scanned the tinted glass case for the telltale sensors, but saw none. The lock was so flimsy, I was certain my bobby pin would be enough to jimmy it open. *Why is he lying about it being protected in umpteen ways, when it is clearly not true?* I wondered. I suppose he wouldn't have to have a particularly dark reason for doing so. Perhaps Alistair simply wanted to ensure that none of his guests tried to steal it.

"I don't buy it. How would you even get your hands on anything this precious?" Mac asked.

"A guy who worked in the props department at one of the major studios owed me money," Alistair replied, causing the quiet woman to choke on her drink. "But he didn't have enough to pay me back, so he gave me this instead."

"Oh yeah, I remember that robbery. The guy managed to sneak a whole bunch of props out of the warehouse," Colin said, as if a lightbulb had just gone on in his head.

Alistair shook his head, as if he didn't want to hear it. "Don't look at me—I didn't ask the guy to steal anything. I only found out about the theft after the fact. That's why I've hung onto the statue for so long. I didn't want anyone to accuse me of stealing it. But the statute of limitations passed a few years ago, so I figure it's safe to sell it off now. And if you all have my back and would be willing to verify that I didn't acquire it illegally, that will help keep the price high."

"You are unbelievable! It's always about you and how we can serve your needs," the now-not-so-quiet woman spat at Alistair. She looked as if she wanted to skin him alive.

Yet when she opened her mouth to speak again, Mac beat her to it. He had moved closer to the statue and was leaning over so that he was standing eye to eye with the bird. "Wait a second, Bogart's version was in black and white, right? Why would they use real gold and jewels for a black-and-white movie?"

"It's Hollywood; not much makes sense there," Alistair teased. "So, folks, why don't you take a look around and see if you see anything your friends might be interested in. Ask if you have questions!"

Alistair all but ran from the office, I assume to get away from the once quiet, now vocal, woman whom I had dubbed Greta Garbo. She started to follow him, but when another glass case holding a necklace caught her eye, she changed direction. She rushed over to the colorful piece, and pressed her nose up against the glass.

The intensity with which she was examining it made me move closer, just in time to hear her mumble, "That's not it."

She seemed to push away a tear, then strode off to one corner of the saloon. The way she kept her back to the rest made me think that she was upset, but didn't want anyone to notice. But why would a necklace make her tear up?

As much as I wanted to find out, I had a job to do first. Luckily, Rhonda was like a kid in a candy store, racing around the room and recounting stories about her favorite scenes from the movie the props were featured in, to whoever was close by. She wouldn't notice that I wasn't by her side.

After I had briefly examined every object in this space, I realized that at least twenty-five of the thirty-three missing items on Myrtle's list were on this ship. The statute of limitations might make it more difficult for my employer to get Alistair into legal trouble, but Reggie did have a way of being persuasive. Knowing him, I suspected that Reggie would threaten to badmouth the sale on Rosewood's social media so that any potential buyers understood the items had been stolen and not purchased legally by Alistair. That, of course, would harm his sale and embarrass him tremendously.

So far, Alistair appeared to have an ego as large as his ship and as easily bruised as a ripe tomato. I expected that Rosewood could easily talk him into returning the stolen items—if they could catch him, that is.

I longed to contact my employer and have them send in the calvary, but my phone was locked up in Captain Jack's safe. Per Myrtle's instructions, I had left it on and enabled the "Find My Phone" tracker, but I doubted anyone would react until I'd sent word that I had verified Alistair's identity and had found the stolen goods. Yet as long as I had no access to my phone, that wasn't going to happen.

Before I could decide what to do next, Rhonda slid up next to me. "Oh, my goodness gracious—Judy Garland's shoes from *The Wizard of Oz* are in that first vitrine!"

"The ruby reds?" I couldn't help but get excited as I followed her over to the case and stared at the heels. It had been one of my favorite films as a kid, though I'd had nightmares about the Wicked Witch on occasion.

"Do you think Judy Garland really wore those?" Rhonda asked, trepidation in her voice. Was she in awe that she was standing so close to something worn by one of her idols? Or was she thinking, as I was, that those sequins sure looked new, and there was absolutely no wear on the heel or sole, even though there should have been, had Judy really worn them on set.

"Huh, I'm really not sure. They don't appear to have been worn much. What do you think?" I knew Rhonda was smitten with our host, and wouldn't appreciate it if I spoke in a derogatory manner about him, which was one reason why I chose my words carefully. But it was also because I didn't want to influence her opinion. She certainly knew far more about collectibles such as these, than I did.

"I've got a funny feeling about these. They don't feel right, somehow," Rhonda said. "But I'd have to go get my glasses out of my suitcase, in order to get a good look at them. I swear, I get more and more farsighted by the week. You know what, I'm going to ask Alistair if these are the genuine article or not."

"Oh gosh, great idea." I couldn't believe that she would be willing to do that. When she scampered off to find Alistair, I wished her luck. It was as if Rhonda was completing my assignment for me, without knowing she was doing so.

So while she had our host occupied, I decided to try to get to know the rest of the guests a little better. They were slowly circling the room, each taking in the many wares for sale at their own pace.

The quiet woman had already caught my attention because, ever since we entered Alistair's office to see the Maltese Falcon, she seemed to only have eyes for a gorgeous art deco necklace made of large blue and red stones, each gem held into place by a thick blob of silver. I wasn't a jewelry person in general, but that one I would have worn in a heartbeat.

Also, the way she'd accused Alistair of theft and the fact that she didn't seem to be friends with any of the other invitees made me wonder why she was here. Now that I thought about it, Alistair had ignored her so far, too.

I held out my hand, eager to find out more about her. "Excuse me, we haven't met. I'm Carmen."

She nodded at my hand, but didn't take it. "Lucy. I would say it's a pleasure to meet you, but I really don't want to be here." Her "I want to be left alone" attitude matched that of her Hollywood doppelganger.

Why did she come to this party? I couldn't help but wonder. "I gathered that," I said evenly, so as to make clear that I wasn't offended, before nodding at the object inside the vitrine—also on my list of stolen items. "I've never heard of the film it appeared in, but it is a gorgeous necklace. I can see why you are infatuated with it."

Her expression hardened for a second as if she was going to deny it, but then suddenly softened. "I suppose I am. It reminds me of a necklace I once longed to own. But I haven't seen anything like it in years."

"It's gorgeous, isn't it?"

I about jumped up in the air when Alistair spoke. He'd crept up behind us and was leaning his head in between ours.

Shoot, I thought Rhonda had his attention. I looked to my friend and saw that she was now hanging on Colin's arm. I couldn't blame her for enjoying his companionship.

"Yes, it is," Lucy said wistfully.

"I'm only asking a half million for this one."

"Are you insane?" Lucy's shrieky reaction surprised me, until she added, "It's paste, Alistair."

Our host's eyes bulged out at her words, before he shoved his face to the glass. "It can't be! The paperwork says that those are real sapphires and rubies."

Lucy laughed bitterly. "You must have stolen the wrong document. My husband made two versions."

Husband? I thought with interest, as Lucy continued, "One was made of glass and was meant to be pulled off of the actress's neck, but the scene was cut. The other was genuine."

Alistair's brows knitted together. "Two—are you certain?"

Lucy pointed at the red stones. "Real rubies don't have mold markings on the corners."

I pressed my nose to the glass, as well, curious to see what she was referring to. "See there? It looks like the director wasn't too concerned about it being seen in the closeup, if he let that slide."

She was right; two of the facets clearly had ruffled edges. Yet my mind was still stuck on Lucy accusing Alistair of lying about the prop's real worth and material composition. Why hadn't he reacted to that comment? And had she said her husband made two necklaces for a film? I only had one of these art deco necklaces on my list. Who was Lucy's husband, anyway? Was he a jeweler, or had he perhaps worked in the props department? I would have to check him out, after I got my phone back. Questioning the wife was also an option, but I somehow doubted she would tell me the whole truth.

Lucy studied him intently. "Both versions were stolen ten years ago, by you, I presume. So where's the second one at, Alistair?"

Our host shook his head. "I received this necklace as part of my payment. I didn't steal anything."

Lucy's eyes darkened before she turned on her heel and walked away, leaving a gaping Alistair behind. "I guess I'll have to get my eyes checked. I really thought this was the real one."

"Haven't you had any of these items appraised?" I couldn't help but ask.

"Why should I waste my money on that? I have all of the original certificates proving that they are genuine. That's all collectors care about."

"So you are certain that these were all 'screen used'?" I asked, proud that I had taken the time to learn about how you appraised movie props before coming aboard.

"One hundred percent."

I studied his face as I considered his smug answer. The articles about authenticating movie props had warned repeatedly about unscrupulous dealers trying to pass off "replicas," copies of original props and costumes, as the genuine article. Alistair was not proving to be the most honest character I had ever met, which made me question some of these pieces' authenticity.

Apparently, I wasn't the only one. Divine tapped him on the shoulder, a scowl on her face. "Have you 'screen matched' any of these? That would significantly increase their value—if they are genuine, that is."

"Of course they are real!" Alistair laughed off her comment as if she was crazy to even think such a thought. "Divine, darling, what do you think about the descriptions I've written for each item? You've been hawking things on television for so long, you probably know better than me how to push them and what kind of information to include or exclude."

"In what alternative reality do you see me hosting your auction?"

Instead of snapping back, Alistair pulled out his phone and turned it towards Divine.

"Let me show you what I'm thinking. I've had a website built for the sale. It should make it easier to attract buyers, and via this link they can browse the entire catalog of items and place a bid."

"Hey, that's not right! I didn't give you permission to use my photo or name on the banner."

I dared to glance over Alistair's shoulder and at his phone. The banner across the top of the page featured a large photo of Divine, smiling at the viewer with her famous "you can trust me" smile.

"It's only a concept." Alistair brushed her concerns aside. "I figured you would take me more seriously if you knew the site was ready to go live."

"If you post that, I will sue you."

Alistair sighed deeply. "If you will just let me explain the commission system I have in mind, I bet you'll come around."

Divine rocked back on her heel. "You still haven't told me what your plan is, but keep assuming that I'll go along with it. I don't work for you anymore, remember? And as I recall, you still owe me quite a bit of back pay, so tone it down, buddy."

Alistair cast his eyes downward. "I suppose you're right. I just can't imagine you will say 'no' once you hear my offer."

Divine began to retort, but bit her lip instead. The way she hesitated, it was clear her fear of potentially missing out on a good deal was too much to bear. She lowered her voice even further. "You do know that I'll need to see the certificates of authenticity before I get involved with this auction, right?"

"Of course! I have those for almost everything."

My eyebrow shot up. Moments ago, he'd claimed that he had documentation for everything on display.

Divine folded her arms over her torso. "*Almost* everything? I swear, if you try to pull a fast one..."

He tittered as he grabbed her arm and pulled her away from the rest. "If we work together, I can pay you double what I owe you. Maybe more."

Divine's attitude transformed from hostile to interested in a heartbeat. "We do need to have that chat. Is there somewhere private where we can talk?"

My ears perked up at the word "private." That was my cue to stay close.

He looked around the room, then nodded towards the narrow hall that connected the saloon to the mess and guest cabins.

"Follow me."

Divine let him take her hand and pull her out of the saloon.

14

Divine Intervention

I waited until they had slipped into the passageway before slowly following. Just as I poked my head around the corner, Alistair pulled Divine into one of the cabins and closed the door. Luckily for me, it was not made of glass, so I could stand outside and press my ear to the wood, without alerting them.

"Come on, Divine, you are known for only pushing high-quality vintage items on your show. Your reputation will lend credibility to the sale, which will bring in more visitors to the website and hopefully jack up the prices. I'm willing to give you a twenty percent commission on all sales made through the website. If we play our cards right, your cut should make up for all the money I owe you, and then some."

"You are dancing around my question. Be straight with me, Alistair—are you trying to pass replicas off as genuine items?" Divine's tone was dark and brooding.

Our host was quiet a moment before answering, "There may be a couple of replicas on display, but only a few of the lower-ticket items."

"I knew it," she seethed. "What about the sales receipts? Can you prove that you purchased everything in the room?"

"Ah, yes, well, that's a little trickier…"

"Stop it!" Divine shrieked.

"Shhh!" Alistair scolded.

"Don't you dare shush me. I should have known that you were lying again—why would you change? You want to use my reputation as a straight shooter to hawk your stolen and fake items. If I help you, and your buyers later discover that they've been fleeced, I will be ruined. Don't you understand that? It's taken me years to rebuild my career after you disappeared with my paychecks. I refuse to allow you to destroy all that I've built up!"

"What about thirty percent?" Alistair pleaded.

"I don't need your money anymore. I'm earning my own now, and it feels great. You shouldn't have invited me to your little party, Alistair."

"You have to help me!"

"Get your hands off of me!" Divine practically shouted. The sound of a scuffle made my hackles rise. If he tried to harm her in any way, I was breaking down that door. Luckily, it sounded like Divine could hold her own.

"If you aren't careful, I'll expose you for the fraud that you are." The way her heel clicked on the wooden floorboards, it sounded like she was headed towards the door—and me.

"You can't do that!" was the last plea that I heard Alistair make before backing my way into the mess. When the kitchen door opened, the cook's eyes widened momentarily, but both he and his assistant were too polite to say anything, only nodding and smiling before continuing with their tasks.

Moments later, I heard Divine's high heels clicking their way back to the saloon, followed soon after by Alistair's more muffled footfall.

What was our host going to do? Divine was clearly not going to be the face of his auction, as he'd hoped. Would he continue on with his online sale or bring them to a reputable auction house? If the props were authentic, there were enough venues that he could use to sell them off.

If he did employ an auction house, Alistair would probably earn more per prop, thanks to their clientele lists and marketing campaigns, even though he would have to pay them a commission. So was their fee the reason he would prefer to sell them via his own website? Or was it because they were not necessarily the objects that he claimed them to be? The fact that he was avoiding the easier and perhaps more profitable route made me further doubt the authenticity of everything on display.

Pop culture was not my specialty, and without being able to either video chat with a reputable dealer or look up a specific item's estimated value online, I would not have a clue as to the true worth of any of the objects showcased in Alistair's saloon. Nor would I be able to verify their authenticity, without outside help.

My only choice was to get my best friend to help me verify the items, without alerting her as to my real motive. She wasn't a pop culture specialist either, but given the nature of her show, she did have a broad knowledge of an object's general worth and was surprisingly accurate in her estimations. So knowing her talents and interests, I didn't think it was going to be a problem to accomplish my goal. All I had to do was ask.

15

Checking In With Rhonda

When I exited the mess, the first thing I heard was, "There you are!"

My bestie had apparently read my mind, for suddenly she was standing right in front of me.

"Hi, sorry, I had to use the bathroom."

"Isn't that the kitchen?"

"It is. I picked the wrong door."

"Alright, well, when you're done, do you fancy a drink?"

"That sounds great. I'll see you back at the bar."

Rhonda had already poured us each a glass of merlot by the time I returned. I took a seat next to her, hoping we were far enough away from the other guests, still circling the items for sale, that they couldn't hear us.

"Say, what do you think of our host?" I said in a low voice.

"He's a fascinating person who probably has a million interesting stories to tell," Rhonda gushed. "It's too bad about his leg, though."

"What do you mean? I hadn't noticed anything other than a slight limp."

"He's been diagnosed with a serious form of arthritis. He's taking medication to help ease the pain, but he's afraid he won't be able to climb the stairs soon, if it keeps progressing at the rate it has."

"Yikes, that is going to be a challenge, living here then." To get around this ship, one was constantly climbing staircases or ladders to reach all of the floors and spaces.

When a rough wave hit and knocked us both into one wall, Rhonda said, "If I were him, I would use whatever proceeds are left from the sale, to rent an apartment on land. All this motion can't be good for his joints." She was quiet a moment before adding, "I wonder if that's why he's selling off all of his possessions now, so he can move back to the mainland, in an apartment or house with no stairs."

"That's a really great point, Rhonda." Her comment put his actions and motivations in a whole new light. Was he really going to use the profits to pay back his friends, or was he intending on using the money to finance a new life on land? So far, almost everything he said had been a lie or twisted version of the truth. I wouldn't be surprised if he was planning on keeping the money. So why did he invite all of these people here, if it was not to set his wrongs right? A foreboding feeling settled in the pit of my stomach as I wondered what else our host had in store for us.

"But Alistair does seem to be nervous about something. I suppose that has something to do with him meeting up with all these people he wronged so long ago."

"He did invite a strange mix of guests," I agreed, before asking what I really wanted to know. "What do you think about the items on offer? I'm frankly shocked by how much he is asking for some of them. Take that art deco necklace Lucy seems so obsessed with. He's asking a half-million for a piece, even though the stones are made of glass. And he wants two million for that Maltese Falcon statue. It's hard to tell through the tinted glass, but that gold looks to be more leaf than solid."

When Rhonda stared at me, I knew I'd made a mistake. "Why is it so shocking that a movie prop could be worth so much? The value of any collectible is in the eye of the beholder. To an avid film buff, something like the Maltese Falcon is as awe-inspiring as a Matisse or Rembrandt is to an art lover. It's not the value of the gems that makes it worth buying, but its role in an iconic film. In a way, it's a tangible object that connects us to a fictious world."

"Well said," I mumbled into my wine. "Yet, I'm still not entirely certain that everything in this room is authentic."

"But Alistair said they were—why would he cheat his friends?" Rhonda blinked at me as if she couldn't believe what she was hearing.

I usually loved her naïve refusal to believe that people were inherently bad, but sometimes she could be a little too obtuse. "Not everyone is as honest as you are."

"If they were, the world would be a better place," she sniffed.

"I don't know, a well-timed white lie now and again has probably saved many a relationship."

"Regardless, as long as Alistair has the certificates of authenticity, then they must be the genuine article." Her tone told me that she was finished with this conversation, and that she refused to believe that Alistair was lying about anything. She did seem to have a soft spot for our host. So instead of pushing, I changed the subject.

"What do you think of the other guests?"

"They are pretty fascinating people. That lady, Lucy, seems alright, although she's been keeping to herself so much, I don't have a real feel for her personality. But she doesn't give me the creeps like that that Mafia-looking guy. Luckily he's keeping to himself, too."

"I know what you mean. He does seem more like an extra for a *Godfather* film than a producer."

"Maybe he sees himself as some sort of tough guy or gangster type and chooses his wardrobe accordingly," Rhonda quipped while putting on her meanest of faces, making me giggle. The Baroness was a great partner, but didn't have a very good sense of humor. It was a nice change to have a little giggle now and again while on the job.

"And what about Colin?" I asked as I batted my eyelashes at her and smiled.

Rhonda slapped me lightly on the shoulder. "He's easy on the eyes, that's for certain. But he seems to be the kind of guy who flirts with everyone, so I'm not getting my hopes up just yet."

"I don't know, I'd say he is quite interested in you. Though maybe not as much as Alistair is. Our host does seem to be smitten with you. But then again, you're a fascinating woman, so that's no surprise."

"Well thank you kindly." Rhonda smiled up at me and squeezed my hand.

As she did, a loud bell rang.

"What is that?" Rhonda cried as she covered her ears.

"Dinner is served," Alistair called out.

"Well, why didn't he just say so?" she grumbled to me. "I'm just going to check my makeup before we eat."

"Me, too. I'll join you." I grabbed my handbag and followed my friend to the bathroom.

16

One Way Or The Other

We were the last to arrive at dinner. Rhonda took the free seat between Colin and Alistair, and I sat down between Lucy and Mac. Divine sat at one end of the table, watching the rest of us over a generous glass of wine. Since her private chat with Alistair, she'd been distant and withdrawn. I could imagine that she felt betrayed by him, yet again.

Our host, on the other hand, was cracking jokes with Colin, his old business partner, as if he didn't have a care in the world. Considering how much her refusal to be the face of his sale would affect his plans, I was slightly surprised to see Alistair in a jovial mood and showing no signs of distress after his disastrous conversation with Divine.

As soon as we were seated, a portly man in a chef's hat rolled a cart filled with food into the galley. On it were fresh loaves of bread that smelled of sourdough, trays of steaming vegetables, and a tureen full of soup—seafood of some sort, if my nose was to be believed.

The cook served each of us a small portion, before parking the cart to one side, and then returning to the kitchen, without a word. So far, the crew of five scurried away whenever any of the guests got close. Only Captain Jack had been reasonably friendly during our short tour of the ship, though he obviously wasn't interested in mingling with us, preferring to remain in the wheelhouse for the duration of the trip.

Alistair rose from the small table and held up his glass of wine. "Dear guests, my chef has prepared a delicious feast of fish stew, marinated vegetables, and organic bread."

"I would have expected something fancier, given the circumstances," Mac said, as if he was trying to bait him.

"Yeah, like caviar and lobster. I heard you batting around some pretty large numbers in there," Divine added. In contrast to Alistair, her irritation was bobbing to the surface. "You clearly think you are entitled to more than they are really worth."

Yep, they were definitely trying to get a rise out of Alistair. Yet our host was clearly doing his best not to let the two get to him. "That's why it's an auction—you never know how much someone will bid for an item. Look, I understand your frustration and will do all I can to address your grievances, as soon as the auction is over. Fred told me this was going to be a difficult process, but one I had to complete if I want to grow emotionally and spiritually."

Without batting an eye, Alistair picked up a stack of papers from the table and handed them out to his guests. "This is a list of the items for sale and a brief description. If you know anyone who would be interested in buying any of these items, I'll give you a ten percent commission for referring them to me."

Mac nodded as if he was seriously considering Alistair's proposal. "Sure, okay. I might know a few people."

"Why should we pay for anything?" Lucy threw down her napkin and rose so quickly, her chair trembled. "You stole everything and framed my husband for the crime! I'm here to clear his name, even if that means taking you and your stolen props in to the police myself."

Gasps circled the table as her words sank in. *Well, the cat's out of the bag,* I thought, realizing this meant I could now discuss the theft with Rhonda, without breaking my promise to my boss.

"We had two young kids at home when the police arrested him," Lucy cried. "Two children who grew up without a father, thanks to your lies."

Alistair, to his credit, did not deny her accusations, but bent over to pat her on the back, as if he was comforting a good friend. "There, there. Let it all out."

"Don't touch me, you monster! My husband's only crime was opening the back door for you, and looking the other way while you took whatever you could get your grubby little hands on. And then you set him up to take the fall!"

"I know you think I wronged your husband, but it's simply not true. Gary was the mastermind, not I." Alistair's tone was serene, as if he'd been expecting this confrontation since Lucy arrived.

"Liar!"

Alistair slowly shook his head.

"You are going to give me the items you took from the WorldWide Studios warehouse so that I can take them to the district attorney. She promised to reopen the case if I can prove to her that someone else was involved. You should pay for your crimes, too. Not just Gary."

Alistair's eyes narrowed, but his serene smile remained firmly planted on his face. "My dear, you have every right to be angry that your husband was sentenced to jail, but I'm afraid he's not as innocent as you think."

When Lucy opened her mouth to speak, Alistair talked over her. "I know you believe that I set up your husband. That's why I invited you here, to try to make you understand what really happened. I've always felt bad that he felt driven to steal, in order to pay me back. Maybe if I'd given him more time to come up with the money, he would not have robbed his employer," Alistair said in a voice fit for a Hallmark movie.

"The robbery was your idea, not his. My husband was only foolish enough to let you in."

Alistair slowly shook his head again, a pained expression now plastered onto his face. "My dear, it pains me to see you so, but you have it all wrong. The keycard used to open the door was his, no visitors were registered during his last shift, the truck used to move the stolen goods was rented in his name, and the security guards had noted that he had been working later than usual the week preceding the robbery, presumably so that he could prepare the objects for transport. Even his own lawyer could provide no evidence suggesting that he had an accomplice. The courts were convinced that he planned and executed the crime on his own. I know it's not what you wanted to hear, but it is the truth."

Lucy stood before Alistair, shaking her head as she pursed her lips. "Stop it! I refuse to believe you, no matter how many times you say it. You deserve to be punished as severely as my husband was. One way or another, you are going to pay for your crime."

Alistair remained impassive as she stormed off, leaving the dinner party and the rest of us speechless.

How did Alistair and Lucy's husband know each other? I wondered. Hollywood was small; they must have worked together at some point. If only I had access to my phone, I could look up both of their filmographies.

After a moment's silence, Colin dabbed at his lips, then tossed his napkin onto his untouched plate. "I see you still have a way with women, Alistair. I'll see if I can repair the damage you've caused," Colin said in his irritatingly snarky voice.

He rose, then paused and turned back to our host. "You know, this reminds me of when we were business partners. I had to clean up so many of your messes, I should have kept a mop and bucket in my car."

"Ha ha, real funny. Fine, go after the broad, but don't make yourself scarce for too long. I want to talk to you, one on one."

Colin smiled wryly. "Do you want to make up for lost time, or are you finally going to explain to me why you drained our company's accounts before you disappeared?"

Alistair's eyes widened for only a fraction of a second, then he seemed to dismiss Colin's comment, ignoring it in favor of grabbing a piece of bread.

Colin exited quickly, letting the door fall closed with a bang.

"You know, I'm not really hungry, either," Divine said as she took off, before any of us could respond.

That left Rhonda and I seated with our host and Mac, two men we barely knew. Before I could start the conversational ball rolling, Rhonda turned to Alistair and whispered, "Do all of your guests hate you?"

Mac apparently heard her comment, too, because he chortled with laughter, baring the sharp teeth filling his oversized jaw as he did. "Great question."

Alistair laughed along with him, though it sounded forced. "That's one way of looking at it. I have caused them all significant pain in the past. Fred warned me it wouldn't be easy to make them see that I am serious about making amends. All I can do is keep trying until they do believe me."

Rhonda patted his hand. "Well, that's mighty nice of you to try. I hope they come around to your way of thinking."

I smiled at my friend, who always tried to find the silver lining in any situation. I, on the other hand, couldn't help but think that we were trapped on this ship with this virtual stranger and surrounded by people who would rather see him dead.

Alistair's eyes narrowed in response to Rhonda's comment. "They will, one way or the other."

17

A New Complication

Mac "Moneybags" Mahoney cleared his throat. "Speaking of which, you and me have something private to discuss. Would you mind terribly if we retired to Alistair's office?"

He glanced over at Rhonda and I as he spoke, but the look on his face made clear that he would not take "no" for an answer.

I sprung out of my chair. "We can certainly give you some space to talk. Tell you what, why don't you two stay here and we'll move to another room."

"But what about my soup?" Rhonda asked. "It's delicious, I'd hate to waste it."

I spotted a serving tray and placed our bowls on it, then handed it to Rhonda. "We can take it with us. There's a small table in the guest room next door. Why don't we finish our meal in there?" I suggested, eager to leave the two men alone so that I could eavesdrop on their conversation.

"That's an excellent idea," Mac said as he held up the bread basket. I smirked at him as I grabbed it out of his hand, then used the other to propel Rhonda towards the door before following her out of the room.

As soon as the door hit the frame, I could hear Mac's deep voice resonating through the dining area, his polite veneer already gone. Rhonda and I both stood stock still, listening. I was so glad that my bestie was a gossip hound, too.

"You got a lot of nerve, popping up after ten years and acting like

93

everything's alright between us."

"I invited you here, remember? If I thought you were going to kill me, I wouldn't have, would I? I have what you want, which is why I reached out."

"Oh yeah? You have a ten-year-old debt to settle with me, and I mean tonight."

"Ah, yes, that is exactly my problem. I am cash poor at the moment. Would you consider a trade?"

Mac snorted. "I don't want a souvenir. Why did you invite me here if you don't have what you owe me?"

"To show you that I am serious about paying you back."

There was a long silence before Mac added, "And?"

Alistair sighed loudly. "I want to make sure that you won't interfere with the auction. Selling off these possessions is the only way I can pay you back the millions I owe you. I figured it was better to get in touch now and explain my intentions, than to have you find out about the auction from someone else."

"Alright, I respect that. However, I'm not leaving until I have something valuable enough to constitute a down payment on your two-and-a-half-million-dollar debt."

"It was two!"

"You forgot to add interest. So what's it going to be?"

"If you could only wait until after the sale…"

"Yeah, right. I answer to Antonio Corozza now, and he's holding up the Giraspi family tradition of never forgiving or forgetting a debt, which means I have to keep an eye on you until you pay him back in full. And after ten years, I'm getting pretty impatient."

"Corozza—when did he take over?" Alistair sounded truly frightened.

I completely understood Alistair's reaction. At the mention of Corozza's name, my knees turned to jelly, and my lungs momentarily stopped working. He was the man I suspected of killing my dear husband, Carlos—and over a pair of cupid statues, no less. Only after his death did we discover that Corozza was not simply an importer-exporter with a passion for Italian statues—he was also an up-and-coming lieutenant in the Italian branch of the Giraspi crime family, which also had a strong foothold in Las Vegas. If Mac was now answering to him, Corozza must have been promoted to the Vegas branch of Giraspi's criminal organization.

It took me precious seconds to recover my ability to think and breathe. The idea that my husband's fate had been decided by a thug like Mac made me want to jump out and strangle him with my bare hands. But Mac was big, and I wasn't certain I would be successful, despite my rage and training. And even if I was, where would that leave me—on the run from the mob for the rest of my life? Killing a random someone from the organization that presumably killed my husband wasn't good enough. I needed to find the biggest fish of them all, and that was Antonio Corozza.

"About a year ago, and he made it quite clear that he was not forgiving any outstanding debts owed to the organization. So what do you propose as down payment? Or must I break your legs?"

"No! Of course you don't have to go that far. What about the ship? It should be worth several million, to the right buyer."

"You said the Maltese Falcon is worth two million. I'll take that."

"It's, uh, maybe not worth as much as I said it was."

"Is it the falcon from the Bogart film, or not?" Mac groused, his impatience shining through.

"From one of the film adaptations. Let's just say I'm not planning on hanging around long enough for the new owners to check their purchase's authenticity."

My brow furrowed, and I looked to Rhonda. What the heck was that supposed to mean? She shrugged, but remained quiet. I wished I had my phone on me so I could record this, or at least could send Mac's name to Myrtle. *Who is this guy?* I wondered. He was clearly not your average film financer, if he answered to the head of a crime family.

"Geez, Alistair. Can anyone believe anything that comes out of your mouth?"

"I can sign the ship over to you right now, and as soon as the auction is over, I'll hand over the keys."

"Sure you will. How do I know you aren't just going to sail away again and disappear with the sale's proceeds? Besides, this is your home. Why would you sell it?"

"I won't be needing it after the auction because I'll be a landlubber again soon. Don't tell the others—it's meant to be a secret."

"Alright, let's go sort out the paperwork. I'll take the boat, falcon, and the necklace that broad keeps eyeing."

"Do you really have to take all three? The statue was supposed to be the highlight of the sale." Alistair sounded put out. "And why would you want that necklace? It's made up of cut glass, not real gems."

"That broad seems obsessed with it. She did say her husband worked in the props department for a lot of years; maybe she knows something you don't."

"Be my guest. I doubt it's worth more than a few bucks."

"Even more reason to take the falcon statue and ship, as well," Mac hissed.

"Isn't there anything else you would consider—"

"No. Now quit stalling. Let's take care of this now, before you get sidetracked again. Lead the way to your office."

A wave of terror rolled over me. Would Mac kill Alistair after he got what he wanted? More importantly, would he then kill the rest of us so that there were no witnesses? I tried to place myself in the gangster's shoes, ultimately realizing the chance that Mac would kill all of us guests and the crew was a billion to one. This wasn't a slasher film, and some of the crew members looked strong enough that they could probably take Mac down. And he had said that the three items were a down payment, meaning he expected more from Alistair in the future.

I let out a soft sigh, as relief washed away my angst and allowed my mind to focus on how I could use Mac to get to Corozza. The mob boss would be protected by bodyguards and his loyal lieutenants, making it nearly impossible for anyone to get close. I needed the smaller fish like Mac to lead me to him.

If I could steal Mac's phone, we might be able to discover how they communicated and ultimately use that information to track Corozza down, I realized. My boss was as eager to punish the man responsible for my husband's death as I was. Carlos had been killed while on a mission for the Rosewood Agency, a fact that Reggie had never been able to forget.

As much as I wanted to talk this out with someone, I realized that, until I could get ahold of my phone, I had to keep this to myself. This information was not something that I could share with my best friend, without compromising my work for the agency. Which meant my mission just got even more complicated.

18

Target Practice

When I heard the sound of chairs being pushed back from the dining room table, I signaled to Rhonda to get inside the guest room next door, and pronto.

Luckily she understood what my frantic nods meant and immediately moved into the cabin, holding the door open with her hip so I could quickly follow. I pushed the door closed behind me, just as the dining room door opened. Seconds later, the pair exited the dining room and presumably headed to Alistair's office where he would sign over his ship, the Maltese Falcon statue, and the paste necklace to Mac.

A sense of both helplessness and excitement boiled up inside of me. Part of me was thrilled that I finally had a lead to Carlos's killer. After my husband's death, Corozza had gone underground, and this was the first real lead we'd had on him in three years. Yet another tiny sliver of my soul was afraid to begin down that treacherous path called revenge. I closed my eyes, wondering how far I would go to find the man who had murdered my husband—and what I would do to him if I ever did get him in my sights.

As much as I wanted to tell Rhonda about finding a lead to my husband's killer, I knew that I could not. She didn't know how Carlos had really died or what he really did for a living. And right now was not the time to untangle a web of lies decades old.

Besides, Reggie would never allow me to expose Carlos or myself over this. So I kept my mouth shut.

"Oh, my—that was exciting!" Rhonda snickered into her napkin to help dampen the noise. "If this had been the Wild West, I swear Mac would have challenged Alistair to a gunfight."

I chuckled along, even though my mind was racing with possibilities. How could I get ahold of Mac's phone without him noticing? And would he have Corozza's contact information on it?

Before I could come up with a witty reply, a series of shouts caused us both to rush towards the source of the noise.

"Is that Divine yelling? It sounds like she's in the saloon."

"I think you're right," I replied as we hightailed it down the narrow passageway.

When we entered the saloon, Divine and Alistair were standing nose to nose in the middle of the space, glaring at each other. Behind them, just in front of the office door, was Mac. To his right, stood Lucy and Colin. All three were staring at the arguing pair, as if they couldn't believe what they'd just heard.

"Stop it, Divine."

"No, Alistair. Your friends"—she made invisible quotes around the word as she smirked—"deserve to know the truth. Why don't you tell everyone the real reason why we're here—to help you hawk your fakes to all of our friends. He can't sell most of this stuff through an auction house because it's not the genuine article, so he wants us to convince our friends to buy his replicas!"

"Don't listen to her," Alistair growled.

Divine's face lit up as she rushed over to the Marilyn Monroe mannequin and turned up the skirt to reveal its label. "Aha! Just as I suspected, it's polyester."

"So?" Alistair replied, his voice full of indignation, yet tiny beads of sweat dotted his temple.

"That fabric wasn't even invented until the 1970s. And *The Seven Year Itch* came out in 1955."

"Divine, I'm warning you. I've offered you an incredible deal, don't mess that up."

All she did was laugh. "I told you before, I don't need your money anymore. I make my own." She continued sauntering around the room until she stopped at the mannequin dressed as a leather-wearing archeologist and pulled the hat off of his head.

"And what about Indy's hat? They were all handmade so they'd fit perfectly on Harrison Ford's head." Divine turned it over and laughed, before showing it to her tiny audience. "Made in China. What a surprise."

Alistair raced to her side, grabbed her roughly by the arm, and began pulling her towards his office. "Could we have a private word?"

"Unhand me!" she cried out and jerked her arm out of his grasp. "We've already talked. I'm just telling them the truth, something you are incapable of doing. I wouldn't want anyone here to feel swindled. But then, it wouldn't be the first time you pulled a fast one on your supposed friends and left them in the lurch. Am I right?"

Alistair wrung his hands. "This is all my fault. I didn't explain my intentions clearly enough. I see that now."

"Oh, no, you made your intentions crystal clear."

He was obviously trying to keep a cool head, but Divine's goading must have been getting under his skin. He ran a hand through his hair before turning back to the rest of us. "I truly do not know what she is talking about."

"Liar! I am going to do my best to ensure everyone knows—"

A whooshing noise sliced the air and cut her comment short. Suddenly, Divine was no longer standing tall, but bent over at an unnatural angle with her mouth hung open and her eyes wide with fear. Even stranger, one of her hands was wrapped around an arrow now sticking out of her side, and her blood dripped down its shaft.

Divine looked to Alistair and stretched out her other arm, as if she wanted to grab ahold of him. "You shot me?" Her garbled words escaped her lips just before she fell forward with a sickening thud.

Rhonda's scream just about ruptured my eardrums. I honestly don't know whether I yelled out. Since I'd arrived in Europe, I'd already had to deal with a dead body; maybe that experience had numbed me. Or perhaps Divine's sudden death just hadn't sunk in yet.

Rhonda, however, was anything but numb. She tore at her face, shrieking so loudly I seriously wondered whether my hearing would be permanently impaired. I wrapped my arms around my friend's trembling body, hoping to ease her pain with my comforting embrace.

19

Mutiny On The La Vida Loca

"What just happened?" Lucy shrieked as she stared at her hands, as if she also had blood on her palms.

Alistair raced over to the mannequin dressed in green. His back blocked the bow from my sight momentarily as he examined his prop. Then he stepped back and pointed at a semi-transparent blob on the bow's string. "I can't believe it. The glue must have come loose."

"After all these years, it comes loose right when Divine steps into its path? I don't buy it," Mac said. "I don't know how, but you did this, Alistair. I can feel it."

I tended to agree with Mac. As soon as I could, I was going to examine that bow. But for now, I was content to examine the body. I lay my finger on her wrist, then her neck, feeling for a pulse but finding none. When I bent over her nose, no breath of air rushed into my ear or along my skin.

"She's gone." I closed her eyelids and said a little prayer.

"That seems pretty obvious; look at all that blood pooling up on the floor. Oh, poor Divine! What a horrible way to die. Despite your gut feeling, Mac, I had nothing to do with this." Alistair knelt by Divine's body and took her lifeless hand. "This is an awful, yet random accident. That's all."

Seconds later, the door burst open, and Captain Jack rushed in. "I heard screaming. What's going on?" The portly man's ragged breathing turned into gasps of air when he noticed the body on the floor.

He removed his hat and placed it against his chest. "Is she still…"

Alistair shook his head. "It was a terrible accident, nothing more."

Captain Jack gulped. "I'll radio it in and set course for the nearest port."

Alistair sprung up. "No—you can't do that!"

The captain froze, midstep. "What do you mean? A woman is dead. The authorities must be alerted."

"It took months of planning to organize this party. Divine's passing is no reason to end it prematurely. We can sail back to shore as soon as my guests and I wrap up some unfinished business. It shouldn't take much longer. But don't you dare radio for help until I tell you to do so."

Jack's eyes about popped out of his head. "Try to stop me!" He raced to the door, Alistair on his heels. The two men jostled up the stairs and onto the bridge. I followed them up, with the rest nipping at my heels.

Jack grabbed the radio and pushed in the call button, but before anyone could respond, Alistair bashed a fire extinguisher into the panel, sending sparks into both of their faces. He continued his onslaught until there was practically nothing recognizable beyond a few bits and pieces of the paneling.

"You're insane!" Jack screeched.

"No, I'm not. I simply refuse to let a little thing like a death get in the way of my long-laid plans. Having the Coast Guard race out to meet us isn't going to bring Divine back, Jack."

"This isn't right," he muttered, but his tone and body position had become more passive.

"We stay on course, until I say otherwise. Agreed?" Alistair's unnatural calm in the face of death made his words sound ominous.

Jack nodded slightly but refused to meet Alistair's eye. Seeing as we still didn't know whether our host had killed Divine, appeasing him seemed like the smart choice.

After a few more coddling words from Alistair, Jack returned to the helm, still shaky but no longer considering mutiny. At least, not as far as I could tell.

20

Old Friends

Alistair shooed us down the stairs and back into the saloon. After closing the door, he leaned back against it before rubbing his hands together quite vigorously. "We have a few more things to hash out before we return to shore. Shall we adjourn to the bar? I could use a stiff drink."

"I don't know what sick game you are playing, but I want off of this ship. If you don't have Jack set sail for the closest haven right now, I will wrestle the wheel from him and do it myself. And once we hit land, I'm going to do all I can to destroy you," Mac growled.

Instead of trembling in fear, Alistair only laughed. "Oh, Mac, you wouldn't be able to sail this thing home even if you wanted to. It takes a crew of at least four experienced sailors to get it moving in the right direction."

He kept chuckling, even as he began to shake his head. "Why can't you believe me when I tell you that my intentions are pure? But no, you have to go and threaten me again. I am going to pay you back in full—you just have to be a little more patient."

"With what—this junk? I think Divine was on to something about it all not being genuine, and now I wonder if anything on this ship is worth as much as you say it is. I'm done trying to be nice. It's time for you to meet with Corozza so you two can work out how to repay your debt to his satisfaction. I promise, you won't like his proposal."

His casual mention of my husband's killer made my blood boil. I just had to get ahold of his phone. He must have Corozza in his contacts if he was threatening to set up a meeting with him.

"There's no need to threaten me with violence. We're both adults. We can talk it out," Alistair pleaded.

Good luck with that, I thought, just as Rhonda whispered, "Who is Corozza? He sounds like trouble."

I closed my eyes and took in a deep breath, glad I wasn't facing my friend. "You got that right."

Mac glared at our host for several seconds before finally replying in a low voice, "You had your chance." The finality in Mac's tone was as clear as a cloudless sky.

When he stormed off towards the door, Alistair trailed closely behind and grabbed his arm just as Mac was about to cross the threshold. "Where are you going?"

Mac shook his arm off. "To ask Captain Jack to sail us to the nearest harbor. I doubt it will take much convincing."

"Oh, no, you don't!" Alistair cried as he followed the much larger man up towards the wheelhouse.

As soon as the two quarrelling men were out of sight, Lucy apparently saw her chance to be alone with the necklace again, and shot off towards Alistair's office. Colin looked over at Rhonda and shrugged, before following Lucy into the other room.

Inwardly I cheered, glad to have a few seconds alone to examine the murder weapon. Rhonda's lower lip, however, shot out and begin to quiver before I could cross over to Divine's body. I followed my friend's line of sight, straight to Colin.

"You do like him, don't you?"

She attempted to shake off her glum expression by smiling at me, but her grin was still tinged with sadness. "Like I said before, he does seem to be a ladies' man. And he's known Lucy for far longer than me."

I paused and cocked my head at my friend. "What do you mean?"

"Oh, I overheard them talking earlier. I wasn't eavesdropping, mind you..." she said as her voice trailed off.

"Yes you were," I giggled, glad my friend was a born busybody. It was tough to not be able to tell her the truth about my interest in Alistair or his stolen goods, but it was a relief to know that I really didn't have to tell her everything. Thanks to Divine's murder, we were all trying to solve the mystery surrounding her death and the questions concerning the authenticity of the items Alistair wanted to sell off.

"Well, they were hemming and hawing about this and that, but I sensed they were sweet on each other, or once had been. I swear, if they'd been kids, they would have been playing footsie."

"That's odd. He was business partners with the man she claims set up her husband. Why would she be hanging around with Colin? Do you think they were a couple—or still are?"

Rhonda paused as she recalled the conversation. "They may have been. I'm not saying that I'm certain they were in a relationship, but he knew her kids well enough to ask about them. And he asked about her house, if she'd gotten a new porch light yet. Maybe they were in a relationship and it ended badly. It sounded like they haven't seen each other in quite a few years."

I patted her on the back. "Either way, well done. That explains why they seem to be ignoring each other for most of this trip. I just figured they didn't know each other well."

My mind filed that fact away, just as I realized we were still alone, but probably not for long. Alistair and Mac were presumably still duking it out upstairs, but their fight couldn't go on too much longer. I hoped that Mac won, and that we would soon be sailing back to the mainland. But as long as we were stuck here, I wanted to clear up one more mystery before deciding whether Rhonda and I needed to abandon ship.

"Say, while we have the chance, let's take a look at Robin Hood's bow. Something doesn't feel right about Divine's death. It might just be coincidence that the arrow fired right at that particular moment, or Alistair might have played a nasty trick on us all."

Rhonda searched my eyes, as if she couldn't believe that I thought our host would harm a soul. "You don't think he somehow caused the arrow to fire? He was nowhere near it!"

I figured Rhonda's infatuation with Alistair would hinder her judgment. Regardless, I skipped over to Robin Hood, hoping to complete my examination before our host returned. It didn't take long to figure out how he'd done it. A tiny servo motor hidden just under Robin's green sleeve released a metal clip, that presumably had held the bow's string taut. It was a long shot that the force would be enough to kill someone, but Divine had been standing quite close, and the arrow had presumably pierced major organs. Based on her blood loss, even if we had been docked when it happened, I doubted paramedics would have been able to save her life.

"Rhonda, honey, could you please come over here."

With obvious reluctance, my bestie dragged her feet over to the mannequin.

"See this device?" I pointed at the small black motorized device tied to Robin Hood's arm, then pulled the string back, to show her that it fit into the metal clip. "This device was holding the string taut. It's wireless, meaning someone could have triggered it from a distance."

"That's just plain silly! Carmen, what is wrong with you? Why can't you just accept that Alistair is an interesting man and that we might be compatible? Just because you don't want to date yet doesn't mean that I can't."

"This has nothing to do with our love lives, Rhonda. I know you don't like to see the bad in anyone, but it sure looks to me like Alistair had a murder weapon set up in his living room." I made a show of looking down at Divine's corpse as I spoke.

Rhonda, however, refused to do the same. "That makes no sense. Why on earth would he do that?"

"That is a great question, and one I hope to soon get an answer to. But preferably after he's behind bars."

"Carmen!" Rhonda huffed as her fists flew to her hips.

I slid over to my friend and wrapped an arm over her shoulder. "Honey, I don't know what game Alistair is playing with his guests, but I don't want us to end up as collateral damage. It's time for us to leave."

"What do you mean, leave? We're in the middle of the ocean."

"We aren't that far from shore, and the lifeboats are equipped with motors—I already checked. If we can get into one of the dinghies without

Alistair noticing, we can at least get far enough away that another ship might spot us bobbing around. It's safer than staying here."

"But why would we need to do that?"

I frowned at her. "Why are you being so stubborn? I just proved to you that Divine's death was not an accident!"

"Until we can talk to Alistair, I refuse to believe that he set that arrow up just to kill one of his guests."

This time we both looked to Divine, crumpled on the floor, the arrow still piercing her side. The blood had stopped flowing but was pooling up around her lifeless body. I looked over at Robin Hood again, wondering why else Alistair would have placed that servo motor there, if not to do away with one of his guests. Yet, when my eyes rolled over to his neighbor, James Dean, I forgot all about the merry archer.

"Where is James Dean's switchblade?"

21

Abandoning Ship

A scream pierced the night. I tore to the doorway, just ahead of the rest. In the passageway was Mac, a switchblade sticking out of the back of his upper arm.

"Help—Alistair stabbed me!" Mac groaned as he stumbled into the saloon. The blood flowing out of his arm left a bright red trail on the floor marking his path.

I faltered, leaning back against the wall to keep myself from falling over, my fears confirmed. Alistair was picking off his guests, one by one.

"Me and Alistair wrestled on the stairs, and when we tumbled into the wheelhouse, Captain Jack screamed and ran off. I turned to push Alistair off of me, when I felt a sharp sting in my arm. Then I saw the knife. Alistair ran off before I could grab him, but he must still be on this ship. We've got to find that psychopath."

"How do we know you didn't stab yourself?" Lucy asked.

"Use your eyes—the knife's sticking out of the back of my arm. How could I have done that?" He twisted around to try to grab the blade, unsuccessfully.

"Can somebody pull it out? It's killing me."

I sprang forward before anyone else could be of assistance. "We'd better get a towel first. And a bandage big enough to cover his wound." I took a closer look, pulling back the torn fabric, none too gently. "Luckily for you, it's not deep, but you are going to need stitches."

Colin found an emergency medical kit under the kitchen sink that was surprisingly well stocked. Luckily for Mac, first-aid courses were required by my employer, precisely for this sort of emergency. My patient was not a crybaby, but he did visibly flinch as I stitched up the hole in his arm. Just as I was admiring my work and about to slap a bandage over it, a loud splash had us all running out onto the deck.

Bobbing in the dark waters next to our ship was one of the two lifeboats, with Captain Jack and our crew of five aboard.

Colin cupped his hands and called down to them. "Why are you all in that boat?"

"I'm not staying here with you psychopaths!" Jack screeched, his hand already on the motor. "I don't know which one of you killed that woman, but I know it wasn't one of my crew. And now Alistair is attacking his guests with a knife? We're leaving before something horrible happens to one of us."

"Divine's death was an accident," Lucy called down. "She wasn't murdered."

I let her comment slide, more focused on the fact that our captain was abandoning ship—with us still on board. "You can't just leave us bobbing around the North Sea."

"Yes I can, if that's what it takes to save my crew! No job is worth dying for. I've sabotaged the other lifeboat so you can't follow us, but I'll alert the Coast Guard once we reach land," Jack screamed back, then revved the engine, drowning out our cries as he sped off towards shore.

"You can't do this!" Lucy shrieked.

My stomach sank when he mentioned the sabotage. "Great, there goes our escape plan. Now we're stuck on a ship with a killer," I groused to Rhonda, but she seemed too focused on our captain sailing away to hear me.

I rubbed my hand along my cheek, wondering how this evening had gone so wrong, so quickly.

If Mac was telling the truth about our host, that would mean Alistair had already tried to kill two of the five invited guests. But why would Alistair murder Divine and try to off Mac? A horrible thought flooded my mind. He'd repeatedly said that he'd invited the five of them here under the guise of making amends, but actually it was to use them to peddle his wares. And the two who had openly threatened to interfere with his auction had been attacked.

Earlier, Rhonda and I assumed that everyone here had a reason to want harm to come to Alistair. Yet he had just as good a reason to want harm to come to them. Was Robin Hood's arrow a backup he'd put in place, in case his guests didn't go along with his plan? If it was, had he set up any other booby traps around the ship?

My mind raced through the probabilities, hoping to think up another reason for Alistair to attack those two. Yet it sure seemed to be a simple case of "you're either with me, or against me." And Rhonda and I were stuck at his killer party. I groaned, realizing if I hadn't invited her to Europe, we wouldn't be here, trapped on this ship.

I looked over at my friend, wondering whether she'd ever forgive me for asking her to come over. Yet now was not the time to worry about that. We had to locate and subdue our murderous host, before he struck again. The ship was not huge, but offered plenty of hiding places. Trying to flush him out would be a dangerous task, if not a deadly one. I couldn't let Rhonda be a part of that.

I turned to Colin. "We've got to find Alistair."

"You're right. Mac and I will search the lower cabins and hold. Why don't you three stay in the saloon until we return." Colin looked to Mac for confirmation as he spoke, getting a nod of approval from the tough guy.

Normally I wouldn't put up with that sort of macho behavior. I was quite capable of taking care of myself, perhaps even more so than Colin. Yet in this particular situation, I was happy to let the men deal with tracking down the killer roaming the ship. My bestie needed me by her side. I just hoped she would forgive me for getting her into this mess.

22

Rose-Colored Glasses

"Why would I be upset with you? I'm having the time of my life! This is so much more exciting than sitting by the pool, sipping iced tea all day long. Heck, I've only been here a day, and we've already met so many interesting people and gotten to sail on a pirate ship! I can't wait to see what happens next."

I blinked, caught off-guard by her response. Here I was, fearing for her life, and she was enjoying herself immensely. *Should I be concerned?* I wondered. Rhonda was not dumb by any means, though she could sometimes be incredibly naïve. Her ability to always find the silver lining in any situation was usually a breath of fresh air, but in this case, it could get her killed.

"You do realize that Alistair tried to murder two of his guests, right?" In my mind, finding our host was our top priority. If Alistair had attacked Mac with the intent to kill him, we wanted to lock our host up, before he could do more harm. Luckily for me, the others were also convinced that Alistair had murderous intentions, although Rhonda still refused to believe it could be so.

While Mac and Colin were searching the ship for Alistair, Rhonda and I were huddled in one corner of the vast saloon, our heads close together. Even though Lucy was busy examining that art deco necklace again, all the way on the other side of the space in Alistair's office, I didn't want to risk letting her overhear a single syllable of our conversation.

"Even though we have nothing to do with whatever is going on, we are on the ship. And if Alistair decides to clean up any witnesses…"

Rhonda blew off my remark with the wave of her hand. "Oh, you're seeing things. When we find Alistair, we're going to ask him about Robin Hood's bow. I bet there's a simple explanation for it."

"Okay, but he also stabbed Mac. How do you think he is going to justify that?"

"You know, I've been thinking—are we sure Mac is telling the truth?"

"Excuse me?" Rhonda's comment threw me for a loop. "I thought it was pretty clear what happened."

My friend leaned back on one heel as she wrapped her arms around her torso. "Alright, well, tell me this. Who seems more trustworthy to you—Mac or Alistair?"

I blew out my cheeks. She had a good point. "Up until Divine's death, I would have said Alistair, hands down. But something is off about that man. And Mac couldn't have stabbed himself in the back of the arm like that."

"Unless he had wedged the knife in between something and backed up into it," Rhonda offered. "If Alistair is arrested for Divine's murder and attacking Mac, chances are that his collection will be confiscated. I bet Mac's hoping to steal it before the authorities arrive."

As obtuse as she could be, sometimes her insight was crystal clear. I was quiet a moment, considering her words, until I came to the conclusion that she was spot on. "I didn't even think about that. I bet you're right. You know, for someone who sees the good in almost everyone, you do have a wicked imagination. I would hate to get on your bad side!"

"Oh, honey, you could never get on my bad side! You're too special to me." When she pulled me in for a quick hug, I had to dodge one of her hair extensions that was starting to come loose. "Now, before we pass judgment on Alistair, let's see what he has to say."

"Agreed." I pushed her hair clip back into place, then turned so I could look her in the eye. "But could you at least stick close to me? If anything happens to you, I will never forgive myself. Nor will your kids."

Rhonda sniggered. "I don't know, you haven't talked to Jules for a while.

She's gotten to be quite the adventurer. In fact, I bet she'd be thrilled to know I'm on a ship full of dangerous strangers. She's always telling everyone what a boring old fuddy-duddy I am."

"Well, Sam sure wouldn't. I bet she'd be worried sick!"

"That's true. She's always been more of a homebody than her older sister, which is why we won't tell her every little detail about what happened so far, right?"

Rhonda's two "girls," as she often called them, could not have been more different, despite having been raised in the same household by the same doting parents. Julie, or Jules for short, was her oldest child, a dark-haired thirty-two-year-old woman who always kept to herself during the family functions I'd briefly seen her at. Although, since she'd graduated from university with a master's degree in international relations, she'd been abroad more than in the States. In fact, when I thought about it, I couldn't recall the last time I'd seen her at a family gathering.

Her five-year-younger sister, however, didn't even have a passport, as far as I knew. The bubbly blonde was happiest in her garden, playing with her two beautiful children and a plethora of animals she'd rescued from local shelters. She was a constant presence at any event Rhonda organized, often responsible for providing the delicious finger foods we feasted on. I always looked forward to sampling her classic seven-layer dip and salmon wraps. Although she seemed like a nice kid, I tended to sidestep her at parties, simply to avoid being trapped in the corner while she talked my ear off about her latest rescue pet.

I loved both women simply because they were Rhonda's children, but knew I could never take their mother's place. And I was one hundred percent certain neither one would forgive me if I got Rhonda killed. Technically Rhonda was the one invited to the party, but I had pushed her to come over to Europe in the first place. If she hadn't been on that plane, she wouldn't have met Colin, and we wouldn't have ended up here.

So on top of everything else going on, I now needed to add "bodyguard" to my list of things to do.

I pressed my hands together under my chin and batted my eyes up at my friend. "Pretty please with sugar on top, will you be more alert and less trusting than you usually are? At least until we get off this wretched ship?"

My bestie ticked her tongue against her teeth. "Fine. If it makes you feel better, I'll try to be more cynical and suspicious—like you."

"Excellent. Thank you."

23

Catching A Killer

Luckily for us, the brigantine was small, and Alistair was easily found. We soon heard his voice echoing through the ship. "Unhand me!"

"No! You killed Divine and stabbed Mac. I'm not letting you go, I'm turning you over to the police," Colin replied. Seconds later, he burst through the saloon door, calling out triumphantly, "I found our killer!"

"What is this nonsense?" Alistair blustered. "I didn't harm anyone."

"Then why were you hiding out in the storage room?"

"I was down in the hold trying to find some more champagne, but we don't seem to have any more crates of it."

"What were we going to celebrate—you killing off a second guest?" I said. "I found that servo you used to release Robin Hood's arrow."

Alistair frantically looked around the room, as if he was trying to find a way out. "You're all crazy! I haven't hurt anyone."

"Mac's still alive, Alistair. You got him in the arm, not the back. He's already caught us all up on your actions, so you can stop lying now."

Seconds later, Mac rushed into the saloon. "You found him?"

When he caught sight of Alistair, Mac rushed towards the Hollywood director, his arms outstretched as if he planned on throttling him. "Why, I oughta…"

Before Mac could carry out on his threat, Alistair collapsed onto the floor, as if the weight of the world was on his shoulders.

"Why did you have Robin's bow rigged to fire? I found the servo, so I assume you have the trigger in your pocket." Alistair glanced away as if he hadn't heard me, but the rest did.

"Are you saying Alistair somehow fired the arrow remotely?" Lucy gasped, her eyes widening in fright as she backed away from our host.

Alistair bolted upright. "No! I set it up like that for a party and forgot to remove the motor, that's all."

My eyebrows shot up. "What kind of party was that?"

"We'd held an archery competition among the mannequins. Robin Hood won. But that was years ago. I doubt it even works."

"Really? Can someone hold him so I can check his pockets?"

Colin grabbed our host and pulled him up, then held Alistair's arms tight, so I could search his elaborate costume. The tiny push-button device was in his pants pocket. Finding the servo brought me no joy, but rather confirmed my worst suspicions and made me fear for my friend's life.

Lucy threw her hands against her cheeks and screamed when she saw me pull the electronic trigger from his pocket.

"You killed Divine! Which means Mac was right. You tried to kill him, too!"

Alistair began shaking his head, as if he was about to deny it, but then suddenly his shoulders straightened and he held his head high.

"If Mac hadn't turned around, I would have gotten him in the back, just as I planned." His voice was stronger than it had been, as if he could finally stop playing whatever game he'd dreamt up.

"I knew it!" Mac raged. "But why? I thought we'd settled our debts."

"Had we? You'd already demanded my ship, the falcon statue, and necklace as down payment. How much more would you expect from me? You and Corozza never would have let me go." Alistair shook his head sadly. "You only have yourself to blame. If you had trusted me to repay you, I wouldn't have had to take such extreme measures."

"Why did you invite us here to this ship—to murder us?" Lucy asked.

Alistair shook his head. "No, to help me sell off my possessions, so I can move back to land. I'm turning seventy-five this year, and my body's starting to give out. But I can't get regular medical treatment if I'm bobbing around at sea. It's time to find a place to settle down, but everything I have is tied up in this boat and my collection. I haven't worked on a film set in ten years, and nobody wants to hire a washed-up has-been. So I have no choice but to sell it all."

"But why ask us, of all people, to help you?" Lucy cried.

"Because I knew you were all still angry with me, and felt as if I'd cheated you, somehow."

Colin snorted. "Because you did!"

Alistair ignored his remark and kept his head held high. "I thought if I could win you over and get you on my side again, you wouldn't interfere with the sale, and maybe even help me rustle up a few clients."

"So you could fund your new life on land," Colin added. "You were never planning on paying us back. Have you no conscience or sense of compassion?"

Alistair glared at him. "What was I supposed to do? If any of you had seen this online, you would have come after me and demanded the profits, or tried to sabotage the sale. I couldn't let you do that."

"But your plan backfired, and Divine was going to destroy you anyway. Is that why she had to die?" I asked through gritted teeth.

Alistair finally let his head hang in shame. "Yes. I thought if she was the face of the auction, she would draw in a less discerning crowd. But she threatened to badmouth me and my props to anyone who would listen. I couldn't let her do that."

"So she had to go?" I finished for him.

All he did was nod.

Rhonda squinted at Alistair as if she was seeing him for the first time. "You've lied about everything tonight! Do you even have a spiritual guru?"

Alistair hung his head. "No, I do not."

"I figured as much. Who'd trust a guru named Fred with their spiritual journey?"

Mac nodded his chin at the glass case closest to him. "So is any of this stuff genuine?"

Our host looked away. "Almost all of it is what I've described. Although, after I'd used up your two million, I did sell off a few of the pricier items to fund my lifestyle and may have replaced them with less valuable substitutes."

"Like the Marilyn Monroe dress?" I asked.

"Audrey Hepburn's, too. And the Indiana Jones accessories, a few of the posters, and a handful of trinkets—bowties, shoes, that kind of thing," Alistair admitted. "I'd kept a copy of their certificates and because they were common items, I figured I could try again."

"That's pretty low. You're asking quite a bit for those items."

Alistair nodded absently. "Most collectors can't tell the difference between an old dress, or a newer one that's been treated to look worn. I must have forgotten to remove the labels from a few items, which was a silly mistake and one I won't make again."

Suddenly Alistair looked up at his invited guests, the twinkle back in his eye. "It's not too late, you know. The auction can still continue on as planned, and I can still give you your cut of the profits. I mean, I didn't actually kill you, did I, Mac? It was more of a scratch."

Alistair remained calm, so much so that I was truly frightened for our lives. He showed no remorse, only a single-minded determination to achieve his goal. Wasn't that the definition of a psychopath? It was clear he was going to keep going, and that those he perceived as a threat would be eliminated.

Why did fate bring us here? I moaned internally, wishing I could somehow snap my fingers and transport myself off this blasted ship, and away from this ruthless killer.

"You know what, Alistair? If you're going to jail for killing Divine and attacking me, then you won't be needing any of your possessions, will you? I think we'll help ourselves to them, instead," Mac said, confirming Rhonda's assessment.

For the first time since we'd caught him, Alistair showed genuine emotion—and lots of it. He began kicking at Colin's legs and screaming. "You can't do that—it's all I have!"

"We have to tie him up," I yelled over his screams, desperate to contain this threat. "And then we have to find our phones and call the Coast Guard."

"Agreed," Colin yelled back as he and Mac wrestled Alistair to the ground. "But I say we lock him in his bedroom. He might squirm out of his bonds before help arrives."

24

Locking Up The Suspect

It took three of us to work Alistair into his room. But after we locked the door, he stopped pounding on it and became strangely quiet, instead. Our host was contained for now, but could we keep him locked away until we got back to shore? This boat was so rickety and in need of maintenance, I wouldn't be surprised if he could kick his way through a wall, if he got agitated enough. It was too bad none of the guests had brought sleeping pills with them. Just for a moment, I wished I had the Baroness by my side. She traveled with enough uppers and downers that her carry-on would be considered a pharmacy in some countries.

Colin held the key to Alistair's bedroom out to my friend. "Here, Rhonda, you should hold onto this. You and Carmen are the only ones with no reason to harm Alistair."

Rhonda kept her hands planted on her hips. "Hold your horses; you have some explaining to do first. Why exactly did you invite me to this party? You apparently knew who Alistair had invited and why. So why did you think I would be welcome here?"

"If I had known what Alistair's real intention was, I never would have gotten you involved." Colin gazed at Rhonda with such remorse, I knew she wouldn't be able to stay mad at him for long.

"The truth is, I dreaded coming to this party, but had to see Alistair again. I thought you being here would help lighten the mood, and maybe prevent him from being his old arrogant self. Plus, he'd already hinted that he was going to sell off some of his collection to pay off his debts to us, which is why I thought fate had intervened when we sat next to each other on the plane."

He cast his eyes down, as shame blossomed his cheeks. "I thought if you could help us verify whether the items were authentic, it would help ease my mind."

"Do you mean to say that you assumed I would be happy to evaluate his collection?"

Colin ran a hand through his hair. "I know, it was foolish of me to assume. But you must understand that investing in movie props requires some faith in the seller's honesty and the authenticity of the item on offer, and I had no illusions that Alistair would change. He would always do anything to make a fast buck, even if it meant screwing over a partner or supposed friend. But if you could prove to me that some of it was genuine, then I could sleep better at night, knowing he really was trying to do the right thing and pay us back."

"That was a low thing you did, lying about why you invited me to this party. I'm not saying I didn't enjoy meeting everyone, but you should have been upfront with me. I probably would have said yes anyway simply because this whole trip over here to Europe is supposed to be an adventure." Rhonda wagged her finger at him. "But I hate it when people lie to me."

"Would you still consider appraising his collection? It would be a great help to us to have a more realistic idea of the items' worth. I don't trust the price list Alistair provided or the descriptions he'd written. You might even be able to weed out the forgeries he referred to."

Rhonda glared up at him, but I knew how much my friend enjoyed testing her skills. "Alright, I'll take a closer look and see what I can see, although I can't guarantee that I can provide you all with a realistic estimate of their worth. But if there are any profits to be made, all three of you should get a share. Carmen and I don't need any of his stuff."

"That's very kind of you. I agree, we should all reap the benefits."

Mac, however, narrowed his eyes.

Rhonda cleared her throat and glanced over at Destiny's body, still lying in front of Robin Hood. The blood forming a pool around her body had now begun to congeal and turn a dark burgundy. Her expression was exactly the same as it had been when she fell, one of terror and confusion, now frozen onto her face forever. I shivered, hoping we wouldn't suffer a similar fate before this night was through.

"I do have one request before I help you all out. We have to cover up Divine's body. I know we can't move her body because of the police, but I can't spend any more time in this room with her staring at me, all glassy eyed. It feels wrong. I buy my hair extensions from her network!"

"I can do that for you," Colin said gallantly. "I'll grab a blanket from one of the cabins in a minute."

"While you're examining the objects, I'll search Alistair's office for the collection's documentation," I said, curious to see whether he had all of the paperwork concerning the items on Myrtle's list. My dear friend was unwittingly helping me verify their authenticity, so it was the least I could do.

"How fun, it's like we're detectives working the case from two angles," Rhonda tittered, her eyes gleaming with delight. How I wished I could tell her how right she was.

"I'll help you, Carmen," Lucy replied. "I want to see those certificates of authenticity with my own eyes."

"Sure, why not? Four hands make for lighter work."

"Shouldn't we call for help first? We are drifting around the ocean without a captain," Colin said.

"You make a good point," I conceded. "That should be our priority. But the radio is down. We'll have to get our phones out of the safe."

"It's in the wheelhouse, right?" Mac asked.

"I believe so. I saw Captain Jack take them up with him, just before we boarded," Colin offered.

Mac pounded on Alistair's bedroom door. "What's the code to the safe you have our phones locked up in?"

The captive laughed heartily before answering. "Do you really think I'm going to give you the combination? Good luck getting the safe open."

25

Safe Crackers

We left Rhonda with the collection, and the four of us climbed the short staircase up to what some guests called the wheelhouse and others the bridge: a small raised room above the main deck that housed the wheel used to steer the ship. From here we had a great view of the choppy sea and smattering of rain, but not of the stars above. I cupped my hands on the glass and looked out past the square masts billowing in the wind, towards the second dinghy. To my dismay, Jack hadn't lied. A harpoon stuck out of the boat's hull, making clear that it was no longer seaworthy.

Mac's attention, however, was focused on the small safe built into the back wall of the wheelhouse.

"What do you think?" I asked the room, but really was pointing my question towards the one person I figured would have some safe-cracking experience. My instincts were right.

"Let me handle this one," Mac said as he made a show of cracking his knuckles.

Colin folded his arms over his torso and leaned in, as if he was examining the safe for weak spots. "Can I help?"

Mac shrugged. "Sure, why not. I might need some assistance."

"Alright, we'll leave you to it," I replied, as I nodded to Lucy. "We'll be in the office."

Mac bent over the safe and examined it for a moment before rising and saying to Colin, "We're going to need a crowbar, some grease, and a drill. If you come across a sledgehammer or blow torch, grab them, too. They could come in handy."

Colin regarded Mac with a mix of respect and fear. "You really do know how to crack a safe."

"Yeah, well, we can't all be born on the right side of the tracks. Are you going to help me search for tools, or not?"

Colin bowed deeply before him. "Lead the way, kind sir."

Mac's expression darkened, but he let Colin's sarcastic remark slide and headed below deck, while Lucy and I turned back towards the saloon and Alistair's office.

26

Big Fat Liar

One of the first lessons I'd learned as a budding art sleuth for the Rosewood Agency was the importance of always carrying a bobby pin with me—which is why I usually tucked a pair into my thick hair at the base of my neck. Seeing as my boss wanted us to stay under the radar and not carry around criminal-looking things like guns or a set of picklocks, I had learned to adapt. Bobby pins, I'd come to realize, were such versatile tools and so inconspicuous. With that bendy strip of metal in my hand, I could pick a lock, interrupt a security laser's beam, or block a window from closing properly. Heck, I bet I could even use it to stab someone in the eye, if need be. Luckily, I had not yet had reason to try the last.

So the simple lock that Alistair used to protect his archival cabinet was no match for my trusty bobby pin. A little jiggling, and it fell open, revealing a well-organized system of folders and dividers. One of the three pull-out drawers was dedicated to his movie memorabilia, and another to his ship and personal finances. The contents of the third drawer surprised me a little: medical records, hospital pamphlets, and expired prescriptions. Alistair had mentioned that his health was deteriorating, but other than a limp, he didn't seem sickly.

"Finding the certificates of authenticity should be our first priority," Lucy said, eagerness in her voice.

"I agree." I couldn't wait to check the documents against Myrtle's list. From what I'd seen, it sure looked as if he still had most of them, but I hadn't had a chance to read every description of the almost two hundred pieces he had displayed in the saloon and his office. The certificates would help me confirm which of the items he still had in his possession. The more information I could provide Myrtle with, the more brownie points I expected to receive.

However, I also knew that Lucy was searching for something in particular, and I had a sneaking suspicion it had to do with that necklace she was obsessed with. So I did the courteous thing and handed all of the files labeled "Collection" and "Auction" to her, knowing she couldn't dash off with the documents because we were adrift in the North Sea. Then I set about examining the rest of the documentation filling the other two drawers.

It didn't take long for me to realize that Alistair was a big fat liar. Ten minutes in, I found my first clue as to our host's ulterior motives in the form of a recently signed rental contract for a condominium located on Spain's Costa Brava. He wasn't considering moving ashore; he already had. Despite his repeated assurances that all of the proceeds from the sale would be used to pay his friends back, the bank account designated for the profits from the auction was the same one he was using to pay his condo's service fees with.

Another folder revealed another lie, one that explained how he'd managed to stay underground for the past ten years. *La Vida Loca*, the ship he had promised to sign over to Mac, was not even registered in Alistair's name, but that of a Spanish film company—and I would bet money that this company was owned by his producer friend.

After I'd finished searching through the two drawers that had nothing to do with his collection, I dove into the third to see what else he'd saved. Lucy had the folders of certificates and those containing information about the auction, but there was also another set of folders marked "Proof of Sale" that we'd yet to go through. Most were quite thin, but there were several, meaning it took me a while to work through them all. In the end, it was time well spent for their contents were highly informative.

Several folders contained a single sheet of paper listing the items Alistair had purchased from an auction house or private collector, as well as the price he'd paid for them. None were worth more than a thousand dollars when he'd bought them, yet all had quadrupled in value since, at least according to Alistair's price list. He was either an incredibly lucky investor with a keen eye, or he was planning on gouging whoever bought them. Knowing what little I knew about our host, I suspected the latter.

Another folder contained a sales contract for a rather large collection of props from old spaghetti westerns that he had bought from another film director seven years ago. When I compared the prices Alistair had paid, to those he had set as his reserve price for the auction, there was a gigantic difference that could not be accounted for by seven years' inflation. Again, it appeared that Alistair had either gotten them for a steal, or was planning on asking far too much for them.

At the very back of the drawer, was a thick folder marked "Mine." Indeed, it was full of the certificates of authenticity from props used in his own movies. Most were the scary masks and futuristic weapons I'd noticed earlier but avoided, as well as a number of smaller items—glasses, headbands, and prosthetic noses—used during filming. A few of the items listed appeared in his earlier, nonslasher films, though, and were more ordinary in nature.

Yet for the props that had come from his own movies, I could find no documents showing that he had paid for any of them. Had he taken the props with him after filming, without asking? Or had it been written into his contract that he could keep a number of the props used? That was a question I did not expect to find an answer to, nor was it really that important in the grand scheme of things. It was, however, evidence that our host may have more illegally acquired goods in his collection.

After I'd gone through all of the files and folders, I realized that what I had not found was quite telling. In his archives, there was not a single sales receipt for any of the items on Myrtle's list. I'd have to double-check his desk in a minute, but it seemed to be another piece of proof that Alistair had acquired them illegally.

Everything I'd found so far only seemed to underscore how right Divine had been. Though she was wrong in saying that most of the objects were forgeries or replicàs, there were certainly enough questionable items in the bunch to give any legitimate buyer pause.

While I was busy digging through the cabinet's contents, Lucy had spent her time muttering under her breath as she flicked through the thick folder containing all of the certificates of authenticity. I couldn't tell whether she was angry or irritated, but figured it was best to let her be. When she'd almost reached the end, Lucy seemed to have found what she was looking for. She didn't say anything, but she suddenly pushed the rest aside and slowly read the page in her hand—word for word, by the looks of it.

Only after she had set the single page back on the desk and let out a long sigh did I dare speak to her. Yet instead of interrogating her about her findings, I decided to lead with my own.

I raised my pile of papers in the air to get her attention. "Alistair wasn't lying about wanting to move ashore, just about the timing. He purchased a condo on the coast of Spain two weeks ago, which explains why he won't need his ship after the auction."

"You are joking!"

"It gets worse. The bank account he's funneling the proceeds of the auction's sale into is the same one he's using to pay several monthly bills."

Lucy's forehead crinkled up so much, I was now certain her face was not filled with Botox. "What are you talking about?"

After I'd caught her up, all she could do was shake her head. "Is Alistair capable of telling the truth or being honest with anyone? No wonder he's been alone all of these years."

She sat a moment, seemingly contemplating something, before rummaging through the pile of certificates again. She soon pulled one out of the pile and held it up for me to see. "What you've discovered fits in well with my own findings. The Maltese Falcon statue isn't from Bogart's version, but that 1975 sequel, *The Black Bird*."

A chuckle escaped my lips. "You have got to be kidding. And here he was acting like it was one of the highlights of the auction. Doesn't he want two million for it?"

Lucy laughed along, but I could tell her heart wasn't in it. Instead, she kept gazing at the document. "It's so strange to see that name again, *The Black Bird*. It was one of the first films my husband worked on as props master, long before we met."

My ears pricked up. Sure, coincidences happened all the time in everyday life, but in my line of work, it was imperative to take note of them. "Seriously? That's quite a coincidence."

"I suppose, but it could mean anything—or nothing," Lucy sighed as she tossed the page back onto the pile.

"I wonder if Alistair has described this statue as being from the 1941 version on his website or not." I grabbed the Maltese Falcon's certificate and began to read through it, when Lucy handed another document to me.

"Divine showed us that the dress the Marilyn Monroe mannequin is wearing is made of a polyester blend, but this certificate says it's made of rayon-acetate crepe."

I nodded slowly. "Is that what it should have been made of?"

"It is, I looked it up online."

Before I could contemplate what this meant, she lifted another paper off the desk. "Then there is this. It's the certificate for that art deco necklace displayed in the office. According to this, the rubies and sapphires are genuine. But that can't be! They are clearly made of glass."

"That is strange." I took a moment to glance over the document. "Either this is a forged document, or Alistair sold off the real necklace and is now trying to sell this one off as the real thing."

"Either way, it looks like he was going to scam whoever bought it. What a horrible man."

I cleared my throat and looked at my companion sideways. "Lucy, I don't mean to pry, but why are you so obsessed with that necklace? I overheard you say to Alistair that your husband made this one"—I nodded towards the glass case holding the jewelry in question—"and another version."

"Shoot, I thought I was speaking softly enough that no one else could hear me, but Alistair got me so riled up, I must have spoken more loudly than I thought. My husband, Gary, promised to give me the real necklace after they'd finished filming. But he was arrested before he could. It was the last film he worked on, bless him."

My eyes widened in surprise. It was a sweet gesture for Gary to say that, but could a props guy really give his wife a gem-filled necklace, one that the studio had paid him to make? I seriously doubted it. Yet it was another reference to a second necklace, even though there was only one on Myrtle's list and Alistair only had one on display. As much as I could imagine Alistair trying to pull a bait and switch with the necklace, as he had apparently done with Monroe's dress, he did seem genuinely surprised to learn that another one even existed. I tended to believe that he didn't have it, simply because if he did have the more valuable version, letting his friends see the genuine gem-filled necklace would have eased their minds that he was serious about paying them back.

"You said your husband made them both. Was he a jeweler?"

"He had worked as a jeweler and sculptor before he began working for WorldWide Studios in their props department. Gary was so talented, it didn't take long to get promoted to props master, which meant he was making all sorts of items for major motion pictures."

Lucy smiled as she pulled that fantastic hairpin out of her long locks and held it up for me to get a better look. "This is the last thing he made for me, and why I've kept my hair long for so many years. I found it in his nightstand, all wrapped up with a card addressed to me, after he'd been arrested. When I asked him about it during my next visit, he was overjoyed that I'd found it. He told me that he'd created it for a key scene, which was ultimately cut from the film, and hoped I would always keep it with me. Wearing it makes me feel complete, somehow."

"May I?" After she nodded her assent, I took it gently from her, surprised to feel its weight. The hairpin was several inches long and almost as thin as a paperclip, yet incredibly sturdy. A scroll of metal at one end served as the handle. Now that I could see it up close, there were several tiny gemstones, probably cut glass, embedded into the swirls. "It's quite beautiful. Gary is really talented."

"It's not worth anything, but it does have a high sentimental value."

When she held out her hand, I returned her pin and asked, "So is that how your husband knew Alistair—from WorldWide Studios?"

Lucy nodded as she twisted her hair back up and pushed the pin in, and I could see a wave of sadness passing over her face again.

When she remained quiet, I added, "I don't want to pry into your personal life"—she stiffened immediately at the mention of "personal"—"but how exactly did your husband know Alistair?"

I was afraid she was going to clam up again, but a glint in her eye told me there was something she'd been wanting to get off of her chest for ages. "What does it matter now? My husband, Gary, had a gambling problem. He and Alistair worked on a few B-movies when they were both starting out. Later, they both bet on horses at the same track. I knew Gary had borrowed money from him a few times, when he was down on his luck. But I thought he'd paid him back."

Lucy's eyes squeezed shut and a tear rolled onto her cheek, but she kept talking. "Until one night, Gary came home late and told me what he'd agreed to do. Alistair needed the money he'd lent Gary, to finance a new film, but Gary owed him almost fifty thousand dollars by then—money we certainly didn't have."

While Lucy wiped away a tear, I calculated inflation. Gary had really dug himself into a hole.

"So he agreed to help Alistair steal several movie props that would be easy to sell off, in lieu of repaying his debt. He was going to crate them up and set them close to the door, but Alistair would remove them from the premises, not Gary."

"How did he get caught, and not Alistair?"

"A few minutes after Alistair left, the police received an anonymous tip that one of the stolen props was in the back seat of Gary's car. He parked it in the employee lot, so it wasn't even locked! Anyone could have put it there, but the police didn't listen. Alistair had already fled the country by the time anyone went looking for him, and there were no other viable suspects. Gary took the fall for all of the thefts, not just that one silly mask."

"I heard you say he was incarcerated. Is he still inside, or has he been…" My voice trailed off when I saw how upset my words were making Lucy.

"He died in prison," she whispered.

"How did that happen? Did he fall ill, or have an accident?" My empathy level shot up to high. Losing a partner changed everything, especially when there were young children involved.

Lucy's head whipped up. "It was no accident. Everyone thought Gary knew where the stolen props were, even his own lawyer. A few months into his sentence, a group of inmates tried to beat the location out of him, but he couldn't tell them, even if he had wanted to. If they'd allowed him to be moved to a proper hospital, instead of treating him in that understaffed jail hospital, he might have made it. But we'll never know for certain now, will we? My two babies grew up without a daddy—that's something I'll never forgive Alistair for."

Alistair was far more evil than I could have imagined. Stealing money from a loan shark or your business partner was one thing, but setting up an innocent man to pay for a crime he did not commit was beyond horrible. Especially when it ended so badly, though admittedly even Alistair couldn't have predicted that outcome.

Her explanation caused me to mentally stumble, though. Here I thought Alistair had somehow owed her money, as he did the rest. He'd even implied that he'd put a price on what each invitee was owed. Yet, it didn't sound like that was the case with Lucy.

"Lucy, why are you really here? Alistair didn't owe you any money, like he did Colin, Divine, and Mac."

She gazed down into her lap, breaking eye contact with me.

"I only accepted the invitation because I thought Alistair had my necklace, the one Gary made and promised to me. It disappeared around the same time as the robbery, and I had always held out the hope that Gary had put it in one of the crates meant for Alistair and was planning on recovering it later."

Lucy threw up her hands as if she knew it was a crazy idea. "But now I discover that it was all for nothing. Alistair either never had the real necklace or has sold it. Otherwise he would be showing it off for us all, especially with Mac breathing down his neck."

I nodded, glad that she'd come to the same conclusion as I had about the chance that Alistair had the other necklace, but was keeping it hidden away.

"But why would you think that Gary had done that? Had he told you that he was planning on including something in the crates for you or your family?"

"Not exactly." Lucy looked away again. "He couldn't tell me explicitly what he meant because he was in prison by then, and the guards were listening in on our conversations. But he kept hinting that I had to find Alistair. At first, I thought he meant so I could help prove that Gary had not worked alone. But that wasn't it; it was more that Alistair had something of mine, but Gary could never be specific about it."

She laughed, but it was bitter, not sweet. "Silly, I know. But this is the first time Alistair has surfaced since, and I thought he would be man enough to hand it over, whatever it is. Especially after what happened to Gary. But if it was the necklace, something must have gone wrong because the one in that vitrine is definitely not worth more than a few hundred dollars. Or Gary hid it in something, and Alistair hasn't yet stumbled across it."

"Or Alistair has an incredible poker face." I paused a moment to consider our host. "Come to think of it, he's lied about pretty much everything since we got here. If it was worth a half million, maybe he set it aside, as a sort of backup plan, in case this auction is a flop?"

I considered our host and his motivations, before recalling another scene between the two. "Wait a second, that story you told about taking everything Gary was accused of stealing to the district's attorney's office…"

Lucy blushed. "That was a lie. I doubt she would have reopened the case even if Alistair waltzed in and confessed. No, she has always been convinced that Gary did it, and that he somehow passed the location of the stolen goods on to me. I swear, it seemed as if the police followed me wherever I went, the first two years after the robbery. They disappeared after that. I assumed they ran out of funding or something else became more of a priority."

I nodded, taking in her words. Man, she'd had a hard time of it. Her husband was accused of a crime he didn't commit; he was killed in prison, leaving her a widow with two small children; and yet the police still kept her under surveillance. That would mess with anyone's mind.

"What are you going to do now?"

"What I've been doing for the past ten years—keep my head held high and my nose clean. I couldn't bear for my children to go through another trial or lose another parent. We aren't rich by any means, but I've managed to give them a good life."

I ached to hug her, but given her aloof nature, I didn't dare.

Instead, I gestured towards the piles of paperwork spread across the desk. "So what do you think was Alistair's game plan? Was he going to pay you all back or take the money and run?"

Lucy shook her head. "I truly do not know. He had already built a website for the auction, so he must have been serious about going through with the sale. But if whoever ended up purchasing the Maltese Falcon had it appraised, surely an expert would be able to tell that it was not made in 1941."

"We can ask Rhonda about that, but yes, I would assume you are right," I interjected.

"And whoever bought my necklace would only have to open the box and they could see for themselves that the gems were fake!" Lucy added.

I paused to contemplate this new information. "Which can only mean that he was planning to disappear again before anyone realized that they had been scammed. And then poor Divine would have been the person they'd try to sue. Even if they didn't win, her association with the auction would have ruined her reputation. Oh, that poor woman. She must have known what he was up to, which would explain why she had to die."

Lucy's whole body shook. "This trip is a nightmare we can't wake up from, isn't it?"

I sighed, wishing I could say anything comforting, but I was at a loss. "You know what, it's time to show these certificates to Rhonda and see what she says. I bet she's had enough time to look over the collection and can tell us more about the pieces' values and authenticity."

Lucy's face lit up. "That would be wonderful. Why don't we ask her now?"

Yet when she rose, she wiped at her cheeks, almost surprised to feel tears on them. "Let me just wash my face first, then I'll join you. I don't want the others to see that I've been crying."

<h1 style="text-align:center">27</h1>

<h1 style="text-align:center">Shattered Glasses</h1>

With Lucy gone to the bathroom, I took the opportunity to search Alistair's desk, before skimming the certificates of authenticity. Of the thirty-three items on Myrtle's list, Alistair had documentation for twenty-nine here in this folder. That was going to make my company contact happy. But what would make her ecstatic was what I had not found. After having searched through all of the paperwork in his archives and desk, I had not found a single sales receipt or other proof of sale proving that Alistair had bought any of the props on Myrtle's list from a private collector or auction house. I couldn't wait to contact her and tell her the great news.

What was strange, though, was that there had to be at least two hundred objects on display, yet I counted only one hundred and eighty-seven certificates. Were the rest authentic props that he no longer had documentation for, or were they the replicas he'd mentioned? Whatever they were, Alistair must have hoped that the buyer would not make a fuss about the lack of paperwork. Yet, from what I had learned before coming on this trip, a certificate of authenticity was an important document for a serious collector to have, especially if they wanted to later resell it via a reputable auction house. I would have to match his current inventory with these documents, to see what he didn't have documentation for.

When Lucy returned to Alistair's office a few minutes later, looking refreshed and with her makeup touched up, she said, "If you don't mind,

136

I'm going to go and see how they are getting on with the safe, while you are talking with your friend. I do hope they can break in soon so we can call for help. I know Alistair's locked away, but I don't like being close to someone this evil."

"I hear you. Give us a shout when they get it open, will you?"

"Naturally."

We walked back through the saloon together until we spotted Rhonda. I chuckled as I took in my friend down on all fours, staring into one of the lower shelves of a glass case.

After Lucy waved to her and swept up to the wheelhouse, I turned to Rhonda. "What are you doing?"

"Trying to get a good look at one of the items on the bottom shelf. The label says it's one of the Christmas ornaments from *It's A Wonderful Life*, but I sure don't recall seeing anything like that in the film, and it's one of my favorites, so I've seen it quite often."

I circled around the case, slid the back open, and handed the ornament to her. "Is that easier?"

"How in the heck did you do that?"

"The only case that's locked is the one holding the Maltese Falcon."

"Don't I feel like a fool. Here I've been crawling around on my hands and knees trying to get a good look at everything!"

I took her hand and helped her up.

"What do you think so far? Are they genuine, or replicas that he's trying to pass off as the real thing?"

Rhonda brushed dust off of her skirt. "I'd say ninety-five percent appears to be what Alistair's description claims it is. I would have to check the certificates to be certain, but on face value, I trust them to be authentic."

"I did wonder if you'd had much experience with these kinds of collections."

"Honestly, not much. If we hadn't had a young man come in with a few props a few seasons ago, I would have been lost. But he'd inherited a pipe and hat used in a TV version of Sherlock Holmes and had no idea how much they were worth. I didn't either, so I asked him to come back during the next show. You know I prefer to appraise everything live in front of my studio audience, but I'm not above doing a bit of research, if it means a more accurate estimate."

She looked shyly over at me, as if she was embarrassed that she hadn't been able to discern the worth of the TV props, simply by looking at them. "Of course. I'm in awe of the fact that you could eyeball-estimate anything and get it right ninety-nine percent of the time!"

My answer seemed to satisfy her. "So I checked to see what similar items had sold for and called a few specialists just to be sure. Boy, am I glad that I'd done that because they weren't worth a few hundred dollars, as I had suspected. Wouldn't you know it—they were worth ten thousand dollars!"

My mouth gaped open. "Ten thousand dollars, for a hat and pipe?"

Rhonda snickered. "I know, I was surprised, too. It just proves that you never know what a buyer will pay for this kind of memorabilia, and it shows how important it is to do your research before you buy or sell anything."

My friend paused for a moment, and glanced around the room. "Having said that, Divine was right in that there are a few items with an inspection sticker or labels stating they were made in China, which is strange considering Alistair's descriptions for those say that they were handcrafted. But most of those are smaller items that he wasn't asking much for anyway, like those posters. Well, except of course, with exception of those two dresses."

She gestured towards the Marilyn Monroe and Audrey Hepburn mannequins. "Both of those gowns are made of fabrics that weren't even invented when they were seen on screen. And he was asking almost a half million for each."

I shook my head. "Geez, he's not just a crook, he's an inept one, to boot. How hard would it have been for him to remove those labels?"

"And take a look at those framed posters." I followed Rhonda over to a row of framed posters from classic and contemporary films, signed by the leading actors.

"I've had a lot of signed photographs, books, and posters across my desk on the show. So many famous people's signatures have been scanned in that you can usually look them up and compare the two. But even if you don't have access to the internet, there are a few things you can check, such as the type of paper used to print off the poster."

I straightened up, understanding what she meant. "For example, if the poster has been printed recently, but the film star died decades ago, the signature is fake."

"Exactly. Which brings us to Alistair's posters. Of the twenty on this wall, I'd say sixteen are the genuine article. But those last four are most likely forgeries. But in this case it's not the paper that gives them away."

I glanced over the four she'd pointed to, posters featuring Steve McQueen, Harrison Ford, Brad Pitt, and Rock Hudson, and then at the other sixteen. "How can you tell?"

Rhonda waved me closer. "Take a good look at the pen strokes."

I did as requested. "Alright. They seem to be the same kind of black felt pen of roughly the same width. What's so strange about that? Pens haven't changed that much over the years, have they?"

"True, but if you look to the other sixteen, the actors used a variety of pen types and colors to sign the posters. Even the pressure used varied; some actors barely touched the paper, and with others, their pens seemed to soak through and bleed a little. But these four are exactly the same color, width, and pressure. It looks to me as if the same felt pen was used to sign them, even though they are from movies spanning several years' time. The chance that the star in question always had access to exactly the same color and thickness of pen is pretty much nil. Which makes me seriously question their authenticity."

"Oh, boy, this is going to complicate things even further."

"Indeed, but again, most of his collection does seem to be authentic, as in they appear to be the correct age and material composition. Yet even those items that do seem genuine are priced far too high." Rhonda pursed her lips as she gazed around the room.

"What are you saying?"

"Five thousand dollars for a movie poster is on the steep side, even if it really was signed by Cary Grant. And that's his reserve price, which is the lowest price he's willing to sell it for, so he's expecting to get more for it. I've had this kind of thing on my show before, and I know these are usually not worth more than a few hundred dollars."

Rhonda then began walking back towards the office, careful to steer clear of Divine's corpse, now covered by a white sheet. "It's the bigger-ticket items from the Hollywood films that he keeps in his office that worry me the most. That necklace your buddy Lucy loves to look at, for example. I'd already noticed that the stones molded into the low-quality silver are made of paste. They aren't even transparent, so it was a poor copy or unimportant."

I nodded. "That makes sense. If it was meant to be torn off an actress's neck, then why go to all that trouble to make it look real? Which is what Lucy said it was created for; her husband made it."

"Oh, is that a fact?"

"But check this out." I pulled the certificate of authenticity out from behind my back, with a flourish. "According to Alistair's paperwork, there are seven sapphires and eight rubies in that silver setting."

Rhonda looked as if I had slapped her. "Are you saying that I got it wrong—that those stones are real?"

I couldn't help but laugh. "The look on your face! No, I'm saying that this certificate must be forged, or he sold the real one already and kept a copy of the paperwork."

Rhonda looked devastated. I could imagine how Alistair's deceitfulness had shattered her rose-colored view of the world. "He seemed so kind and sincere, but really he was a horrible man, and this party had nothing to do with penitence or seeking forgiveness. He was planning on using his friends for their connections to push his fakes. Or he set all of his hopes on Divine's television buyers being dumb enough to buy them. I wouldn't be surprised if he was planning on disappearing again, after the sale."

I sucked in my breath. "Are you clairvoyant? He already signed a lease for a condo on the Brava Coast in Spain, and it is pretty pricey."

"Is there anything he didn't lie about? Is that Maltese Falcon real, or is that a fake, too? I can't tell for certain, but the gems embedded into its head sure look fake. The case is locked so I can't get in to examine it."

"Let me help you there."

Using my trusty bobby pin, it only took a few seconds to free the bird. I removed it from its case, surprised at how light it was for a statue supposedly made of solid gold, and set it on the desk. Rhonda and I took in its jewel-encrusted surface and shiny gold feathers.

Even from this distance, something about it seemed off, but Rhonda was the expert when it came to kitschier things like this, so I kept my mouth shut so as to not influence her opinion. Of course I already knew that it was not what he had claimed it to be; I wanted to see whether Rhonda would discover that for herself.

My friend carefully lifted the statue from the desk. Good 'ole Rhonda, I thought, bless her for being so careful and considerate of old things.

"It doesn't look like real gold to me, more like a thick layer of gold leaf. But I would have to damage the surface in order to be certain. But it sure is light for something that should be solid."

She turned it over and stared at the base, before lying it down so the bottom was pointed at us. "Aha! No wonder it's so light. See these pinholes? They're pretty well covered up by the gold leaf, but it looks like there are four of them. Those are usually made by wax tubes, left in the mold when casting with molten metal. They act as ducts, releasing the noxious gases and let the rest of the wax run out of the center. Usually they are filled in later, but then, if the base never came into view, there would be no need for the props maker to do so."

She continued her inspection, turning the statue over in her hand, her forehead creasing into a ripple as she did. I loved watching her work; her concentration level was astonishing. "One of the easiest ways to spot a fake is to look at how an item has aged. Even when they are well cared for, a certain amount of rust and dust can get caught up in seams and whatnot. If this was made in 1941, I would have expected to see more aging here and here."

She pointed to the deep grooves lining the bird's back, and several more under its beak. "However this one seems to be in mint condition for something that old. I would say this has been cast more recently."

Rhonda turned to me. "And another thing doesn't add up. According to the description, this is one of the genuine Maltese Falcons and is decorated with all sorts of gems. But they aren't anything more than well-cut glass."

She laid it back down on the desk, somewhat less carefully this time. "It's quite a puzzle. If I didn't know better, I would say it is not the same piece Alistair describes on that little card next to the case. It's a well-made prop, but its material worth can't be more than a few hundred dollars. And that's being generous. Whether it was used in a film or not, I cannot tell. A specialist would have to look into that."

I stared at the statue. "Wow, he really was trying to screw over everyone he knew, wasn't he?"

I showed her the statue's certificate of authenticity, proving that it had been made for the 1975 version, and not the film brought out in 1941.

"I've got to hand it to you for seeing through his deceit. You've got an excellent eye, Rhonda."

"It's too bad. Alistair seemed like such an interesting fellow," she sighed. "But really, he was a liar and a cheat."

She scanned the paperwork one more time, then turned her attention back to the statue. "It being made in 1975 makes a whole lot more sense. There doesn't seem to be much dust on it, at least not as much as you would expect to find on something that's more than eighty years old."

She ran her hand over the statue's head, regarding it with a mixture of disappointment and sadness. "You know, it's too bad that Alistair had to throw a few fakes into the mix. Their presence taints the authenticity of the rest. Even though I would stake my reputation that most of the items on display are genuine and valuable, the forgeries' presence makes me question everything he's said about the sale so far. Without doing a whole lot of research, I wouldn't dare to set a price to anything on this ship."

She sighed as she glanced around the room. "I know I promised the others that I would give them estimates of these items, but this just isn't my area of expertise. Once we get our phones, I could look at a few online databases and see what I can find out about their provenance. The Smithsonian has a fantastic database filled with this sort of pop culture. But to do a thorough search would take weeks, if not months. He's got such an extensive collection, it'll take time to work through it all."

Before we could discuss it further, Colin and Lucy burst into the office.

"Hey, what are you doing with that?" Colin asked, pointing to the statue on the desk, still on its back.

"Are you trying to steal the falcon? I just showed you the documentation proving it's not even the right one," Lucy said.

I pooh-poohed away her remark. "Of course we aren't stealing it. You asked Rhonda to appraise the collection, and that's what she's doing."

"How did you get the lock open? Did Alistair give you the key?"

Rhonda blushed as she stuttered a gibberish response to Lucy's question.

"What my friend is trying to say is that it wasn't that hard to open. It's a cheap lock; all I had to do was hit it with a stapler and jiggle it a few times, and it fell open."

Colin studied the lock, then my face. "Who are you exactly?"

"Just a childhood friend of Rhonda's."

"Huh." The pair of invited guests circled the statue. "It doesn't look like it's made of solid gold, does it?" Colin said, disappointment in his voice.

"It's from the 1975 version. Alistair lied about everything," Lucy explained.

"Is it even one of the props used in that film, or is this some sort of replica?" Colin asked Rhonda.

My best friend shook her head. "I don't know. This is getting out of my league. I would have to research how many copies were made and what they were made of, before I could even venture a guess. But it is clearly not solid gold, and those are not real gems. But it still could have been featured in the 1975 film." Rhonda bit her lip, as if she was considering the statue's condition as she spoke.

"Once we're rescued, someone more familiar with authentic props will have to examine these. I wish I could help you more, but a specialist would have to do some serious research into their provenance to know how much they were worth."

"Sure, and they'll expect a generous commission and proof that we own them. Lucy said you didn't find sales receipts for all of the items," Colin groused.

Rhonda nodded. "Without the right documentation, it will be challenging, if not impossible, that's true."

"We still appreciate your help with this, Rhonda." Colin kept his eyes on the bird as he spoke, as he squeezed my friend's shoulder.

"It was my pleasure." She looked up at him, trying to meet his eye, but his mind was apparently elsewhere.

"Shall we return the falcon to the glass case?" Lucy asked. "Do you mind if we keep pretending that it's locked up, at least for now? Mac is determined to get his due before we dock. If he knew the lock was busted, I bet he'd steal it in a heartbeat—whether it's genuine or not."

If he did take such extreme measures, would Rhonda and I still be safe here? Killing a whole crew and a half dozen guests was a massacre. Picking off a quartet might be less of an issue for him, especially given his employer's penchant for violence.

Rhonda and I looked at each other and nodded. "Sure thing. We're happy to play along."

"How is Mac doing with the safe?"

"He's almost through," Lucy said.

"I'll go check on him." I rose and crossed to the door, hoping Rhonda would not follow. It was time to confront my past, and I couldn't do so with her present.

28

Italian Roots

I went up to the wheelhouse to find Mac, eager to deal with a part of my past I had thought to be long buried.

My husband had the bad luck of attempting to verify a pair of Cupid statues on the deck of Corozza's yacht, a vessel the gangster used to smuggle art between European ports. The proceeds from their sales were funneled back to the Las Vegas branch of the Giraspi crime family through the Italian one.

Only after Carlos disappeared did my boss discover that Corozza was a rapidly rising star on the Italian side of the crime syndicate, and was skyrocketing his way to the top by killing off anyone who got in his way. Reggie and I had to assume that my darling Carlos was collateral damage, nothing more.

Would Corozza even remember Carlos or the statues that he'd been trying to verify? I somehow doubted it. Men like Corozza didn't have a conscience and considered men like Carlos nothing but cockroaches to be squished under their heels.

I also knew the chances were slim that Mac would tell me anything that might lead me to Corozza's current location. But I did have the advantage of having insider knowledge. Hopefully that would be enough to convince him to answer me honestly. Well, as honestly as a mobster could.

I stood outside the bridge door, trying to center myself before entering. Once it had sunk in that Carlos wasn't coming home, I had spent my days and nights thinking up ways of exacting revenge on his murderers. But all it did was wear me out, especially when we discovered that the most likely suspect was someone we would never be able to capture. Corozza had greased the palm of pretty much everyone who might be able to put him behind bars, and as such, enjoyed a level of protection rarely seen, even in this kind of criminal environment.

So I gave up, at least on the idea of my husband's killer ever being caught and tried for what he had done. But now that I'd heard his name aloud, and from the mouth of that Mafia type, all of my repressed anger was boiling back up to the surface again. I only hoped I could control my emotions long enough to get some sort of useful intel out of Moneybags Mahoney.

When I pushed the wheelhouse door open, Mac was bent over the safe, drill in hand. He looked up and nodded his chin towards the lock. "You're just in time. One or two more holes, and I should be able to pop it open."

"Hey, that's great. Say, I heard you mention the name Corozza earlier."

Mac raised his eyebrows. "You did?"

"That's a rather unusual name, and the same as a relative of mine, out of Sicily. Do you know Antonio Corozza?"

I couldn't tell whether it was a smile or a smirk that crossed his face, but he definitely recognized the name. "If I knew a guy like him, I wouldn't be swinging his name around. He's not the kind of person you want to mess with."

His not-so-veiled threat was not lost on me.

Instead of feeding off of his implied terror, I decided to play dumb. "What do you mean? I remember from family parties that he has a short temper, but he used to love bouncing me on his knee when I was a kid."

That was a stretch I knew, I didn't think Corozza was more than ten years older than me, but I had to throw in some sort of familial reference.

For a split second, I swear fright crossed his face. "You, ah, are related to him, huh?"

Even Mac wasn't dumb enough to risk insulting me, in case I was family of the mob boss.

I stiffened my spine and crossed my arms, as if I was annoyed by his response. It was a gamble, claiming to be a distant relative of one of Italy's most notorious gangsters. "Yeah, I am. Haven't seen him in a while though. He tends to live off the grid, if you know what I mean. My mom wants me to try to look him up while I'm over here. Any ideas on where I should look?"

He locked eyes with me, and the questions racing through his mind were almost audible. Was I a hit woman searching for my target? Or was I truly a distant relative, meaning Corozza would kill him if he blew me off?

After a long few seconds of deliberation, he finally answered in a neutral tone. "I haven't seen him in a while. Tell you what, if he does get in touch, I'll let him know you're looking for him. How about that?"

That was better than nothing, I thought. The answer coming out of my mouth was much politer. "Sure, do that. Tell him his second cousin Carmen's in town. Maria's daughter." I grabbed a name out of the air, figuring that among his cousins, there were at least one Carmen and one Maria, if not several of them.

"Alright. Now, if you will excuse me, I have a safe to crack."

"How did you learn to break into one, anyway?"

"You ask a lot of questions, lady."

"Yeah, well, I've got an inquisitive nature."

"The Bronx. I grew up in a rough neighborhood and picked up a few skills along the way."

"And now you're a Hollywood producer. Who would have guessed, right?"

"I'm more of a financer than a producer. My name doesn't appear on screen, and I like it that way."

He picked up the drill and revved the motor.

"Good luck," I said before stepping back and covering my ears.

29

Contact Restored

Ten minutes later, Mac's cries of joy echoed throughout the ship. After having drilled out the pins of the lock mechanism, he was able to turn it open with a flathead screwdriver.

When the door to the safe popped open, we both cheered.

I grabbed my phone, glad to see there was a little power left. Myrtle and Sophie had sent several messages asking for an update, but Rosewood had not yet sent anyone to look for us. Which made sense when I looked at the time. It felt as if we had been on this boat for days, but it had only been a matter of hours.

Colin, Lucy, and Rhonda raced up to us, and eagerly grabbed their phones out of the now-open safe.

"Do we call the police or the Coast Guard?" Lucy said.

"I say we call them both—I'll do the Coast Guard," I replied.

"Wait a second—why should we involve the authorities straightaway?" Mac said. "If we sail the ship back and sneak Alistair's stuff off it before we call for help, we can divvy up the collection as planned. Otherwise we're all out of luck. The cops aren't going to let us waltz off with any of Alistair's things, not without proof he sold it to us, which we don't have."

Rhonda held her hand up, as if we were back in grade school. "Did you say we would sail this ship back to shore?"

Mac shrugged, as if he'd often had to sail a brigantine back to shore. "Why

148

not? It can't be that hard."

"I bet there's a motor," Colin added. "It can't be that difficult to steer, at least once we lower the sails. Can anyone read the radar or sonar?"

"A crew of six jumped ship, so apparently it takes a lot of hands to work those sails," I said, trying to interject a little realism into their fantasy world. "Those ropes race through your fingers, and if one of those beams hits you, you're a goner. I have no idea how to raise or lower them safely—do you?"

"I say we call for help, right away. We have a dead woman in the saloon and a murderer locked up in a bedroom. There's no reason to dillydally!" Rhonda cried.

"Fine, be boring. Where is your sense of adventure, Rhonda?" Colin chided.

"It disappeared when the first body fell."

"Come on, how hard can it be?" Colin pleaded with her. "We can look everything up online now that we have our phones."

"You go right ahead. I'm calling the Coast Guard." I held up my phone for emphasis.

"No, you are not, Carmen," Mac said in a tone that made clear there was no room for argument. "I don't want the authorities to get wind of this, not yet. Alistair killed Divine and stabbed me. He's going to jail, and his collection will be confiscated, if it's still on board when the police show up. If that happens, nobody wins. I say we get the loot off the boat first."

"I agree with Mac," Lucy said, to my surprise. "Alistair deserves to pay for his crimes, and we deserve payback for all the pain he's caused."

"You're both right," Colin said. "I'll look up how to lower the sails and start the motor."

Rhonda gasped. "Are you serious?"

"Yes, quite. Alistair stole from all of us, and we deserve something in return. Mac is right; why should we let this opportunity pass us by?" Lucy said before taking Rhonda's hands in her own. "I know it doesn't feel right, but I am begging you to let us try to make Mac's plan work, before you call the authorities. If we can't figure out how to turn the ship around, we'll reach out for help. I promise."

Lucy's sincerity obviously won Rhonda over. "Alright, we'll wait until you give us the go-ahead."

"Thank you."

When Colin then turned to her, a smile on his lips, my stomach sank. "Rhonda darling, you could help us divvy up the props in an equitable manner. I realize that you two don't belong here, and that is my fault. I'm happy to give you part of my share to make up for your troubles."

"We don't need anything. All we want to do is get back to shore and forget all about this ship and party," I replied for her.

Colin locked eyes with me. "Good, then can I ask Rhonda to assist us?"

Before I could make up an excuse as to why she could not, Rhonda spoke up. "Actually, there's not much I can help you with. As I said before, this just isn't my area of expertise. I'd say you'd be better off using Alistair's price list as a guide. That'll at least give you an indication of an item's worth, even if it's inflated."

"Alright, so our guess is as good as yours, correct?" Colin looked to Rhonda for confirmation.

"Correct," she said and yawned.

"Say, since you two don't want a cut, why don't you take a nap and let us worry about getting back to land. It's quite late, and it's been a long day. There are several bedrooms on the other side of the kitchen."

"That sounds like a great idea," I said, perhaps too enthusiastically. "We'll leave you to it. Wake us when we're close to shore, would you?"

"Will do," Colin said and moved in to kiss Rhonda on the cheek. She suddenly feigned another yawn, and just missed clipping his chin with her fist as she stretched her arms above her head. "Oh, gosh, sorry about that. I guess I'm just wiped out after all this excitement. You sure Alistair's locked up tight?"

"You betcha. You've got the key, so only you can let him out."

'That's true, and quite the relief. Alright then, good luck!"

We rushed out of the room as if we were running from a death squad. When I glanced back, Mac was staring at us so intently it felt as if he was measuring my casket with his eyes.

As soon as we were inside the first cabin, Rhonda grabbed my arm. "I know I was all excited about having an adventure, but I've got a bad feeling about this whole situation. We should have called the police straight away."

"I agree. They are crazy to think they can sail this ship back to shore. But don't you fret, we shouldn't have to wait too long on help. As soon as I contact my editor, Myrtle, she'll send in the calvary, or whatever they call it in Belgium. But until we are rescued, I say we go along with whatever they propose. I don't want any of them to think we are going to stand in their way."

"I agree," Rhonda said with a shiver. "But Mac made pretty clear that he doesn't want you to call the authorities just yet. And I do sympathize with Lucy. It's not fair that everything would be confiscated and they would be left in the lurch, again."

"I understand her point, but I owe Myrtle an explanation. The last thing I want is for her to think we aren't going to be able to make the Luxembourg show," I fibbed, before adding truthfully, "And frankly, I'm more worried about how she is going to react than Mac."

30

Friend Or Foe

Once we were inside the guest cabin, the first thing I did was ping my location to Myrtle along with this text message: "We're on board *La Vida Loca*, Alistair's brigantine and home. Most of the stolen items are here. Alistair destroyed the radio and killed a guest. We now have him locked up in his stateroom. The captain abandoned ship and harpooned the remaining lifeboat. Please send help." Considering Myrtle's new fondness for emojis, I added a wide-eyed sad face to the end.

Myrtle returned a thumbs-up followed by a face surrounded by kisses. I guess she was happy about the stolen goods, and had somehow overlooked the part about the dead body and killer on board. At least she added, after a heartbeat, "Calling Coast Guard."

Captain Jack had said that he'd call them once he reached shore, but I had my doubts that he would keep that promise. It wasn't that I couldn't call the emergency services myself, but I knew from experience that that sort of call was usually quite lengthy, and I didn't want Mac to hear me reach out for help. He was dumb enough to let us take our phones, but I figured he was relying on his physical scariness to keep us in line. Considering how volatile he was, I still wasn't certain how far he'd go to get his share of Alistair's things, and I didn't want to give him any reason to harm Rhonda or myself.

Before I could tell my friend that help was on its way, my phone rang, scaring the bejesus out of both of us. Admittedly, I had intentionally set the ringer to the highest volume while we were on the boat riding out to Alistair's ship, but had forgotten to turn it down once we arrived on the brigantine.

Rhonda about sprung off the bed. "Are you trying to give me a heart attack? Turn that thing down."

"Sorry." I did as requested, then accepted the call.

"There you are—finally! You haven't responded to a single one of my messages since you left."

I had never been so happy to hear my partner's voice, despite her dressing down. "Oh, gosh, sorry, it's been a crazy few hours. I didn't see your messages because my phone was locked in a safe, which we just broke open."

"What's going on? Why was your phone in a safe? I told you it was a bad idea to go that silly party. Movie props—as if they were important enough for Rosewood to concern themselves with." Her voice still sounded abnormally high; my guess was she was still flying high on painkillers.

"Our host required us to turn in our phones before we were admitted entrance. He claimed that he didn't want anyone to post to social media about the party, but I think he wanted to be able to commit murder without anyone being able to call for help."

"Excuse me? Is it the medication, or did you say that Alistair McPhee killed someone?"

"You heard me right. He invited everyone here onto his boat to show us his collection of stolen movie props. Then we chatted with an actress, a loan shark, and a producer over a lovely fish stew, before Alistair shot one of the guests with a bow and arrow. Well, technically Robin Hood did." Why did I tell it like the setup for a joke or giggle at the end? Maybe it was the stress of everything that was going on and my partner's need to downplay this excursion as pointless, but no matter the reason, it felt cathartic.

"It sounds like you and Rhonda are having a grand time."

"Excuse me?" Sophie usually got my sarcasm, but this time she seemed to have missed it by a mile.

"Myrtle can't stop talking about how wonderful Rhonda is and how Reggie thinks she could be a great asset for the company. Apparently both of them just love her show." Her words were rushed, as if she had been waiting to get this off of her chest for far too long. I don't know whether it was her being stuck in a hospital bed or the idea that a celebrity could replace her, but the Baroness was upset, and this thing with Rhonda had been festering for a while, probably since I suggested my friend take her place.

I rose, knowing I couldn't have this conversation in front of Rhonda. "Give me one sec, Sophie. I'm going to take this in the next room."

I made a "she's acting crazy" motion by swirling one hand close to my ear, before covering the phone and adding in a whisper, "She sounds pretty loopy, so our conversation might get weird. I would rather talk to her in private. Is that alright?"

"Of course, please tell her that I hope she feels better soon," Rhonda said.

"Sure thing." I winked, knowing that I would do no such thing, then popped into an empty guest cabin two doors down. It was quiet in the passageway; the rest must have been dividing up Alistair's props, I figured. How to do so when their worth was still unclear was thankfully not my problem.

"Okay, I'm back." I had to pinch my nose in order to keep my tone even. "Sophie, darling, did you hear anything that I just said—killer, dead body? This is not the right time to act jealous. I have enough on my plate right now, like trying to ensure that Rhonda and I survive the night."

"You like Rhonda better than me," the Baroness sniffed.

That stopped me in my tracks. "Seriously—are we going to do this now?" I demanded, but got no response. Three years of pent-up frustration flowed out of me. "Well, yes, in fact, I do. She's always been there for me, not just when it suits her. That's why I consider her to be my best friend." I knew I was needling the Baroness, but it had to come out.

Sophie's inability to show compassion, empathy, or sympathy in any form had caused an enormous tear in our relationship. Once, she had been my favorite partner, and we'd made an excellent team, until my husband's death changed it all. Three weeks ago, I'd flown over to Europe to ground myself in work again, as well as to hopefully repair what was broken between us while we were on assignment together. Yet, neither one of us had yet dared to address the elephant in the room. As much as I wanted to talk it out with her, I was also afraid I might say something in the heat of the moment that would make things worse, not better. And I suspected that Sophie felt the same. In her high-class world, open displays of emotion were not valued. If she dared to let that emotional dam loose, who knew what would happen.

"And what am I to you?"

"We're partners."

"Not friends?"

Her pettiness, on top of the murder, my fears for Rhonda, and the uncertainty about how this evening was going to play out, was too much to bear. "Why would you think that we are friends? You're a great partner, Sophie, but I've never seen your house, met any of your high-society friends, been invited to any of your charity events, or even gone to one of your garden parties. Heck, I don't even know the name of your butler."

"Jeeves."

"How original."

Sophie cleared her throat a few times before she spoke again. "I know you don't really enjoy those kind of events…"

"Alright, but a true friend would have invited me anyway and done her best to make me feel comfortable."

Sophie's silence spoke volumes. Finally, after all these years working together, I understood why. "I should have known! You weren't worried about *me* being uncomfortable. I'm not good enough for your friends, am I? Hanging around with someone like me when you're off-duty would be bad for your image. That must be why you could never attend any of the birthday parties or anniversary celebrations that I invited you to."

By the way she sighed softly into the phone, I knew I was right. The pain of knowing I had never been good enough cut deep. So much so that I did my worst, wanting to hurt her emotionally, as she had done to me. "You know, there was a time when I thought we might one day be friends. But then Carlos died and you disappeared on me. That was when I realized we were just co-workers, and nothing more. You should have come to Carlos's funeral, Sophie. A real friend would have."

There, I said it, I thought. A strange feeling of relief overtook me. Even though it was harsh, it had been building up since the funeral, more than three years ago.

To my amazement, the Baroness began to snivel into the receiver. I'd never heard her cry, at least not out of sadness. "I've always been quite fond of you and did hope that you were coping with his loss. It was simply too painful to reach out. I suppose I haven't come to terms with my husband's death. It was too soon and too sudden."

"And Carlos's death was not? We never did find the body, did you know that? I had to bury a sack of rocks, Sophie."

"I heard about that, yes," she whispered into the phone.

"You know, as much as I would love to hash this all out with you, now is not the right time." I knew I was being unforgiving, but I was so angry with her. This selfish behavior was so typical of Sophie. It was always me, me, me—even when another's life was in jeopardy. "If you will excuse me, I have to figure out a way to get me and my best friend off of this ship alive."

31

Navigating By Star

"Unbelievable!" I muttered as I hung up the phone. What was wrong with the Baroness? How could anyone be so selfish and cold? *It must be the medication,* I told myself again, before taking a few deep breaths. When I was feeling calmer and more centered, I returned to my friend, popping my head back into the other guest bedroom without knocking first. Rhonda was stretched out on one of the beds, listening to an audiobook with her eyes closed. I figured she was already asleep, but she propped herself up on one elbow and pulled her earphones out as soon as I entered.

"Is Lady Sophie feeling better?" Her genuine concern was heartwarming, and helped me let my partner's irritating behavior go. The last thing I wanted to do was take my frustration with the Baroness out on Rhonda.

But when I sat down on the edge of the mattress, it reminded me of my last visit to my partner's hospital room and how fragile she'd looked. As mad as I was with her, I had to cut her some slack. Not only was her body in bad shape, Sophie must be going crazy lying in that room all by herself for most of the day.

"No, she sounds horrible and completely doped up. I think they're giving her too many painkillers. She was saying some really off-the-wall things; that's why I thought it was better to have a little privacy."

I didn't want Rhonda to get the idea that the Baroness was badmouthing her, even if it was true.

"Well that's too bad. I do hope I can meet her after this is all over. When she's feeling better, of course."

"Sure, once she's more herself. Say, I'm going to check on Colin and see if they've figured out how to sail this thing."

Rhonda laughed. "I'm not holding my breath on that one. At least the wind isn't strong right now."

"True. Though it does look like we're being pulled farther away from shore." I couldn't read the ship's sonar, but my phone's map function worked, even at sea. I pointed my telephone's screen in her direction, showing her the blip that was our ship, quite a ways off of the coast.

We'd been sailing down the Dutch coast towards Zeebrugge, Belgium, when Captain Jack jumped ship. From the looks of it, we were still north of our intended destination and being pulled out towards international waters, presumably because we were adrift at sea with our sails out. The only shining point right now was that the rain had subsided and the winds were lessening.

"Oh, my, that's not good. Hopefully Mac and Colin will come to their senses and call for help, if they can't figure out how to work the sails soon." The way Rhonda yawned and stretched her arms out over her head reminded me of a cat waking from a nap.

"You don't have to come with me. I'm just going to pop up to the wheelhouse, then come right back down."

"Alright, then I think I'm going to rest my eyes."

Rhonda was asleep before I pulled the door closed behind me. Between the jet lag and excitement of the evening, I could imagine she was exhausted. When I climbed the ten stairs to the bridge, I stared up at the skies above, through the skylight over the staircase. The clouds had dissipated, and the stars were out in force, lighting up the night. I searched the heavens until I found Orion and the Big Dipper. Knowing that wherever I was on this planet, I could find those familiar star patterns, was somehow reassuring and comforting. I wished I could read them well enough to navigate us back to shore by star. As I scanned the dark waters around us, I also realized there were no other lights bobbing on the surface. The good news was we wouldn't run into another ship; the bad news was there was no one close by who might notice our strange sailing pattern or whom we could signal for help.

Just as I was about to open the door to the wheelhouse, my phone vibrated in my pocket. It was Myrtle, letting me know that the Coast Guard should be two hours out. Her message was a huge relief and meant this nightmare of an evening was finally coming to an end. Whether we got the boat turned around no longer mattered, although I couldn't tell the rest of the invited guests that. As far as they were concerned, Captain Jack had called in the calvary, not me.

Through the glass door, I could see Colin scrolling through something on his phone, before looking at the control panel in front of him, and flipping a few switches.

I knocked twice before entering, so as not to startle him. "Hey, Colin, how's it going?"

"Oh, you're up! It's going pretty well." He sounded jazzed up and hopeful. "I think I've figured out how to start the motor, but we should lower the sails first. I'm waiting for Mac to return, then we're going to give it a go."

"Fantastic! I couldn't sleep so I thought I'd check in. It's great to know that we'll be back on land in no time." I made a show of looking around the tiny space. "Say, where is Mac?"

"He's getting a drink, I think he said a glass of milk."

"Really—milk? I would have taken Mac for a whiskey drinker."

"Yeah, well, maybe he's worried about dozing off. We have a lot to do tonight, if we want to get this ship back to shore and unload all of Alistair's props, before we call the cops. Lucy's downstairs packing up as much as she can. We found a few empty boxes in the hold."

"Is there anything I can help you with?"

Colin looked pretty upbeat. "No, I think we have this situation in hand. With a little luck, we'll be sailing into Brussels before breakfast."

"I'll keep my fingers crossed." I smiled, knowing there wasn't a real chance that Colin and Mac would get this ship turned around. The two obviously didn't know much about sailing or European geography. Brussels was pretty far inland; Antwerp was probably what he meant to say. Though I wasn't certain that the city had a marina deep enough for *La Vida Loca*.

I copied Rhonda's earlier stretch and yawn, playing it up for Colin before making a show of looking at my watch. "Gosh, it's already eleven, which means it's way past my bedtime. Say, if there's nothing else you need from me, I'm going to go back and try to sleep. Rhonda's already out. But please do give us a shout if you need our help."

"Sure thing. But you two don't need to worry about anything, Mac and I have this situation under control."

"Thanks, Colin."

He smiled broadly at me, his twinkling eyes briefly locking with mine, before returning his attention to his phone. My knees began to wobble and my heartbeat seemed to accelerate, under his gaze. I now understood what Rhonda meant when she'd said he could make you feel like the center of his world just by looking at you.

32

Loose Ends

I skipped down the stairs towards the guest cabin Rhonda was asleep in, still reveling in the afterglow of Colin's adoring gaze, when Mac's deep voice made me freeze. It was coming from the mess, only a few feet from the door I was heading to.

Considering I had already told Colin that I was on the way back to my room, I had a legitimate reason for being there, meaning Mac couldn't get upset if he caught me walking past the kitchen, I reasoned. I approached the closed door on my tippy toes, glad the soles of my Jimmy Choo wedges were made of rubber.

Luckily for me, the deep timbre of Mac's low voice traveled easily through the wood. He seemed to talk, then pause, before speaking again. Because I could hear no one else in the room, I presumed he was on the telephone.

"Yeah, it's not clear what the exact worth of everything is, but there's enough here to settle his debt with us."

A long pause ensued before he chuckled, then continued. "We won't have to worry about Alistair coming after it. Trust me, he won't be a problem for long. I've got to tie up a few loose ends, then I'll contact you when it's all done. How soon can your men get to Belgium?"

A few beats later, Mac grunted. "Excellent. See you then."

My breathing was so ragged, I was worried Mac would hear me hyperventilating outside of the door. I edged my way down the hallway to our cabin

161

and slipped inside. Rhonda was thankfully still asleep, snoring like an old man again, giving me time to process what I had just heard.

I sucked in as much air as my lungs could inhale, then breathed out very slowly. I'd only been privy to half of the conversation, but Mac's words were quite telling. He was planning on stealing Alistair's collection of movie props, and Alistair wouldn't cause trouble or be able to reclaim his props, presumably because Mac was planning on killing him before leaving the ship.

Yet my mind kept tripping over the "loose ends" he needed to tie up. It didn't seem like he was referring to Alistair, considering he'd already mentioned him specifically. So were the other invited guests the only ones who concerned him? Or were Rhonda and I also lumped in with that group of loose ends that needed to be dealt with?

As the gravity of our situation sunk in, I threw my hands over my mouth to muffle the scream building up inside of me. When I looked over at my dear friend, all I could think was how quickly our situation had changed. When she'd fallen asleep minutes earlier, we both believed that the worst was behind us, we were about to be rescued, and her daughters would never have to know what happened aboard the *La Vida Loca*.

How wrong we both were.

33

Escape Plan

Figuring a way off of this ship, without alerting Mac, was our top priority. We'd all seen the harpoon sticking out of the dinghy, but perhaps it wasn't that large of a gash and could be easily repaired. Yet even if that was so, how could I fix the hole without Mac noticing? And let's be honest, I was no handyman, at least not when it came to making something waterproof. The last thing I wanted was for the boat to sink before Rhonda and I got back to shore or were rescued.

Swimming back wasn't an option, either. The ocean's temperature was far too cold for us to use the life jackets and spring in; we'd die of hypothermia long before anyone could spot us. Short of begging Myrtle to send a helicopter to rescue us, I didn't see another way off this ship.

The fact that the sails were still raised meant Colin and Mac weren't having much luck getting the ship turned around. According to Myrtle's last update, the Coast Guard should be here within the next two hours. On the one hand, that seemed pretty fast. On the other hand, everything horrid that had happened—Divine's death, Mac's stabbing, and Alistair's crazy confession—had occurred in roughly the same space of time.

Yet before I could worry about getting us off of this ship, I had to figure out another way out of this room, in case Mac did try to break in and kill us in our sleep.

My eyes scanned the space, doing a quick inventory check. As softly as

I could, I lifted the squat nightstand made of oak and placed it under the door's handle. It wouldn't prevent Mac from getting inside, but it would slow him down. The next step was figuring out how to get into the room next door, even if that meant breaking through the wall somehow. Otherwise we would be trapped in here.

The thin walls separating the cabins seemed to be made of plywood panels that had been glued onto the beams. If I could find a loose seam, there was a tiny chance that my plan would work. This ship was in such poor shape that if I could loosen one of the panels, it might bend enough to allow me to slide through and into the neighboring room. Rhonda, on the other hand, wouldn't be able to fit her bust or buttocks through any such hole, meaning I might as well forget the idea, unless I could figure out how to remove one of the panels completely.

As unrealistic as my plan felt, I didn't have much else to do, other than listen to Rhonda snore and feel sorry for myself.

Which was how I discovered a rather ingenious system that had already been put in place, I assumed by the Spanish film crew, to make filming inside of these cramped quarters possible. The entire back wall of the built-in closet was on a sliding railing. When I pulled down the coat rack screwed into the side wall, it retracted completely, allowing me easy access into the neighboring room via its closet. Best of all, Rhonda could easily fit through.

I checked the next room and found the same railing system on the opposite wall. It was a load off of my mind, knowing that if Mac did try to attack us, we could quietly exit from our room to the next while he was attempting to break in through our blocked door. With a little luck, we could travel via closet through the row of cabins and stay ahead of him. What we would do after that remained to be seen.

Perhaps it was the comforting knowledge that we had an escape route of sorts, or simply that the adrenaline from the evening's events had worn off, but as soon I stretched out on my bed, I was out. Luckily it wasn't a deep sleep, for soon after I nodded off, another scream pierced the air.

I sat up with a jolt and flipped on the light, afraid someone was inside of our room. All I saw was Rhonda blinking her eyes, as if she had also been startled awake, as well.

"What was that?" she asked, her voice as thick as syrup.

"You heard it, too? It sounded like a man screaming. I wasn't sure if it was a horrible nightmare or not." I jumped up off the bed and moved the nightstand out of the way.

"Why is that in front of the door—did we hit rough water?" Rhonda asked.

"No, I was barricading us in. I'll explain later. But right now, I want to see what's going on. Why don't you stay here?"

"Are you kidding—after everything that's happened so far? I'm coming with you. There's safety in numbers," Rhonda exclaimed. "But first, tell me why you thought it necessary to blockade the door."

I scowled, not wishing to scare her, before realizing that she deserved to know what I'd learned while she slept. "Alright, here's what you missed."

While she pulled on her shoes, I told her what I'd overheard Mac saying. Her assumptions about his intentions mirrored mine, and she was as concerned as I about our presence on this ship and inability to get off of it.

"Do you still think we're safe because we aren't friends of Alistair?" I asked.

"I don't know what to believe anymore. But Mac doesn't seem like the type to take risks. I bet he'd err on the side of killing too many witnesses than not enough," Rhonda contended.

"I agree completely. We really have to watch our backs until the authorities arrive."

I opened our door a smidgen and listened. Raised voices coming from the saloon caused us both to tiptoe over to the entrance and poke our heads inside.

The red velvet curtain covering the doors to Alistair's office and bedroom was pushed aside so that both were visible. The bedroom was still closed, but the door to the office was wide open and the three remaining invited guests were huddled inside, staring down at something.

"They're all in Alistair's office. Let's sneak a little closer so we can see what's going on before we enter," I whispered to Rhonda, who promptly nodded in agreement.

However, when we reached the open door and I saw what the trio were staring at, I strode straight inside. The Maltese Falcon sat on Alistair's desk, hunched over and glaring at me. Drops of blood dripped off of its bejeweled head and onto the desk's surface. At its feet lay Alistair's crumpled body, a trail of crimson oozing out of a nasty head wound.

"Oh, no! Is that blood on the statue?" Rhonda cried from the entrance. When she finally noticed Alistair, her screams filled the room.

I rushed over and pulled her in for a hug as she stuttered, "Who would do such a thing?"

"I don't know," I murmured softly as I rubbed her back. "But I'm going to find out."

"Has anyone checked for a pulse?" I asked the rest.

Colin, Lucy, and Mac were still staring at the body, speechless. Was it shock that made them mute, or were they afraid their words would give away their joy in seeing him dead? He didn't look like he was breathing, and there was so much blood on the floor that the chances that he was still alive was pretty much nil. Still, I had to be certain. In spite of his horrid and psychopathic behavior, I would never forgive myself if we could have saved him and did not. He was human, after all.

As expected, I found no pulse or other sign of life. Being so close to him, though, did allow me to get a better look at the wound. There were flakes of gold leaf in it, which seemed to confirm that he had been killed with the Maltese Falcon. After shaking my head, signaling to the rest that he was dead, I patted down his jacket and pants pockets, but felt no keys, phone, or even a slip of paper.

When I rose, I turned to Colin. "Who found him?"

"Gosh, I guess we all did. I was down in the engine room, trying to figure out why the motor won't start, when I heard a scream. When I got here, Mac and Lucy were in the saloon, but had not yet entered the office. The door was still closed, so we hadn't seen Alistair's body yet."

"I had gone down to the hold to get more boxes, when I heard it. I guess I was just ahead of Colin on the stairs," Lucy explained.

Mac cleared his throat. "I was up in the wheelhouse, trying to figure out how to steer the ship, once Colin got the motor running. I came down when I heard someone yell out. I saw Lucy a few steps ahead of me, running through the saloon."

I blew out my cheeks. "So none of you were inside the saloon at the time, but all of you were close by."

Mac shrugged. "I guess so. Where were you when he screamed?"

"Rhonda and I were lying down in one of the cabins. Are we certain it was Alistair who yelled out?"

Lucy gazed down at our host's lifeless corpse. "I assume so."

I looked again at the scene before me, when a new thought struck. "Wait a second, what is Alistair doing inside of his office? We locked him into his bedroom. Rhonda, do you still have the key?"

My friend rummaged around in her purse until she pulled out the large silver key. "Yes," came her soft response, before she wiped a tear away. When I realized she was taking the death of Alistair—a man she admired and had a little crush on, I suspected—pretty hard, I wanted to run over to hug her again. But there were more pressing matters to deal with.

"I already tried the bedroom door, it's definitely locked," Mac confirmed.

"Then how did he get out of there and into the office?" Lucy asked.

"He must have had another key," Colin concluded.

Or his closet was also rigged, I almost said aloud, but decided to keep that tidbit of information to myself for now. I wasn't ready to tell the others about the sliding panel in my closet. "He may have, but I didn't feel one in his pockets. Regardless of how he got in there, I think the more pressing question is, was Alistair trying to escape, or was he freeing himself so he could get rid of the rest of us before calling for help?" I suggested, in the most dramatic voice I could muster. It was time to shake the tree and see what fell out.

"I don't know what to think. First Alistair killed Divine, and now someone offed Alistair?" Mac muttered.

"There must be a stowaway on board! We need to call the Coast Guard and get them to send out a boat to rescue us, right away," Lucy cried.

Colin snapped his fingers. "Lucy might be right about a stowaway. Did all of the crew leave with Jack? Oh, bother, I didn't pay attention to what they looked like. Maybe one of them stayed behind to settle some sort of score with Alistair, and it ended badly?"

I gazed at Colin and the rest, my eyes narrowed in suspicion. How did we get back to this point—adrift at sea with a murderer? I didn't think that there were any stowaways on board, but was fairly certain that one of the three was the killer we sought. Which was why I told myself to ignore them and focus on the crime scene.

It didn't look like anything had been taken from Alistair's desk or archives. The folders of papers that Lucy and I had left out on the desktop were still there, but now sprinkled with flecks of red. The letter opener and blotter had been shifted, but that could have happened during the fatal attack. What did strike me as interesting was that flakes of gold were also covering most of the desk. *Did the gold fall off of the statue when the murderer set it down on the desk?* It very well could have, I realized, if they'd handled it roughly. Which they obviously did, if they'd used it to kill a man.

I looked again to the statue, its head and beak still covered in blood, when it hit me. The gold should have come from there, the striking point, yet the flakes spread across the desk didn't have any blood on them.

I leaned forward to get a better look at the statue, hoping to see if there were other sections where the gold had flaked off completely, when Colin yelled out, "Don't touch it— the killer's fingerprints might be on it! The police should want to dust it for prints, I would think."

"I wasn't going to pick it up," I pouted. "There just seems to be a lot of gold on the desk, is all. Did someone drop it earlier?"

"The murderer must have, because it was locked up in that case up until a few minutes ago," Mac said, then looked at the vitrine again. "Wait a second, how did the murderer get it open without breaking the glass?"

"Maybe the killer found the key. Or Alistair had already removed the statue from the case before his murderer entered," Lucy offered in an innocent voice.

Or they knew that it was already unlocked, I thought. She knew, as well as Rhonda and Colin, that I had already picked open the lock.

"Maybe the killer dropped the statue before they used it to murder Alistair.

You know, they struggled first, and it fell, and then the killer picked it up and finished him off." Colin gazed off into the distance, as if he was imagining a possible scenario.

"Yes, I'd say that I've hit the nail on the head. A disgruntled crew member must have snuck into the office to steal something, but found Alistair there and the falcon out of its case. They fight, he hit Alistair over the head with the statue, and then fled—easy-peasy. You don't need to be Agatha Christie to figure this one out. Look at his head wound, there's gold leaf in it." When Colin finished, he looked quite pleased with himself.

I waved my hand towards the glass vitrines still filled with props. "But why? If theft was the motive, why not take the statue—or anything else, for that matter? It doesn't look like anything's missing."

"That a great question. Maybe they were spooked off when Alistair yelled out? It's a real mystery," Colin replied.

"It's not fair!" Lucy wailed. "Alistair got off easy. He was supposed to suffer, just like Gary did."

Colin walked over to comfort her, and she let herself fall into his arms and weep her heart out.

Something about her words made me pause. Though he hadn't had to suffer the humiliation of a trial, Lucy had gotten what she'd wished for. Alistair had ultimately suffered the same fate as her husband.

34

Rhonda Comes Clean

While Colin comforted Lucy, I pulled Rhonda over to a far corner so we could talk more privately. "Honey, how are you doing?"

She looked as white as a ghost, which was quite a feat considering how much bronze foundation and powder she had applied to her face.

"Not so good. Someone killed Alistair, Carmen, and I don't believe it was some rogue crew member. I think it was one of them." Her eyes were so wide and her tone so low, it was clear that her rose-colored glasses had finally come off.

"I'm sorry to disappoint you, but I'm glad you've seen the light. We have to figure out who killed him before something horrible happens."

"Again, you mean?"

"No, I meant—before something horrible happens *to us*."

"Right." Rhonda began to tremble. "Oh, Lord, I can't die today! I need to see my babies one more time. Oh, Julie! It's been too many years. Why did I let her slip away, Carmen?"

Her words caused my forehead to crinkle. "What are you talking about? You said Julie was back at Christmas—that was, what, five months ago?"

Rhonda choked back a sob. "Carmen, I can't meet my maker, knowing I lied to you!"

"What are you talking about? You detest lying or being lied to."

"I know! But I was so ashamed to admit the truth—I lied to you about

Julie and me. We aren't close at all. The truth is, she hasn't been back to the States since Ralph's funeral. A week after we buried him, Julie accepted her first international assignment at an embassy. Since then she's been hopping from one diplomatic post to another. She was always closer to him, but it still hurts that she won't return my calls or answer my emails. It's like she wants to forget about me!"

I leaned back, stunned to hear my bestie's confession. She'd never let on that there was anything amiss with their relationship. The last time I'd seen Jules was at her dad's funeral, and she had indeed been too overwhelmed with grief to hold a conversation. Based on the two girls' emotional reactions, I would say that Rhonda was right. Not that Samantha was dry-eyed during the service, but she was nowhere near as emotional as her older sister was.

I looked over at my best and oldest friend—someone I'd known since her sixth birthday party, held shortly after her family moved onto our street—trying to understand why she couldn't be completely honest with me, of all people. "Why did you lie to me?"

"Why do you think—I was embarrassed to admit that my oldest daughter pretends I don't exist. I know you think I'm this perfect mother, but it's not true. I'm a failure!"

Her comment threw me for a loop. "A failure—what are you talking about? You were the one who always told me that you have to give your kids room to develop into their own persons. It sounds like she's a strong, independent woman. In my mind, you've done your job well, even if she didn't turn out how you expected."

"Good gravy, Carmen, deep down I know you are right. Julie does love adventure and to push herself, and that's partly thanks to her dad and me trusting that she could take care of herself. She's certainly not a homebody like her sister. But I just wish she'd leave *some* room for me in her life. When my Ralph was alive, she called home every week."

I took Rhonda's hand. "You're right—that's got to hurt. I guess all I can say is keep letting her know that you are there for her, whether she wants you to be or not."

"I suppose." Rhonda's voice trailed off as if she was considering my words.

"And it does sound like she's into building up her career right now. There's nothing wrong with that," I said, recalling with pride my own professional successes. "That's what I did after graduating with top honors from university, and with a lot of hard work, I made it to the top of my profession as art history professor in record time."

"Until burnout soured your love of teaching," Rhonda added.

"Now that I think about it, maybe working so hard for so long wasn't such a great idea," I conceded. That was one of the problems with having a best friend you'd known since childhood—you couldn't lie to yourself about your past. She'd been there to witness it all and had no qualms about setting me straight when I looked back a little too fondly on my previous achievements.

"I know there's nothing wrong with throwing yourself into your career, but she's got to find a balance. She's already thirty-two, and if she wants to have kids, she's got to make time to find a boyfriend." Rhonda wiped away a tear. "Or girlfriend. Honestly, I wouldn't care which one she brought home, but I do want to see her happy. Not that a relationship is a ticket to happiness, but it is nice to share your life with someone special."

My throat constricted as Rhonda's comments brought my darling husband Carlos to mind. I still missed waking up to hear him softly snoring next to me, holding his hand as we walked through busy streets, and inhaling the scent of his musty cologne.

But as much as I wanted to get lost in old memories and continue comforting my good friend, I had a more important task to fulfill. Until I figured out which one of the remaining guests was a killer, neither me or my bestie was safe. After overhearing his ominous phone call, my money was on Mac.

"Rhonda, I am not mad that you didn't tell me everything about your relationship with Julie, not in the slightest. I'm more sorry that you felt you couldn't confide in me earlier. Once we get out of this mess—which we will," I added quickly when I noticed her bottom lip trembling, "I'll help you think up a way to get back in touch with her. I promise."

"Really? Because I think you two might have more in common than me and her. Maybe we could visit her after your assignment is finished? Prague's not that far from here."

"After we're done with this, I will be happy to talk through all the possibilities. But right now, I need to figure out how Alistair got out of a locked room. Are you comfortable staying here alone or—"

"No way! Not with another killer on the loose! I'm sticking to you like glue until we get off of this darned ship!"

35

Now You See It

"How did Alistair get out of his room? Who killed him, and why?" Rhonda asked, echoing the questions racing through my mind.

"I'd bet good money that Mac killed Alistair and is planning on taking all of the props with him. He was up in the wheelhouse, which means he could have snuck down the stairs without us hearing him. And he's the most financially motivated of the bunch."

"But only after he ties up the loose ends—that's us, isn't it?" Rhonda asked in a quiet voice.

"It sure looks like it."

A shiver of fear traveled through her body, mirroring how I felt inside. "But how did Mac get to Alistair? He was locked in his bedroom, and when we were in the office just now, the door was still closed."

"That's what Mac said. But I want to check and see if it is really locked or not."

Rhonda nodded slowly. "Alright. And if it is?"

"Then I have a pretty good idea of how Alistair got out of his room and into the office. But how Mac knew he would be in there still baffles me."

"Really?" A glimmer of hope shimmered in my best friend's eyes. "How?"

"Follow me, and I'll show you."

When we reached the staircase leading up to the wheelhouse, I could hear Mac, Colin, and Lucy arguing about the position of various buttons and levers. We walked quietly through the saloon, hoping not to alert the rest to our presence in the space. When we reached Alistair's bedroom, I tried opening the door, but the handle refused to budge.

Rhonda handed over the key to Alistair's room, allowing us access to the locked room from which our deceased host had escaped.

"It makes no sense. We locked him into his bedroom, and it was still locked when he was found dead in his office," Rhonda said.

"True. He could have had another key, unlocked the door, relocked it so we would think he was in there, and then snuck next door. But I don't think that's how he did it."

I crossed over to the closet and pushed back the clothing hanging inside. Screwed into the side wall was the lever I was searching for. "While you were napping, I stumbled across something interesting in our cabin."

With a triumphant grin, I pulled down the clothing hook and exclaimed, "Ta da!"

When the back wall slid open, I was so relieved that I began to babble. "I bet the Spanish crew did this, so they could film the scenes in the cabins from outside the room..."

However, my friend was not listening. Instead, she was staring through the opening, her mouth hanging open.

"What is there, Rhonda?"

She bobbed her head towards the opening. "That's bad news."

"What are you talking about?" I chastised. "This is great news! Now we know how Alistair escaped from a locked room without any of us noticing."

"True, it is good to have solved that puzzle. However, it appears we have yet another mystery on our hands."

"What are you talking about?"

Rhonda pointed into Alistair's office. "Do you notice anything different, since our last visit?"

I poked my head through the hole, so I could see what she was referring to. The sight before me caused my irritation to dissolve into disbelief. "The Maltese Falcon is gone."

"Ten points for Carmen."

36

Now You Don't

"One minute, the statue is there, the next, it's gone. That's it—I've had enough!" I yelled, so loudly that the rest came running.

"What's going on now?" Colin puffed as he entered Alistair's bedroom.

"I heard a scream!" Lucy added.

"Are you hurt, Carmen?" Mac asked, rather indifferently.

I glared at all three. "Can we stop with these games? Neither Rhonda or I care about your friend's collection, nor do we want to have anything to do with it—or you—after we get back to shore. But enough is enough."

"What are you talking about?" Colin asked.

"Look." I pointed through the closet, to the empty desk in the next room. "Who took the statue?"

"Oh, not again!" Lucy cried. "It wasn't me or Colin. We were in the wheelhouse, trying to get that darned motor to start."

I turned to Mac and raised an eyebrow. The hulk of a man shook his head. "Don't look at me. I was out on deck, trying to figure out how to release the sails without losing a hand."

"You were? I didn't see you," Lucy said. "You told me you were going down to the hold."

"I guess you heard me wrong because I was out on deck," Mac replied as his eyes narrowed again. "And anyway, why would I take it? Alistair had already promised it to me."

"What are you talking about? We already agreed to divide the collection equally," Colin said. "Besides, it's not worth anything."

"What did you say?" Mac's growl deepened.

"Carmen and I found the certificates of authenticity in Alistair's office. It's not from the 1941 film, but the one from 1975. It's not worth more than a few hundred bucks, if that," Lucy replied.

Something about her statement gave me pause for thought. Yet before I could meditate on what bothered me, Mac roared, "I don't believe you. Alistair wouldn't have put it under lock and key if it was worthless. I think you're bluffing."

"Really? Well guess what, I don't care what you think," Colin said. "Lucy saw the certificate, and I believe her. Why don't you go look for yourself, if you don't trust us? But besides that, we already agreed to split everything in Alistair's collection three ways."

Mac laughed. "Yeah, right. Here's what's going to happen. I'm taking what's owed to me, and you two can fight over the rest. And that's that."

"Oh, really?" Colin pushed his torso into Mac's.

I positioned my body so that I was standing between Rhonda and the rest, in case things got ugly. The idea that harm would come to my friend terrified me. Which was why I decided to inject myself into the situation.

"Gentlemen! Please try to control yourselves," I yelled out, hoping to defuse this situation immediately. "We all need to calm down and figure out how to get control of this ship before we hit a rock or another boat. Have either of you figured out how to lower the sails?"

I looked to the pair; both shook their heads.

"And can you get the motor to start?"

Also a no, I noted.

"Isn't it time we call for help?" I asked in as casual of a tone as possible. It didn't matter what they did; the Coast Guard should be bearing down on us fairly soon. Yet if Mac knew help was on its way, he would hopefully be less inclined to murder us all.

"No, we don't call for help," Mac said, resolutely.

A wave of terror washed over me. I'd almost forgotten that he had also requested help, though from the criminal underworld. They were already on their way to Belgium, so in theory Mac could contact them and ask them to pick him up. Given the connections the Giraspi family had, getting ahold of a fast boat shouldn't be much of a problem for Mac's buddies. For all I knew, Mac had already done so, and his friends were currently speeding towards us. Would the authorities arrive before those thugs did? And once Mac's people had the props, would they let us simply float away?

Colin ticked his tongue against his teeth. "I don't know, Mac, we aren't having much luck. Carmen might be right. We don't have the right experience to sail this ship, and right now, we're just bobbing around the open ocean."

"We just don't—that's why."

The resolve in Mac's voice made me even more nervous. I hoped and prayed that the Coast Guard would hurry up.

"Now, if you'll excuse me, I have a call to make."

A soft cry escaped my lips, loud enough to cause Mac to glance over and narrow his eyes at me. If he hadn't already called his buddies, I'd bet money he was about to.

I looked to my bestie. Whatever it took, I was going to ensure that Rhonda got off this ship alive.

We all waited until Mac stormed out of the office. Lucy and Colin appeared to be just as anxious as I felt. Rhonda was a sniveling mess of emotions. When her rose-colored glasses came off, and reality came crashing down, it was always messy. She had such a hard time accepting that others could be cruel or hurtful. That someone in her presence was most likely a murderer was a step too far.

Colin and Lucy turned to each other, and a glance passed between them that I couldn't place. Was it love or something else, perhaps more sinister?

I leaned over and whispered into my friend's ear. "Rhonda, we need to get away from the others."

Luckily, she understood and followed when I shuffled my way out of the office, through the saloon, and back to our cabin. Colin and Lucy only had eyes for each other, or at least pretended not to notice our departure.

"Who did this, Carmen?" Rhonda asked, her teeth chattering so badly she was difficult to understand.

"I'm ninety-nine percent certain that Mac killed Alistair, but was interrupted by the rest of us before he could sneak away with the statue, which is why he came back for it. He's made it pretty clear that he's not planning on dividing everything equally with Lucy and Colin."

Rhonda's eyes widened even further, but she nodded along. "I think you're right. That guy is scary. So what do we do now?"

I sighed deeply, wishing I had some sort of crazy invention in my pocket that could whisk us out of here. Unfortunately, I did not. "I guess we can barricade ourselves in here again, until the Coast Guard arrive. I'm going to message Myrtle and ask for an update on their estimated arrival time."

"Oh, Carmen, I've never been so scared in my life. I want to call my girls, but I'm afraid that I'll break down and cry if I do. And that'll only frighten them. I just have to see them again! Do you promise me that we're going to get out of here, alive?"

"You better believe it!" I exclaimed, though a tear trailed down my cheek. "I owe you a trip to the French Riviera, remember? As soon as we get back to land, I'm booking us into the fanciest hotel I can find. Does that sounds like a deal?"

Rhonda tried to force a laugh, but it came out as a whimper. "What, no spa treatment?"

My belly laugh told everyone where we were, but I didn't care. "I think I can convince my employer to spring for facials."

Rhonda arched an eyebrow.

"And massages."

"Sounds great to me." Rhonda fell into my arms, her body still trembling from the fright.

As we hugged each other tight, both worrying that we might not survive the night, I tried to reassure her, but couldn't do much to counter the terror we were both feeling. All we could do was hope and pray that the Coast Guard arrived before Mac's friends.

Were these our last hours on the planet? If I was going to go out like this, at least it was comforting to know I had my bestie by my side. It was only too horrible to think that it meant her demise, as well.

"Rhonda, I just want you to know that you are my best—"

Before I could tell her how much she meant to me, my phone rang and ruined the moment.

37

Poor Timing

"Are you serious?" I looked at my phone's screen, and after a moment's indecision, ended the incoming call.

Rhonda, still wrapped around me, had seen the screen. Her eyes about bugged out of her head when she saw what I'd done. "You don't hang up on someone like that—she's royalty!"

I rolled my eyes and gritted my teeth.

"Well, I do," I grumbled. "She was acting so loopy last time, I'd rather not talk to her right now. I might say something I regret."

When my phone began to ring again, seconds later, Rhonda wagged her finger at me. "Maybe she has important news to share. I don't know what she said to upset you, but you need to take her call—she is your partner, after all."

Rhonda's tone and expression made clear that she was not to be trifled with. Before answering, I half turned so I didn't have to see her angry glare while I talked to my partner.

"Baroness, your timing is quite poor." I did keep my tone even, but boy was I seething on the inside. My partner was the last person I wanted to speak to.

"Yes, well…" Her voice trailed off, irritating me further.

"Since we spoke last, there's been another murder, and we are now hiding from a killer. I have no time for your shenanigans. Spit it out or I'm hanging up."

"You are right, I should have reached out after Carlos's death, as a true friend would have. My own feelings about Richard's death should not have colored my judgment."

As mad as I was at her, I had to applaud her for getting up the nerve to say she was sorry. "I do appreciate that, Sophie. I really do. But can we talk about it after I get off this ship?"

"Alright, but I do have one question about an item in Alistair's collection."

"What's that?"

"I was curious to know if you had found an art deco necklace with seven sapphires and eight rubies in a silver setting. I noticed it on Myrtle's list, and it actually belongs to a friend of mine. She bought it from the film's producer, but it was supposedly stolen the day before he was to deliver it to her."

My jaw dropped, and I swear steam shot out my ears. "Are you kidding me? Our lives are in danger, and you're worried about your friend's necklace? You are truly unbelievable, Sophie. Don't expect me to ever work with you again."

"Wait, Carmen, don't hang up," she shrieked. "Myrtle told me to call!"

I was about to do just that, when the Baroness's words finally sunk in. "Wait, an art deco necklace with seven sapphires and eight rubies in a silver setting. I know that one. Lucy can't take her eyes off of it," I muttered more to myself than my partner, before adding in a louder voice, "But the gems are made of glass, not rubies or sapphires."

"That's what Myrtle said and why I'm calling. It makes no sense. My friend would not have paid a million dollars for a movie prop. She only wanted to buy it because Elizabeth Taylor wore it at a gala event they both attended, and she's a fashion icon."

"Did you mean to say that your friend had already paid for it—are you certain?"

"Positive. I recall that she had threatened to have the producer arrested for theft, if he didn't deliver the necklace as promised. We were all certain that she'd been swindled, but he insisted that when he went to pick the necklace up from the props master at WorldWide Studios, the employee had said that he couldn't find it. The producer wanted to report it as stolen, but the props master said not to, that he would personally search every item in the warehouse until he found it. When the producer came back the next day to see if he'd had any luck, the security guards told him the props master had been arrested."

"There really are two necklaces," I muttered softly, but Sophie didn't hear me.

"The producer did file a police report, though we assumed it was to satisfy the studio's insurance company. Later we discovered that the props master had absconded with several items that night, including my friend's necklace."

I pinched my nose, taking in her words and their deeper meaning. "Gary Thompson again."

"I don't know either of their names. I can ask my friend, if it's important."

There was no way the studio would have let Gary give his wife the expensive necklace, but he had crated up the props for Alistair to steal. Yet as Lucy already suggested, it would have been easy for Gary to have slipped the gem-filled necklace into one of them, and not told Alistair about it, in the hopes of retrieving it later. Gary didn't know Alistair was going to set him up, or that he would be convicted for the crime and ultimately die in prison.

The Baroness's story confirmed Lucy's version, and added in a few important details. It sounded like Gary had been planning to steal the necklace all along, meaning he was not as innocent as Lucy thought, after all.

I still felt certain that Alistair had been surprised to learn of the second necklace's existence. Which means Gary must have hidden the jewelry inside of something. Could Alistair have had it on this ship, all these years, and not realized it? It was entirely possible. But where had Gary hidden it? I would have to recheck Myrtle's list and see which items were large enough to have hidden a necklace inside of. I wasn't certain why, but this felt important.

"Thank you for offering, but the names don't matter. You know, Baroness, I could kiss you right now. This information was a huge help." I might have been exaggerating a tad, but after our last conversation, I wanted to end this one on a positive note.

"Well, it's a good thing I'm not there then," she replied in her hoity-toity voice, but I heard a hint of a smile.

"Before I let you go, I have one more question, and I need you to be honest with me. Did Myrtle really ask you to call? Or were you checking in, on behalf of your friend?"

"Myrtle truly did. Of course, my friend will be thrilled if you do find her necklace, but that could have waited. When I asked if you'd mentioned which pieces you'd found, and then told Myrtle the story about my friend's necklace, she told me that the version on her list of stolen items was made of cheap silver and glass, not expensive gems. She thought it was strange, so she asked me to let you know, in case it helped you in some way."

"She was right about that. And you are certain that the expensive necklace was missing the day before the robbery?"

"Absolutely."

"Then that explains why there is only one on Myrtle's list, not two."

But why did we find the certificate for the genuine necklace, if Alistair stole the cheap version? I asked myself, knowing the Baroness could not help me answer that question. I didn't know exactly how or why, but this mix-up with the certificates seemed important, as well.

"Carmen, are you still there?"

"Yes, and thank you for calling, Sophie. When I get back to shore, why don't we sit down and chat, just two ladies and a cup of tea." I couldn't bring myself to say the word "friend," though I hoped our confrontation might just be the breakthrough we needed to repair our relationship.

The Baroness sniffed loudly, and I could hear her throat choking with emotion. "Earl Grey?"

"With lemon."

Her sniffles threatened to turn into real tears. I knew, in order for her to save face, we needed to wrap this conversation up. "I have to go unmask a murderer. Please tell me help is almost here."

"According to Myrtle's last update, the Coast Guard should be less than an hour out. Stay safe, Carmen."

"Thank you. I very much hope to see you again—and quite soon."

38

Carmen Gets To Work

I hung up the phone and momentarily held it to my chest, certain I had learned something important. Before I could tell Rhonda what the Baroness had shared, a commotion in the other room caused us to race through the passageway and cautiously peer into the saloon via the open door.

"Unhand me—it's not what it looks like!" Mac yelled out as he broke Colin's grip on his arm. They stood in front of Alistair's desk, where the Maltese Falcon sat, now clean of blood.

"Sure it is. You killed Alistair for his collection. You were never going to share any of it with us."

"Oh, yeah—then why am I putting the bird back?"

"I don't know, to throw suspicion off of yourself?" Colin guessed.

"Alistair owed me two and half million dollars, and I'm guessing that's a lot more than he owed either one of you, so I figured I deserved a bigger cut. I just wanted to see if that statue was worth what he said it was or not. But those gems are glass, the bird is hollow, and solid gold don't flake off."

"I told you earlier that Carmen and I found the paperwork proving it was not one of the more valuable statues," Lucy chastised.

"Yeah, but I didn't believe you or that certificate. Why did Alistair lock it up in a glass case if it wasn't worth anything?"

"To make it seem as if it was valuable," Colin suggested.

"Yeah, well, I know that now. When I told Alistair I wanted it as part of my

186

down payment, he made a big deal about it being worthless, which made me think he didn't want to give it to me because it was really valuable. Alistair lied constantly, so I figured he was lying about that, too. But for once, he told the truth."

Colin and Lucy locked eyes and nodded, as if Mac had just confessed to murder.

"Wait a second, I'm not the killer! There was no need to get rid of him; he'd already promised to give me his ship, the bird, and a necklace as down payment. They're mine. We can split the rest."

Colin laughed. "Sure, he did."

Figuring they wouldn't concern themselves with me while arguing, I moved behind the desk, hoping to get a closer look at the statue. There was very little gold missing from the bird's head or beak. So where did all of that gold leaf on the desk come from? When I picked it up to examine it better, Colin cried out, "What are you doing?"

I blushed, yet kept the bird in my hands. "Mac's already wiped the statue clean of prints and blood, there's no harm in examining it now."

"Geez, Mac, now the police aren't going to be able to trace the killer's fingerprints. Why did you clean it off?" Colin complained.

"How could I get a good look at it, with all that blood on it?"

"You did that on purpose, didn't you, so the police can't prove that you killed Alistair." Lucy's eyes widened and she stepped backwards towards the door, her hand on her heart. She looked like a gazelle about to flee her lion attacker. "I bet you are planning on killing all of us, too."

Colin stepped in front of Mac and spread his arms out wide. Whether it was to block him from attacking Lucy, or to try to contain the much larger man, was unclear. "We should lock him up in Alistair's room, and then call for help!"

Mac responded in kind, broadening his shoulders until he was as wide as a fridge. "I'm not letting you lock me up anywhere. My guys on are their way to meet the boat and unload Alistair's collection. So you have about three hours to explain to me why I should share any of it with you two."

I felt my shoulders relax. If his buddies were three hours out, the Coast

Guard should arrive first.

"Your guys?" Lucy muttered.

"They're coming here, to this boat? As in, to rescue us?" Colin asked.

"No, stupid, to take me and the props back to shore."

While Mac tried to turn the tables on his would-be captors, I turned my attention back to the statue. I laid it gently down on the desk and turned it over, surprised to see that very little of the gold leaf had flaked off its back or wings.

When I picked it up and turned the base towards me, Mac called out, "I didn't bust that lid open; it fell off when I pushed on it."

"Lid?" I asked, my brow furrowing in confusion. Tucked into the base of the bird was a lid, partially pushed into place. A ring of chipped gold leaf exposed its perimeters. Someone had to have chipped it off, to get the lid open, I realized. When I looked closer, I noticed the tiny holes in the base again, the ones we had assumed were a result of the sculpting process. The dark metal around one was exposed, presumably because something had scratched off the gold surrounding it.

As carefully as I could, I removed the lid and placed it onto the desk. The statue was indeed hollow. I could just fit one hand inside. I rubbed my fingers along the inside and felt a rough, raised section close to the opening that felt as if it might be a pattern or inscription. I stretched my fingers farther up towards its head, where they bumped against something that was wedged up into the falcon's head. It felt like paper. I gently pulled it out, to find a sheet that had been folded multiple times. Whatever it was, it hadn't aged well.

Keeping my body between my findings and the rest, I unfolded it as carefully as I could. After what felt like an hour but was probably a second or two, I had it open. That's when I slowly turned around and smoothed the sheet down onto the desk's surface to better read its contents. It was the certificate of authentication for the necklace Lucy admired, yet this one was for the cheap version. I stared at it in confusion, wondering how the heck this document had gotten inside the falcon.

Before I dwelled on that further, I used my phone's flashlight function to shine inside the hole. The rough edges I'd felt close to the opening was indeed an inscription, one that confirmed my suspicions about its maker: "G.T. 1975." Gary Thompson, Lucy's husband, must have made this prop for *The Black Bird*, the 1975 film based on *The Maltese Falcon*, a film he worked on as a props master.

But why would Gary have crated this worthless statue up for Alistair to steal, all those years ago? I closed my eyes to meditate on what I'd learned, when a flash of insight made my heart tighten in my chest as the pieces of the puzzle finally fell into place: Gary Thompson's desire to give his wife a million-dollar necklace, the closet walls that could slide open, and the hairpin cut from the key scene that Lucy only learned about after he'd been incarcerated.

I was pretty certain that I knew who had killed Alistair and why.

39

Unmasking A Killer

"Rhonda, I think I know what happened to Alistair." I had trouble keeping the sadness out of my voice. My suspicions brought me no joy, only sorrow.

She leaned in so close her hair tickled my nose. "It was Mac, wasn't it?"

"As much as I want it to be him, I'm no longer certain it was." I glanced over at Colin and Lucy, raising my eyebrows towards the pair for emphasis, but I don't think Rhonda noticed. The trio were still bickering about who should get what. Thankfully that was not our problem, and it meant they weren't paying attention to us, either.

She moved in so close, her mouth was practically in my ear. "Then who do you think did it?"

"Let me rephrase, I think I know why he died, but I still have two suspects to consider. Although I really hope I'm wrong about one of them."

I could tell Rhonda finally got the hint because she whipped her head around so that she was staring at Colin and Lucy. I moved so that I was in front of her again. "I don't know how they are going to react when I confront them. Can you please stay behind me?"

"If you insist," Rhonda replied, thankfully without arguing. She must have noted how serious my expression was. She huddled behind my back, then leaned over my shoulder to ask, "What exactly are you planning on doing—confront them now or wait until the police to arrive?"

"I don't think we have a choice but to do it now. Help might come too late.

190

I don't want to provoke the killer, but I don't want to sit around and wait to be murdered, either."

"Fair enough. How do you want to play this?"

In response, I cleared my throat. The threesome kept bickering and ignored me completely until I clapped my hands together as hard as I could. My palms stung more than expected, but the result was what I'd hoped for.

The trio stopped and stared at me.

"I have a question for Lucy. Did your husband tell you that the real necklace was inside the falcon statue, or did you puzzle that out yourself?"

Lucy glared at me, her brows knitted together as if I was speaking gibberish. "What are you talking about?"

"I didn't figure it out until I saw the gold leaf missing from the bottom of the statue. You'd told me your husband, Gary Thompson, had worked on *The Black Bird*, the 1975 film, but you didn't mention that he'd made this prop. I found his initials inscribed inside. So Gary would have known that it wasn't worth much, yet he crated it up for Alistair to take."

"Really, you are grasping at straws..." Lucy laughed, but the sound was as hollow as the Maltese Falcon.

Mac's face paled as a lightbulb seemed to go off in his head. "So her husband made the falcon statue? Does that mean she gets to keep it?"

"I don't know about that, but it does mean that she might have known about it being hollow. Which accounts for the gold leaf on the desk—it came loose when she opened the lid." I tilted the falcon so he could see the base, and where the gold leaf had chipped off.

"But it was this certificate that really clinched it for me." I raised the folded piece of paper, now smoothed out, up for my tiny crowd to see. "It's the certificate of authenticity for the cheap version of the necklace your husband made, not the expensive one."

Colin gasped. "Where did you find that?"

"Inside this statue."

"But how could it have gotten in there?" he asked.

"I think Gary was nervous and mixed up the certificates when he hid the necklace inside the statue. I bet he never even noticed that he'd grabbed the wrong one."

"What are you talking about?" Mac groused.

"Lucy, would you care to explain?"

I had a good idea of what had happened, but might not have been able to fill in all of the details. But Lucy didn't know that. Instead of refusing to talk, she bowed her head and began to tremble, but didn't start weeping. At least, not yet. "I hadn't thought about that movie in ages. *The Black Bird* was the first one Gary had worked on as props master, but the film flopped, and it soon became something he was ashamed of and rarely mentioned. It was only when we discovered the paperwork for this falcon in Alistair's office that I remembered he'd created it. He'd been so proud of how it turned out, he'd asked me to come to his work to see it."

Her voice faltered and her eyes glazed over, as if she was trying to recall something from long ago. "When we saw it in Alistair's office, I noticed the base was covered, and that bothered me, but I couldn't figure out why, at first. It took me a while to work out what had troubled me—the falcon statue Gary showed me had been hollow in the middle. He'd said that it was easier to cast that way."

Her voice trailed off again. Whether it was because she didn't want to tell the rest of the story, or it was too painful to remember, I wasn't certain. I was, however, ready to get this confession over with, so I helped her out a little more.

"Key scene?"

Lucy nodded glumly.

Rhonda looked to me. "What do you mean by that?"

I, in turn, looked to Lucy, hoping she would explain it to all of us. "That phrase, 'a key scene,' always bothered me. But I never understood what he meant, until we got here," she said, seemingly more to herself than the rest, before raising her voice. "Gary had told me often enough that he took more time with props handcrafted for key scenes because they were important to the storyline. Which is why they rarely cut props that had been specifically created for key scenes—it was a waste of time and money to do so. When Gary said my hairpin had been cut from a key scene, he was trying to tell me something. But I didn't understand what he meant, until a few hours ago, when I saw the pinholes in the base of the falcon."

I held out my hand and Lucy pulled that gorgeous vintage pin out of her hair, albeit reluctantly, releasing a wave of gray-streaked locks that fell past her shoulders.

I put the lid back on and held up the pin for all to see.

"There's more gold missing from around this hole. It looks like it might be a sort of release mechanism."

I inserted the hairpin into the thin slot and heard a click before the lid popped back off.

"Gary never would have been able to give you that necklace; it was worth far too much. So he must have hidden it in amongst the props Alistair was going to steal, thinking he could get it back later. I bet Gary put this lid and lock into place, so Alistair wouldn't find the necklace before he could retrieve it."

Lucy nodded. "That's what I think, too."

I locked eyes with her, hoping she was a less accomplished liar than our dead host. "Did you mean to kill Alistair? Or did he surprise you when he jumped out of the closet?"

"No, I did not! And how did you know about that sliding door? I only wanted to see if that necklace was inside the falcon. And it was. I'd just gotten it out and was replacing the lid, when we heard a strange sliding noise. The next thing we knew, part of the wall had opened up and there was Alistair. When he saw the falcon on the desk, he lunged for me. I'm ashamed to say I froze." Lucy hid her face in her hands.

"After all he'd done to destroy her life, I couldn't let him harm her, as well," Colin continued. "Which is why I grabbed the statue and hit him as hard as I could with it."

Colin cast his eyes downwards, as if he could still see the blood on his palms. "There was so much blood, I was certain that I'd killed him."

"I couldn't seem to do anything but stare at his lifeless body," Lucy whispered. "I'm so ashamed that Colin had to harm him, to protect me. I knew we had to get out of there, because he'd screamed when Colin hit him. But my hands wouldn't stop shaking, so Colin replaced the lid for me. He'd just set the statue down on the desk, so he could open the glass case more easily, when we heard footsteps. So we went back out to the saloon, circled around the glass cases and rushed into the passageway, so it appeared that we'd just entered the room."

Lucy suddenly turned to Colin and grabbed his shoulders. "Oh, Colin, my kids! What if the police think we killed Alistair for the necklace? How could I be so stupid? They already lost their dad. I can't go to prison for being involved in this; my children would never recover from it!"

When Lucy began to weep again, I leaned over to my friend. "Do you buy their story, that Colin hit Alistair?"

"I don't know. Lucy sure does seem to think she's going to pay for the crime, but she might just be acting paranoid, because of what happened to her husband. Unless she was the one who'd hit Alistair and Colin is covering for her."

I couldn't help but pat Rhonda on the back. "I'm glad to see you approach this situation a little more cynically."

"I suppose it doesn't matter if they are telling the truth or not about who swung the statue, as long as they stick to their story. A man is dead; one of them is going to have to pay for the crime."

"Do they? He was an evil man who killed one of his former employees and tried to murder another man," I reasoned.

Lucy dabbed at her eyes as she regained her composure. "All I wanted was that necklace. If Alistair hadn't snuck up on us, I would have gotten it back, and no one would have been the wiser. It certainly wasn't our intention to kill him, but I'm not sorry that he's dead. My husband paid for Alistair's crimes with his life; it's only fair for him to suffer a similar fate."

She squeezed Colin's hand as her head dropped, a single tear rolling from her eye and onto her blouse. He squeezed back, then wrapped her up in a hug, kissing her cheek as he did.

My jaw dropped open. "Wait a second, are you two in a relationship?"

Lucy slowly pulled out of his embrace. "We were once, albeit briefly. We didn't mean for it to happen, but we spent so much time together after my husband was arrested, we ended up falling in love. But nothing happened between us until after Gary was killed."

"But why did you spend time with Colin? His business partner set your husband up!" I cried.

"In the beginning, I was keeping an eye on him, in case Alistair ever got in touch. One thing led to another, and soon we were meeting for dinner every week to discuss any new leads to Alistair's whereabouts. If I could have proven that he was the actual thief, then there was a chance of getting my husband released. And Colin wanted to find him, so he could get back at least some of the money Alistair had stolen."

Lucy paused and looked away. "After Gary's death, Colin was a great comfort to me. But after a while, I realized there was no reason to find Alistair anymore, except to exact revenge. And being with Colin reminded me of that, constantly. I didn't want my life to be about that, so I broke up with him. Honestly, I've regretted it ever since."

She took Colin's hand and smiled up at him with so much love in her eyes, I blushed and turned away. "This is the first time we've seen each other since and I wasn't certain how he was going to react, when he saw me. But he wasn't upset with me, as I'd feared he would be."

Colin kissed her cheek. "Not at all. I hadn't stopped thinking about Lucy, either, but never dared to reach out to her again. I just wish we'd been reunited under better circumstances."

When they turned and leaned in so their heads pressed together, Rhonda squealed, "Oh, you two make such a cute couple!"

"So where is the necklace?" I asked, breaking the romantic mood that had been building.

Lucy disengaged herself from Colin and pulled her purse open. When she gently removed the necklace, its beauty momentarily took my breath away.

"Wow—that is gorgeous! Your husband was quite a craftsman."

By the way the gems sparkled in the light, I could tell that they were real, even from across the room. I moved in closer to better examine the intricately designed settings, the high-quality cut of the gems, and the sturdy clasp holding it all together. "Rhonda's right, it's spectacular."

"Yes, it is gorgeous." Lucy looked at it for a long second before running her fingers over the stones and settings. Then she took Colin's hand and looked over at Rhonda and me.

"Now that you know the truth, our lives are in your hands."

40

A Suitable Punishment

Mac, Rhonda, and I stepped into the passageway to confer.

"Sending Colin or Lucy to jail won't bring Alistair back. Colin was simply trying to protect her, not kill Alistair," Rhonda asserted.

"If you believe what they say…" I added.

"Stop being so cynical! Lucy's finally found love again after such a difficult time. And it sure doesn't sound like either one of them meant to harm Alistair. If he hadn't snuck up on them, Colin wouldn't have hit him," Rhonda pleaded. "He was a bad seed, and his reasons for bringing them all here were untoward. I'm not saying he had it coming to him, but he should have thought his plan through a little better, before he messed with all of those people's lives again. It's no surprise something bad happened to him."

I was glad to see she'd finally accepted that Alistair was not the kindhearted person he appeared to be. Yet I had to be the voice of reason. "I appreciate your sentiment, but we can't lie to the police. Someone obviously killed him, and if we don't tell them who did it, we'll all be suspects. But we don't necessarily have to tell them why."

"What do you mean?" Mac asked me.

"Alistair was off his rocker. He was dressed up as a pirate and trying to swindle his friends. He killed Divine and stabbed you, Mac. The police don't need to know about the necklace, do they? All that would do is complicate the story and give us a whole lot more explaining to do. It could make it seem that they had intentionally killed Alistair, in order to retrieve the necklace," I explained.

Rhonda tapped her chin. "I see what you mean. We could spin a simple self-defense story out of this without going into details. We can still tell the police that Alistair lunged at Lucy, and Colin hit him to protect her, without mentioning the necklace or hole in the falcon statue. Colin had every right to be scared for her life, as well as his own."

"Exactly. We stick with the truth, well, at least most of it."

"And the cops lose interest in Alistair and his things?" Mac added.

"Precisely," I nodded, glad Mac had seen the light.

"I like it. We're going with that story," Mac said, making the executive decision for us all.

We returned to Lucy and Colin, still holding hands, and explained our idea.

They listened with rapt attention, and immediately agreed wholeheartedly. By pleading self-defense, there was a chance that Colin could do time, but considering Divine's death, we figured a jury would believe that he was in genuine fear for their lives. Most people would have done the same, if someone they loved was being threatened like that, we figured.

Lucy breathed a sigh of relief. "Thank you. This trip has been a nightmare from start to finish, even without having to worry about being arrested. But at least coming here did bring me some peace. I finally know what Gary had been trying to tell me, all those years ago. That was worth going through everything we've withstood tonight."

For a moment, melancholy took over her face, but when she grabbed Colin's hand again, a smile brightened it back up. "In fact, for the first time in years, I don't feel like dwelling on the past anymore. I'm looking forward to seeing what lies ahead."

Colin pulled her hand up to his mouth and kissed it gently. "Me, too."

Rhonda wiped back a tear, and grabbed my arm, squeezing it tight. "Isn't it beautiful—two people finding each other, even so late in life? There's still hope for you and me, you know."

I laid an arm over her shoulder. "For you, anyway. Hey, thanks again for coming all the way over here to help me out."

"You bet. Though I do hope that your Luxembourg assignment will be less exhilarating. One brush with death is enough for a lifetime."

I chuckled along, wishing I could say the same.

"But don't forget about your promise to me—after we finish your assignment, it's hello French Riviera," Rhonda added.

"Of course. Trust me, I am happy to oblige. I haven't been to Nice or Cannes in years!"

Mac cleared his throat before announcing in his gruff voice, "It's great you're all feeling good about this, but I do have one caveat to our plan—I was never here."

"What do you mean?" Lucy asked. "We have to tell the cops about you being here. Alistair did try to stab you."

"So? He missed, and I'd rather have what he owes me than help the cops wrap up their investigation. He killed Divine; that's enough reason for Colin to have whacked him, when he threatened Lucy—especially when the cops find out they are an item. You don't need me here, and I'd rather not alert the authorities to my presence. So it works out for all of us if my friends pick me up before you call the Coast Guard, right?" His menacing expression made clear that we had no real choice but to agree with him.

"Sure, that's fine," I replied for all of us.

Mac turned to my bestie and smiled, exposing his pointy teeth. "Say, Rhonda, do you think I could bend your ear for a few minutes?"

I worked my way between her and Mac. "Sure, as long as you don't mind me coming along."

"Sure, Miss Inquisitive, you're welcome to join us. In fact, you can help me pack."

41

Coast Guard To The Rescue

"Is that the Milky Way?" Rhonda asked as she tilted her head back to better see the thick patch of stars she was pointing to.

"It sure looks like it," I replied, mimicking her movements so I could also take in the mass of celestial beings bundled so close together, yet millions of years from our tiny little planet called Earth.

Lucy, Colin, Rhonda, and I were on the deck, enjoying the starry night, when the Coast Guard found us an hour after Colin confessed to killing Alistair.

"Ahoy, anyone on board," a male voice yelled up in lightly accented English.

"We're rescued!" Rhonda clapped.

"Everyone got their stories straight?" Colin asked.

"After Alistair killed Divine, Captain Jack took the crew and left us," Rhonda answered.

"But not before cutting the second boat loose so we couldn't follow him," I added. In fact, it was filled with Mac's half of the collection and currently sailing away from *La Vida Loca*. With a little luck, he'd sink before his buddies could find him.

Mac didn't want to risk anyone spotting us and offering help before his friends arrived, so he hunted around the ship's hold until he found an emergency repair kit, consisting of a thick plastic blanket and a whole lot of glue. Once he'd repaired the gash the harpoon had made, he loaded up half

200

of Alistair's collection and sputtered away.

He'd let Rhonda choose which items to take, and without my prompting she pointed out the least valuable pieces in Alistair's collection. Reggie may be right, Rhonda might be a perfect agent for the Rosewood Agency. She certainly had the right mindset and streak of mischievousness for the job.

What I couldn't tell Rhonda—without having to break my confidentiality agreement, that is—was the best news of all. Mac might have been a bigshot Mafia type, but he hadn't noticed me pickpocketing his phone moments before he boarded the dinghy. I finally had a lead to my husband's killer; how I wished I could share this wonderful news with my bestie. But I was going to keep that can of worms firmly closed for now and instead simply revel in the thought that I was a step closer.

"And after Jack jumped ship, Alistair attacked me in his office. That's when Colin hit him with the Maltese Falcon statue, in order to protect me," Lucy finished.

I smiled at our little group. "Excellent. I think we're ready to be rescued."

42

Landlubbers

I looked out over the vast ocean, taking in the white-capped waves rolling towards us, glad we were no longer bobbing around the North Sea. From our hotel room's sixth-story window, the choppy blue-gray water did not look inviting in the slightest. As far as I was concerned, we were done with boats for the rest of this European adventure.

After the Coast Guard had boarded and searched the vessel, they decided it was best to leave Alistair and Divine's bodies where they lay, so the police could better investigate the crime scenes after they'd docked in Zeebrugge, Belgium, the closest port to our current location.

A skeleton crew then boarded and prepared to sail the *La Vida Loca* back to shore. Thankfully we were invited to hop onto the much faster vessel that had sped out to rescue us, and we'd made it back to land several hours before Alistair's brigantine had.

After the police briefly questioned us, we had been driven to this off-the-beaten-path hotel and been checked into halfway-decent rooms, where we were requested to remain until they could conduct a longer interview with each of us. Given that it was already dawn by the time we hit the sack, I was grateful they'd scheduled our interviews for later in the day. They were merely a technicality, the police had reassured us. Yet the fact that they'd taken our passports meant they didn't trust us completely. At least, not yet.

As the only two guests who didn't know Alistair well, the police had quickly worked out that we had the least to share and, therefore, pretty much no motive to harm the party's host. Which meant we would be the last to be interviewed, giving me time to take a wonderfully long and relaxing bath.

While the water drained, I snuggled into the hotel-provided bathrobe and grabbed a towel to dry my hair, before stepping back out into our room.

"That was heavenly," I sighed and plopped down into one of the overstuffed wingbacks. None of the furniture was worth much, but it was incredibly comfortable, which was also a valuable asset, and one overlooked by many a designer. "I think we still have enough time for you to take one, too."

"Maybe, after we're done with the police. I'm feeling pretty good, even without a bath."

"I know what you mean. I'm glad everything did work out, but that party could have been our death," I huffed.

"But it wasn't. And to face death like that was just what I needed to call Julie. It took six tries before she finally picked up, but I'm sure glad she did. Life is too short to waste time sitting around feeling sorry for yourself or wishing you'd done something sooner. We chatted for a whole hour while you were in the bath. She's doing great and seems really happy with her current assignment in Prague."

I grabbed her hand. "I'm so glad."

"She said she's going to ask her boss for some time off, so we could meet up soon, maybe even before I fly back to Seattle. And this time, I got the feeling she really meant it. That's good enough for me."

She squeezed my hand and released it. "I'm just sorry you won't be able to write up anything about our adventure on *La Vida Loca* for your magazine. I was hoping you could interview Alistair, but now that he's dead…"

"Honestly, my editor probably wouldn't believe my version of the evening's events, even if I chose to write it up. But I don't know that I could, without exposing Lucy and Colin."

Rhonda nodded. "Then you should let it go. You still have the Luxembourg assignment this weekend; that should make her happy."

I rubbed the towel over my hair, hiding my grin. "I think you're right. She's quite excited to see what I can find out about the smuggling ring.

That should satisfy her." In truth, my "editor," a.k.a. Myrtle, was thrilled with both Rhonda and me for finding Alistair and most of the items he'd stolen. Anytime she could mark a case as closed was a good day, usually for Rosewood and the art world in general.

Even though Mac had absconded with more than his fair share of movie props—including some Alistair had stolen from WorldWide Studios—I didn't have to worry about disappointing Myrtle. Shortly after the Coast Guard had boarded our ship, I pulled one of our rescuers aside and explained that Mac and several boxes of stolen movie props were bobbing around in a poorly repaired dinghy, waiting to be picked up by criminals, presumably wanted by the law. He was more than happy to radio in the news, and from what I gathered, a helicopter and several speedboats filled with police officers were on their way to intercept Mac and his friends.

Rhonda took a long sip of her coffee before staring outside, as if she was still mentally wrestling with something. "Were we wrong to lie to the police?"

"Did we? We told them almost all of the truth, but didn't lie about anything. It's more that we left information out. The police didn't need to know about Mac or the necklace."

"Oh, it irks me that he got away with so many of Alistair's props, when Lucy and Colin didn't take a thing."

I had to hide my smile, knowing I couldn't tell her about Mac being arrested, at least not right now. We had promised the others that we would not mention his presence, and I didn't want to get into a moral discussion with Rhonda about me breaking that oath. With a little luck, it would be a story in the newspaper soon enough. "Frankly, I'm just glad he left peacefully. And Lucy didn't keep the necklace, so it will go back to Lady Sophie's friend, which means there is no reason for the police to know where it had been hidden, or why. My gut tells me that neither Colin nor Lucy would intentionally harm anyone else. If Alistair hadn't popped out of the closet when he did, she would have gotten what she came for, and he would still be alive."

"And in the end, Lucy didn't get the necklace, but got something even better."

I nodded. "Justice, although ten years too late."

Rhonda shook her head as she waved away my remark. "No—love, silly! She and Colin found each other again. That's worth its weight in gold."

"True, for some."

Rhonda only laughed. "So, when is our police interview?"

I checked my watch then sprung back out of the chair. "In about an hour. I suppose I better dry my hair and change. Lucy and Colin are at the station now, but I don't expect either one of them to be arrested. Whether or not he really did swing that fatal blow, he seemed to be maintaining that he did it to protect her, at least on the boat ride back."

"Good. Lucy and her children had suffered so much loss. She deserves a little happiness in her life. I can't imagine the police will arrest him for trying to protect her."

"I agree."

"So?" She grinned over at me in anticipation.

I gulped, dreading what Rhonda was about to ask. I feared that granting her request would be akin to opening Pandora's box, and I would never be able to close the lid and reset things back to normal. I had spent almost two decades of my life keeping my personal and work life separate for a reason. Honestly, before Rhonda's arrival in Europe, I had never really considered what would have happened if the Baroness had said yes to one of my birthday party invitations. Would my friends have welcomed her snobbish behavior with open arms? Probably not.

Rhonda wasn't one to put up with people who put on airs, and I knew she hated it when anyone thought they were deserving of special treatment because of their social standing or wealth. Heck, she was the multimillion-dollar-earning presenter of one of America's favorite television shows, and yet she still refused to skip ahead in lines or ask to be let in the back door so no one would recognize and bother her. Would Rhonda be able to stand being in the same room as my partner for more than a few minutes?

"What did Sophie say?" Rhonda asked, excitement building in her voice.

I suppressed a sigh, and instead answered as brightly as I could. "We are welcome to stop by anytime."

Rhonda began to clap. "How exciting—my first royal visit! That is going to be a day to remember!"

I hid my smirk with the back of my hand. That it would be, but hopefully for the right reasons, I thought.

"Let's make Lady Sophie our first stop after we're back in Amsterdam. Oh, wait, no, I'll need to buy something fancier before I meet her ladyship. Nothing I have will do."

Instead of reassuring her that she had plenty of clothes that would be appropriate, I let Rhonda babble away, reveling in her excitement and the chance to meet a real royal, up close and personal.

43

A Royal Meeting

"Are you certain she's feeling better?" Rhonda smoothed down her new frock, a floral sundress with fringe around the bustline, for the hundredth time, clearly nervous to meet Lady Sophie.

We were standing outside of my partner's hospital room, while my friend took a few deep breaths in preparation for her first royal visit. I handed her the bouquet of black irises and tiger lilies, the Baroness's favorites, and slapped Rhonda on the shoulder.

"Everything's going to be fine. She's going to love you!" I fibbed, hoping this meeting would not include any screaming or hissy fits on the part of my partner. She had been in better spirits during our last conversation and had even insisted that I bring Rhonda along on my next visit. But I still wasn't entirely certain that meeting in this way would be good for them. But my countersuggestion to wait until she'd been released from the hospital was pooh-poohed away as nonsense.

So here we were, my best friend and favorite partner about to meet, face to face, for the first time. Knowing what I did about their personalities and interests, I gave it a fifty percent chance of success.

"They scaled back her medicine some and the last we spoke, she sure did sound more like her old self. But her jaw is probably still pretty sore. She's a little hard to understand because of it."

"That's no skin off my nose. I'm just so excited to meet her!"

I hoped and prayed that my partner would be on her best behavior. After what Rhonda and I had been through on Alistair's ship, I didn't think I could take it if Sophie was catty or condescending to my bestie. Luckily Rhonda was so excited to meet her first royal that if the Baroness was distant, she'd probably consider it becoming of the nobility.

I knocked once, then pushed the door open, glad to see Lady Sophie was sitting up in bed, and looking as regal as one could when wearing a hospital gown. Her foot was still raised up in a sling, but her jaw was starting to yellow, which was a good sign—the bruising was finally dissipating. Resting comfortably on top of her tousled bob was her trademark tiara, the plethora of tiny diamonds sparkling under the bright hospital lights.

"You must be Rhonda Rhodes," her ladyship said in her most posh tone.

"It is an honor to meet you." My bestie curtsied like a pro.

Lady Sophie waved her towards the bed. "Please come closer."

I held my breath, wondering what my partner had in store. I knew that I wouldn't be able to work with Sophie again, if she intentionally hurt my friend's feelings.

Rhonda approached hesitantly, but when she was almost to the bed, the Baroness grabbed her hand tight and pulled her even closer.

When Sophie looked up at my astonished friend with a genuine smile and gratitude in her eyes, I blinked away a tear.

"Thank you for taking such good care of my friend," she said, just before wrapping Rhonda up in a highly uncharacteristic hug.

As I gazed upon my best friend and favorite partner locked in a loving embrace, I had trouble holding back a waterfall of tears.

Everything was going to work out just fine, after all.

THE END

Thanks for reading *A Statue To Die For*!

Reviews really do help readers decide whether they want to take a chance on a new author. If you enjoyed this story, please consider posting a review on BookBub, on Goodreads, or with your favorite retailer. I appreciate it!
Jennifer S. Alderson

I hope you will join Carmen De Luca for her next adventure in *Forgeries and Fatalities*.

Can Carmen track down a fake painting before a real killer paints her out of the picture—permanently? Join in her for another adventure—this time in Luxembourg and Italy!

Acknowledgements

Many thanks to my wonderful family for helping me create time to write, as well as for encouraging me to keep developing these new characters. I am so grateful for their love and support.

I am also indebted to my editor, Sadye Scott-Hainchek of The Fussy Librarian, for her outstanding work and advice. The cover designer for this series and my Travel Can Be Murder Cozy Mysteries, Elizabeth Mackey, continues to amaze me with her gorgeous and fun designs.

The idea to center this book around movie props came to me when I happened upon an article about a real and ongoing mystery surrounding the disappearance, reappearance, and authenticity of several versions of the Maltese Falcon statue that were all supposedly used in the 1941 film. The information Alistair McPhee shares with his guests about the different statues' values and famous owners is true.

The Maltese Falcon was originally a book written by Dashiell Hammett and published in 1929. The first film adaptation was brought out in 1931, and the second, titled *Satan Met A Lady*, in 1936. The most famous version, starring Humphrey Bogart, was released in 1941. In 1975, a comedic sequel called *The Black Bird* was released. In it, the son of Sam Spade is a detective who is also searching for the Maltese Falcon.

Though I do reference real movies, I did embellish on the truth on a few occasions. I have no idea what the material composition of the Maltese Falcon statue used in *The Black Bird* is. I am also certain that there was no props master named Gary Thompson working on that film, because I made him up. WorldWide Studios and director Alistair McPhee are also figments of my imagination.

While doing research into collecting props, I came across repeated warnings that there are a whole lot of unscrupulous dealers out there trying to pass off forgeries and replicas as the real thing, and that this is a serious issue for collectors to consider when buying any item purportedly used in a movie. These warnings helped to shape this mystery.

There is one more tidbit that I feel is important to share. The "Giraspi family" was the name of an Italian-American organized criminal organization based out of Las Vegas from the 1940s through 1975, when it was declared defunct. Their existence helped to inspire my own international crime family. As far as I know, there is no crime boss named Antonio Corozza. And if there is, I mean no disrespect.

I do hope you enjoyed this brief glimpse into the world of movies and props, as well as getting to know Carmen, Rhonda, and the Baroness a bit better. Their adventures will continue soon in *Forgeries and Fatalities*. Until then, happy reading and safe travels!

About the Author

Jennifer S. Alderson was born in San Francisco, grew up in Seattle, and currently lives in Amsterdam. After traveling extensively around Asia, Oceania, and Central America, she lived in Darwin, Australia, before settling in the Netherlands.

Jennifer's love of travel, art, and culture inspires her award-winning Zelda Richardson Mystery series, her Travel Can Be Murder Cozy Mysteries, and her Carmen De Luca Art Sleuth Mysteries. Her background in journalism, multimedia development, and art history enriches her novels.

When not writing, she can be found perusing a museum, biking around Amsterdam, or enjoying a coffee along the canal while planning her next research trip.

Visit Jennifer's website [http://www.jennifersalderson.com] to learn more about her books and sign up for her mailing list. Subscribers receive updates on future releases, as well as two FREE short stories: *A Book To Die For* (cozy mystery) and *Holiday Gone Wrong* (mystery thriller).

Books by Jennifer S. Alderson:

Carmen De Luca Art Sleuth Mysteries
Collecting Can Be Murder
A Statue To Die For
Forgeries and Fatalities
A Killer Inheritance

Travel Can Be Murder Cozy Mysteries

Death on the Danube: A New Year's Murder in Budapest

Death by Baguette: A Valentine's Day Murder in Paris

Death by Windmill: A Mother's Day Murder in Amsterdam

Death by Bagpipes: A Summer Murder in Edinburgh

Death by Fountain: A Christmas Murder in Rome

Death by Leprechaun: A Saint Patrick's Day Murder in Dublin

Death by Flamenco: An Easter Murder in Seville

Death by Gondola: A Springtime Murder in Venice

Death by Puffin: A Bachelorette Party Murder in Reykjavik

Zelda Richardson Art Mysteries

The Lover's Portrait: An Art Mystery

Rituals of the Dead: An Artifact Mystery

Marked for Revenge: An Art Heist Thriller

The Vermeer Deception: An Art Mystery

Standalone Travel Thriller

Down and Out in Kathmandu: A Backpacker Mystery

Death on the Danube: A New Year's Murder in Budapest

Book One of the Travel Can Be Murder Cozy Mystery series

Who knew a New Year's trip to Budapest could be so deadly? The tour must go on—even with a killer in their midst...

Recent divorcee Lana Hansen needs a break. Her luck has run sour for going on a decade, ever since she got fired from her favorite job as an investigative reporter. When her fresh start in Seattle doesn't work out as planned, Lana ends up unemployed and penniless on Christmas Eve.

Dotty Thompson, her landlord and the owner of Wanderlust Tours, is also in a tight spot after one of her tour guides ends up in the hospital, leaving her a guide short on Christmas Day.

When Dotty offers her a job leading the tour group through Budapest, Hungary, Lana jumps at the chance. It's the perfect way to ring in the new year and pay her rent!

What starts off as the adventure of a lifetime quickly turns into a nightmare when Carl, her fellow tour guide, is found floating in the Danube River. Was it murder or accidental death? Suspects abound when Lana discovers almost everyone on the tour had a bone to pick with Carl.

But Dotty insists the tour must go on, so Lana finds herself trapped with nine murder suspects. When another guest turns up dead, Lana has to figure out who the killer is before she too ends up floating in the Danube.

Excerpt from *Death on the Danube*
Chapter One: A Trip to Budapest

December 26—Seattle, Washington

"You want me to go where, Dotty? And do what?" Lana Hansen had trouble keeping the incredulity out of her voice. She was thrilled, as always, by her landlord's unwavering support and encouragement. But now Lana was beginning to wonder whether Dotty Thompson was becoming mentally unhinged.

"To escort a tour group in Budapest, Hungary. It'll be easy enough for a woman of your many talents."

Lana snorted with laughter. *Ha! What talents?* she thought. Her resume was indeed long: disgraced investigative journalist, injured magician's assistant, former kayaking guide, and now part-time yoga instructor—emphasis on "part-time."

"You'll get to celebrate New Year's while earning a paycheck and enjoying a free trip abroad, to boot. You've been moaning for months about wanting a fresh start. Well, this is as fresh as it gets!" Dotty exclaimed, causing her Christmas-bell earrings to jangle. She was wrapped up in a rainbow-colored bathrobe, a hairnet covering the curlers she set every morning. They were standing inside her living room, Lana still wearing her woolen navy jacket and rain boots. Behind Dotty's ample frame, Lana could see the many decorations and streamers she'd helped to hang up for the Christmas bash last night. Lana was certain that if Dotty's dogs hadn't woken her up, her landlord would have slept the day away.

"Working as one of your tour guides wasn't exactly what I had in mind, Dotty."

"I wouldn't ask you if I had any other choice." Dotty's tone switched from flippant to pleading. "Yesterday one of the guides and two guests crashed into each other while skibobbing outside of Prague, and all are hospitalized. Thank goodness none are in critical condition. But the rest of the group is leaving for Budapest in the morning, and Carl can't do it on his own. He's just not client-friendly enough to pull it off. And I need those five-star reviews, Lana."

Dotty was not only a property manager, she was also the owner of several successful small businesses. Lana knew Wanderlust Tours was Dotty's favorite and that she would do anything to ensure its continued success. Lana also knew that the tour company was suffering from the increased competition from online booking sites and was having trouble building its audience and generating traffic to its social media accounts. But asking Lana to fill in as a guide seemed desperate, even for Dotty, and even if it was the day after Christmas. Lana shook her head slowly. "I don't know. I'm not qualified to—"

Dotty grabbed one of Lana's hands and squeezed. "Qualified, shmalified. I didn't have any tour guide credentials when I started this company fifteen years ago, and that hasn't made a bit of difference. You enjoy leading those kayaking tours, right? This is the same thing, but for a while longer."

The older lady glanced down at the plastic cards in her other hand, shaking her head. "Besides, you know I love you like a daughter, but I can't accept these gift cards in lieu of rent. If you do this for me, you don't have to pay me back for the past two months' rent. I am offering you the chance of a lifetime. What have you got to lose?"

* * *

If you are enjoying the book, why not pick up your copy now and keep reading? Available as paperback, large print edition, eBook, and in Kindle Unlimited.

The Lover's Portrait: An Art Mystery

Book One in the Zelda Richardson Art Mystery Series

"*The Lover's Portrait* is a well-written mystery with engaging characters and a lot of heart. The perfect novel for those who love art and mysteries!" – Reader's Favorite, 5-star medal

"Well worth reading for what the main character discovers—not just about the portrait mentioned in the title, but also the sobering dangers of Amsterdam during World War II." – IndieReader

A portrait holds the key to recovering a cache of looted artwork, secreted away during World War II, in this captivating historical art thriller set in the 1940s and present-day Amsterdam.

When a Dutch art dealer hides the stock from his gallery—rather than turn it over to his Nazi blackmailer—he pays with his life, leaving a treasure trove of modern masterpieces buried somewhere in Amsterdam, presumably lost forever. That is, until American art history student Zelda Richardson sticks her nose in.

After studying for a year in the Netherlands, Zelda scores an internship at the prestigious Amsterdam Historical Museum, where she works on an exhibition of paintings and sculptures once stolen by the Nazis, lying unclaimed in Dutch museum depots almost seventy years later. When two women claim the same painting, the portrait of a young girl entitled *Irises*, Zelda is tasked with investigating the painting's history and soon finds evidence that one of the two women must be lying about her past. Before she can figure out which one it is and why, Zelda learns about the Dutch art dealer's concealed collection. And that *Irises* is the key to finding it all.

Her discoveries make her a target of someone willing to steal—and even kill—to find the missing paintings. As the list of suspects grows, Zelda realizes she has to track down the lost collection and unmask a killer if she wants to survive.

Excerpt from *The Lover's Portrait*
Chapter 1: Two More Crates

June 26, 1942

Just two more crates, then our work is finally done, Arjan reminded himself as he bent down to grasp the thick twine handles, his back muscles already yelping in protest. Drops of sweat were burning his eyes, blurring his vision. "You can do this," he said softly, heaving the heavy oak box upwards with an audible grunt.

Philip nodded once, then did the same. Together they lugged their loads across the moonlit room, down the metal stairs, and into the cool subterranean space below. After hoisting the last two crates onto a stack close to the ladder, Arjan smiled in satisfaction, slapping Philip on the back as he regarded their work. One hundred and fifty-two crates holding his most treasured objects, and those of so many of his friends, were finally safe. Relief briefly overcame the panic and dread he'd been feeling for longer than he could remember. Preparing the space and artwork had taken more time than he'd hoped it would, but they'd done it. Now he could leave Amsterdam knowing he'd stayed true to his word. Arjan glanced over at Philip, glad he'd trusted him. He stretched out a hand towards the older man. "They fit perfectly."

Philip answered with a hasty handshake and a tight smile before nodding towards the ladder. "Shall we?"

He is right, Arjan thought, *there is still so much to do.* They climbed back up into the small shed and closed the heavy metal lid, careful to cushion its fall.

They didn't want to give the neighbors an excuse to call the Gestapo. Not when they were so close to being finished.

Philip picked up a shovel and scooped sand onto the floor, letting Arjan rake it out evenly before adding more. When the sand was an inch deep, they shifted the first layer of heavy cement tiles into place, careful to fit them snug up against each other.

As they heaved and pushed, Arjan allowed himself to think about the future for the first time in weeks. Hiding the artwork was only the first step; he still had a long way to go before he could stop looking over his shoulder. First, back to his place to collect their suitcases. Then, a short walk to Central Station where second-class train tickets to Venlo were waiting. Finally, a taxi ride to the Belgian border where his contact would provide him with falsified travel documents and a chauffeur-driven Mercedes-Benz. The five Rembrandt etchings in his suitcase would guarantee safe passage to Switzerland. From Geneva he should be able to make his way through the demilitarized zone to Lyon, then down to Marseilles. All he had to do was keep a few steps ahead of Oswald Drechsler.

Just thinking about the hawk-nosed Nazi made him work faster. So far he'd been able to clear out his house and storage spaces without Drechsler noticing. Their last load, the canvases stowed in his gallery, was the riskiest, but he'd had no choice. His friends trusted him—no, counted on him—to keep their treasures safe. He couldn't let them down now. Not after all he'd done wrong.

* * *

If you are enjoying what you are reading, why not pick up your copy now and keep reading? Available as eBook, audiobook, and paperback.